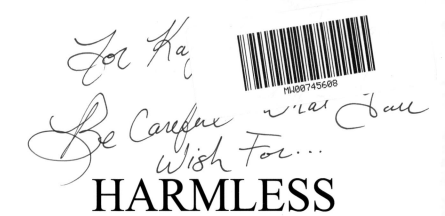

For Ka...

Be Careful what you
Wish For...

HARMLESS

Katherine Dell

Maroon Vixen Publishing Inc.
Calgary, Alberta, Canada

This edition first published in Calgary, Alberta, Canada by Maroon Vixen Publishing Inc. in 2017.

Library and Archives Canada Cataloguing in Publication

Dell, Katherine, 1979-, author
        Harmless / Katherine Dell.

Issued in print and electronic formats.
ISBN 978-0-9959989-0-2 (softcover).--ISBN 978-0-9959989-1-9 (PDF).--
ISBN 978-0-9959989-2-6 (Kindle).--ISBN 978-0-9959989-3-3 (Kobo).--
ISBN 978-0-9959989-4-0 (iBook)

        I. Title.

PS8607.E4855H37 2017   C813'.6   C2017-903710-2
                                               C2017-903711-0

Book cover design by Brianna Schretlen.

For more information, visit www.katherinedell.com

For Orrin, Carter, and Sidney.

Thank you for believing in me.

Journal of Rachel Barnes

January 25

Well, here goes. I'm writing in the journal you gave me. Honestly, I think this is a pretty crappy replacement for not being able to see you anymore, but you're the doc. You've brought me back from some pretty dark places, and I'm grateful for that, but I don't think I can do this. It might be too big a step.

Maybe moving away from Vancouver is a mistake? Maybe you could move too? Uprooting your whole practice would be a lot of work, though. Kidding. A little. Just putting it out there.

I know I can't stay here. And I can't bring myself to move in with my dad and his new girlfriend just to stay. Living on my own while trying to finish high school isn't the answer either. My parents got divorced years ago, but seeing my dad dating still feels weird.

Like you said, a fresh start will be good for me. I'll move with Mom to Hazelton. She's been talking up the place for weeks now. She says I'll love it. I've only been there twice, so I guess I'll have to take her word for it. It's where she grew up—maybe you knew that. Going from a big city to a small town won't be an easy adjustment, though.

I just wish there weren't going to be so many miles between us. You said I'm ready to stop seeing you, but for over three years that's all I've done. I'm not over what happened to Eric. I'll never be over it. You say it's something time will dull. I keep hoping you're right.

You're the only one who's ever really listened to me. I know that's your job, but I'm not sure if I've ever said thanks for that. I'm even going to miss the way you relate emotions to analogies about the weather. I've started doing that, too, by the way. Only in my head, but I'll keep it. It takes me back to a safe place.

I know you'll never read this, but you're right about writing things down. I guess it's a way to get things out so I don't bottle them up. I'll try to keep up with it . . . for you.

I'll miss you, Dr. Doppler.

You'll always be my Weather Lady.

Outlook for the days ahead: cloudy with a chance of rain.

Rachel

CHAPTER ONE

There was a time when stuff like this didn't bother me. It shouldn't bother me. But that was then, and this is now. A stormy gale rears inside me. The weather is unpredictable tonight.

Thousands of tiny dust particles become airborne as Julie rips the packing tape from the sealed cardboard box. I cringe as though it's been torn from my own skin.

Breathe, Rachel, just breathe. It's only one box.

"I can't believe you haven't unpacked yet," she says. "You moved here at the start of second semester, so it's been like"—she mentally counts as she speaks—"almost five months? And you—"

I cut her off before she can say anything else. "Yeah. I have this system of dealing with stuff." *Not a total lie.* "Plus I've been reorganizing things a bit. But it should be in there."

Julie claws into the box marked *Tunes, Trinkets, and Other*

Crap like a tiger scratching at the underbelly of a recent kill.

Say something! Make her stop.

It occurs to me that people might react strangely to the towering collection of unopened boxes in my bedroom. But these boxes are something I don't talk about. I never even told the Weather Lady about them, though my mom might have mentioned them to her once.

My mind flits back to the tiny apartment Mom and I shared after my parents got divorced, the first apartment of many. We moved in about two years after my brother, Eric, died. My mom unpacked all her stuff the instant we got there. Then she started buying new furniture and things to decorate the place. Everything was new and fake. At least it felt fake to me. There was barely a trace of who we used to be in there. I guess it was her way of returning to some sense of normality.

The boxes were mine.

"I can't find your iPod in here." Julie slows her sifting to an occasional paw. "Or the speakers. Come on. I'll dump it out in the living room. There's more space."

Her suggestion pulls on the thin threads of my sanity, but I manage to give her a quick nod.

We head down the short hallway to the kitchen, where everyone is getting drinks. Mason, Ryan, and Chloe: these are my friends—or friends by association. Moving around so much has done a number on my social life, not that it was great to begin with. But in Hazelton, I found my group—or Julie's group—right away. Either way, it's nice to be around people. Loneliness was getting old.

Julie and I met on the very first day I started at Hazelton Secondary. At first I thought she might be one of those goth kids, because she wore so much makeup and had blue and purple stripes in her hair. But it turns out that hair, makeup, and fashion are just her outlets of expression. Every few weeks she changes the color of her chunky highlights. I'm actually super impressed with what she can do with shoulder-length hair.

We're in the same grade-twelve graduating class. She was assigned to show me around for the first few days and make sure I settled in all right. It's like we've been best friends forever, or what I think that would feel like. Julie's been the glue holding things together since I had to leave the Weather Lady. Not that she knows anything about that. My years of seeing a shrink aren't something I plan to discuss with any of my new friends.

I watch as Mason clanks a case of beer beside the bottle of rye on my grandma's kitchen table. I thought this was going to be a few rounds of late-night cards. How much booze do we need?

Mason and I see each other every day at school, but it feels like we're almost strangers. I think he's nice-*ish*—in an unapproachable, hockey-jock sort of way. Julie said he might be into me, but I don't see it. He's out of my league anyway—and not my type. It doesn't matter. He never talks to me, and I wouldn't know what to say if he did.

"Are you sure you guys wouldn't rather go to Chloe's place?" I look over at Chloe. "You said your mom is probably over at her boyfriend's anyway, right?"

But she stares right through me, like I don't even exist. I don't get her. She can be so cold to me sometimes. From what I can tell, most everything about her is an act, from her nails to her heavy makeup to her over-processed hair. She's Julie's BFF, and according to her, there can only be one. It's useless trying to figure her out, but I can't help myself. It's another side effect of too much professional therapy.

"It's simple logistics, Rach," Mason says. "Your mom and grandma are out of town until tomorrow. So we can party at your house till . . . whenever." He gives me the smile he saves for his groupies. He must see the look on my face, because he wraps his arm around my shoulder, giving me a squeeze. He's almost a head taller than me. I feel like a doll being tossed around. "Relax. I'm kidding. There are only five of us. It's more like a friendly gathering."

As Julie and Chloe go into the living room to set up the music, I don't move from my spot in the kitchen. All of this feels awkward. Ryan searches for glasses in the cupboards. Julie has scattered the contents of the box on the living room floor. And Chloe sits cross-legged beside her, picking at the wrapper of a fresh pack of cigarettes.

Please don't smoke in the house. Not those glasses, Ryan! And Julie . . .

"So, how about giving me a tour?" Mason asks. This is probably the most attention I've received from him since I moved here.

"My grandma's house is tiny. There's not much to tour." My neck and shoulder muscles are so tense they might cramp up if I move the wrong way. Maybe that's why his hand falls away from my shoulder.

Let a breeze clear your skies. There's a sunny day around here somewhere.

"So? I'm still curious," he says. "Like, where's your room?"

Is he flirting with me? This is new and uncharted territory. With his fingers, he combs his dark waves of hockey hair away from his face. I'm not sure if the shaggy look is in, but he pulls it off without even trying.

"Down the hall, next to my grams' room." I try not to make eye contact. For me, there's something way too personal about looking into someone's eyes. "The kitchen and living room are here. Obviously. And if anyone needs the bathroom, it's across the hall from my room. Oh, and my mom's room is in the basement."

"You picked the room next to your grandma's? I would've taken the room in the basement for sure. More private, you know?"

No, I don't know, Mason. Why don't you explain to me how being farther from parental supervision helps with your sexual prowess? Except I don't say that. My inner voice always stays inner. Just another weirdo coping mechanism the Weather Lady tried to cure.

"Are you kidding? It's super dark down there. You can barely see your hand in front of your face when the lights are off."

"Aw, is somebody scared of the dark?" The impish grin that spreads across his lips tells me I walked right in to that one. When am I going to learn? Teasing is like a sport around here. You either join in or get a thick skin.

"Um, no." Was that convincing? "It's just way darker here than in the city. You guys must all have some nocturnal gene that lets you see in the dark." God, I suck at this. That comeback couldn't have been any lamer.

"Hey, give it a rest, Mason," Julie calls from her circle of debris in the living room. "You want her to get rid of us the first time she has us over?"

Julie saves the day. She always sticks up for me like that. Sometimes it's nice. Other times I feel like I have no voice in the group, like I'm just taking up space.

"Hey," Ryan says to me. "I made you a Ryan Wagner special."

He hands me a big glass, and the smell of alcohol wafts towards me, like there isn't even pop in there.

Ryan and Mason, although both stereotypical jocks, look nothing alike. Ryan is super tall with a buzzed haircut, and he's a little on the thin side, like he's been stretched out. You'd think his sport would be basketball, but he plays soccer, which is really popular around here.

"Easy on the new girl, Ryan. I don't think she's much of a drinker." I hear the hint of venom in Chloe's voice.

"I'm just trying to break her in, Chloooeee."

"Right, or something like that," Chloe shoots back. If looks could kill, Ryan would be a good six feet under right now.

Everyone heads into the living room and I'm glad to be alone for a second. *Calm down. This is what normal teenagers do. They hang out. I can handle this.*

I swirl the ice in my drink and take a sip. Maybe it'll help take the edge off—*holy crap!*—or it'll burn the roof of my mouth. Wiping a tear from my eye, I swallow it down.

I compose myself and walk into the living room. Finding a spot to sit between Mason and Ryan, I do my best to get comfortable without touching anyone in embarrassing places. I don't want to get too close to Ryan, aka Chloe's boyfriend. At least, I think he is. The way they're forever breaking up and getting back together, it's hard to stay current. They aren't a horrible fit for each other. With his preppy hair and clothes, Ryan's trying just as hard as Chloe to be something he's not. He's shuffling the cards like a pro poker player right now. He's always showing off. Tonight it's cards. Later, who knows?

I can hear the *flip, flip, flip* of the cards, the music playing low in the background, and Julie pawing through the box.

"Hey, what's this?" she asks.

Rummaging inside the cardboard box, Julie pulls out an intricately carved wooden box. Its vivid scent of cedar mixed with age takes me back to my twelfth birthday, the day Grams gave it to me.

"I forgot where I put that." The wooden box teeters precariously between her fingers as she turns it in her hands. "Careful with it, it's really old. Here, I'll go put it back in my room."

"Just a sec. I want to look at it. It's a Native piece, right? It looks like the carvings you see around here."

"It might be. My grams is full blood, and so was the person who gave it to her."

"Seriously?" Mason says. "With your blonde hair and blue eyes? I wouldn't have guessed."

"I get the blue eyes from my dad. And my hair is actually

a little darker than this. My mom dyes it for me sometimes." I twist a strand of poker-straight blonde hair around my finger before I let it fall back.

"So what is it?" Julie asks, still holding the box. She runs her fingers over the deep grooves carved into the sides. "Is it from around here?"

"I'm not sure, really."

I remember the day Grams gave it to me, and all the warnings that came with it. Over the years, I resigned myself to keeping it hidden away.

"I could ask my cousin about it," she says. "He spent a summer working at the 'Ksan museum. I bet they could tell you something."

"My grams tried that. They said stories like that are usually passed down through the Native elders. But they couldn't find anyone who recognized the carvings." I remember something Grams told me once: "History is told by those who survive it." I don't think she got the quote right, but it makes sense for this box.

We shouldn't be playing with it.

I reach across the table to grab it from Julie.

"What are you doing?"

"I'm gonna put it away."

"Just a sec," she says, still looking at it. "It's so beautiful.

Is it a jewelry box or something?"

"Uh, no. My grams called it a spirit box."

"Really?" Chloe pipes up. It's the first time she's paid attention to me all night. "Cool. What does it do?"

All their eyes are on me. I didn't ask for the attention, but it looks like I'm getting it. I settle back down in my spot between Mason and Ryan. They smell like cologne mixed with laundry soap, and the scent swiftly becomes overpowering. My leg is going numb from the effort of keeping it away from Ryan. Everyone's too . . . close. My personal bubble is on the verge of—

"Rach?" Mason touches his hand to my knee. "How does it work?"

Pop.

"Um . . . right. See these carvings? My grams called them spirit animals. There's a bear, a crow, a deer, and a wendigo." I turn the box again. "And see this? It's sort of hard if you don't know what you're looking for. But there's a stripe that weaves all around the box, intertwining the animals together. My grams told me it represents the force that interconnects everything in the world. But here's the cool part."

I press lightly on the heart carved into the chest of one of the animals. I hear a quiet *click* as I open the lid and take three small white carvings from the box. Each is about the size of a chess piece. Smooth and white, they look like they're carved from petrified bone.

"My grams called these the Great Spirits," I say, standing each one up. "A white bear, a white deer, and a white crow. Just like the ones carved on the outside of the box."

"I think you're missing a piece," Julie says. "There are four animals on the outside of the box."

"There's another one." Gently pulling the tiny knob inside the box, I lift out the false bottom. Inside is a figure carved from what looks like black, charred bone. "This is the last one. She called it a wendigo."

"It sort of looks like a wolf," Chloe says. I'm surprised. I didn't think she'd be interested in all this.

"My grams said a wendigo is more like a creature than an animal."

"I know what a wendigo is," Mason says. "At sixth-grade camp, the counselors told us about them." His hand brushes mine as he reaches for the piece. I have a million preconceptions about Mason Allen: that he's a jock, an inconsiderate jerk, and maybe even an asshole. Yet the butterflies inside me are happy to flutter at his touch. "Is it okay if I take a closer look?"

"Yeah, sure. Just be careful with it."

He bites a little on his lower lip as if he wants to say something, but he doesn't. *Down, butterflies! Down!* He settles back, examining the carving in his hand.

"According to my oh-so-reputable sources—the camp counselors—there's a legend about a wendigo."

"It's probably total bullshit," Ryan says.

"Are you gonna let him tell the story or what?" I notice the flush in Chloe's cheeks as she speaks. Wow, she's pounded half her drink already.

"I'm getting to it. Don't get your panties in a bunch." Mason smiles a teasing grin, putting the wendigo piece with the others. "So at this camp, one night my friends and I decided that the epic thing to do would be to go on a panty raid of the girls' cabins. So we bravely set off in search of their undies. But it was so late, we got totally lost in the woods. After about twenty minutes of nothing but darkness and trees, we came across a bonfire. Turns out our camp counselors had a little raid of their own that night—on the camp organizer's liquor cabinet.

"They should have marched us back the moment we showed up. But they were drunk, and obviously in no condition to be shaping young minds. So we hung out for a while. I had my first taste of apricot brandy that night." He makes a face as he remembers. "They should've left that bottle with the old lady who owned it."

Everyone laughs but me.

"Anyway, it was late and the fire was dying down. Everyone started to huddle together for warmth. That's when one of the counselors starts, 'A long time ago, before you were even born, these mountains were haunted.' He started telling us this story about a husband and wife that were camping near Hagwilget Peak."

"Where's that?" I ask.

"If it wasn't so dark you could see it from here." He motions to the bay window, but the night is black and I can't see a thing.

"The campers weren't from around here, but they'd been coming to Hazelton for years to hike the back country. So the locals knew them. They used to stay the whole season, checking in with the rangers every week or so."

I think about the people in his story, alone in the dark woods. *No thanks.*

"This went on for years—until one day they didn't check in. A search party was sent out to look for them. Their camp wasn't hard to find. They were set up in one of their usual spots. But here's the weird part. They found the couple sitting upright on a fallen log, stone-cold dead, next to what would've been their campfire from the night before. The woman was holding a full cup of cold cocoa. The man's cup had fallen beside him and spilled on the ground. They were slumped together, holding each other up, like they'd fallen asleep that way."

Mason pauses for a minute, taking a sip from his drink. The ice clinks against the walls of the glass like tiny icebergs.

"But there was something else. The searchers said there was a third cup, set on the log beside them. And the fire pit was wet, doused with water. It looked as though there were a third person who'd finished their drink and put the fire out—after the couple died."

The story brings me back to a warning Grams gave me about the spirit box: the wendigo is tainted and dark, and in many ways we are not equipped to understand it. I should have put the box away when I had the chance.

"The authorities didn't find any evidence of foul play, no poison, no reason for their deaths at all. So the case was eventually filed as unexplained. The thing is, every few years since then another dead camper shows up around here. The bodies are all found in the same peaceful state, just like that couple years ago. People say it looks like their souls have been snatched from them. Rumours started to spread that what killed them all was a wendigo."

I swallow loudly, and Mason looks over with a small smile. "You scared?"

"No, of course not," I lie.

"Well, we sure were. Because right then one of the counselors jumped out from behind a tree and howled like a maniac. Maybe we got lost the first time we ventured out of our cabin, but we sure as hell made it back." Mason raises his glass as if to toast. "In record time too."

"You ran back without the counselors?" I say. "I would have just turtled and waited for the wendigo to get me."

The sound of Chloe almost snorting her drink through her nose flushes my face red. *What's wrong with me? Inner voice!*

Mason looks over. "Don't worry. If there's ever a wendigo, I won't let it hurt you."

I'll come a-calling if I ever see one, then.

"So that's it?" Julie chimes in. "That's your wendigo story? It sounds like some random psychopath in the woods got them."

"What else is a wendigo but a random psycho in the woods?"

"The wendigo isn't a psycho," I say. "My grams told me it brings the balance back, but that you should never ask it for anything."

"What do you mean, ask it for stuff?" Chloe says between crunches of ice. She's holding the white crow piece, running her finger along its wing.

"She said that the Great Spirits grant wishes. Wishes that can help when you need it, but that can also curse. Because nothing asked of the Great Spirits is ever harmless."

"Have you tried it?" Julie asks. "Or is it totally hokey? Like throwing a penny in a well."

"I don't know. It's probably not real or anything. Just a

story."

I see Chloe's lips moving as she holds the crow in front of her face then nestles it back into its groove inside the box.

"Chloe, what did you just do?"

"I made a wish!" she says. "I just whispered what I wanted and put it back in the box. Is that how you do it?"

I have no voice. All my thoughts are swirling around, dying to get out, but I will not let the storm escape.

"It's just a box, Rachel. Chill." All I see are her sticky, candy-pink lips. But her words *snick* yet another string inside me.

"Come on." Julie's hand feels ice-cold against mine as she reaches across the coffee table. "We'll make a game of it. Let's make a rule that says the wishes have to be good. You can't wish harm on anyone. And they have to be about Hazelton." She gives my hand a little squeeze. "And then you can put it back and we can get to playing cards."

I thought a funnel cloud was on the horizon. I thought the night might get torn apart, but the sky is only as cloudy as I think it is.

"I'm not sure. It's not a toy. Maybe we should just put it away."

"Come on. It'll be fun. What are you going to wish for?"

I'm annoyed she can't recognize the angst I'm having about all this. *You've opened my boxes! We shouldn't be messing with this!*

"I don't know. You can give my turn to Ryan. I don't really want to."

Ryan puts both hands up. "No thanks. I made it a rule not to fool with stuff like this. Ever since that psychic at the fair last year, anything like this gives me the creeps. Remember, Mason?"

Mason nods but says nothing, holding the black wendigo piece in his hand.

Julie picks up the white bear and hands me the white deer. "It's your game. You have to play."

"I told you, it's not a game."

"Whatever. You know what I mean. I'll go next. While you think of your wish."

We all watch as Julie brings the white bear close her face to make eye contact then whispers to it. She then places the piece back in its groove inside the box.

"OK, your turn."

Everyone is watching me. I can't concentrate. What would I wish for if I could have anything? *Just think of something.*

I turn the piece over and over again in my hands, feeling its smoothness, trying to think of something unique, something cool to wish for, but I'm drawing a blank.

Until I know. Or don't know, if that makes any sense. I'll wish that I knew what I wanted, and that I'll find it here, in

Hazelton. It fits Julie's little rules. And if it comes true, I'll have gotten exactly what I wanted without having to think about it too much. I'm a genius at wishing. I could write a book on it!

I concentrate on my obscure wish, whispering it to the little white deer cupped in my hands. Placing it in the box, I look over at Mason. He's watching me again, a small smile on his lips. Why would a guy like him pay any attention to me? *You're dreaming. You probably have a nugget of grossness on your face.* As nonchalantly as possible, I brush my hand over my face before speaking. "Your turn, Mason."

Mason straightens up a little taller as he looks at the carved piece in his hand. "Okay. I wish that my dad's company would make some progress around here. It's been a major dry spell for ages. Bringing some new jobs back to town would be good for everyone."

My wish was pretty selfish compared to his. I would never have guessed he'd wish for something like that. Maybe he did it for my benefit, to show he's not just some self-centered jock?

There you go again. Why would he care what you think? He's not into you. You're not his type.

Hesitating slightly, Mason places the wendigo piece back in the box. "Not that it's ever gonna happen. It would take a miracle."

"Why?"

"Because people don't like oil and gas projects around here. Haven't you noticed all the billboards?"

I've seen the signs, but I'd never put much thought in to them. "Yeah. But I don't really keep up on that sort of stuff."

Mason doesn't say anything, just takes his hand away from the box, leaving the wendigo piece there.

"Wait." Chloe's voice breaks the silence. "My wish sucked compared to Mason's. I need a do-over."

"That's not how it works, Chloe. You can't change your wish." The tone of Ryan's voice is harsh, insinuating that she's stupid without saying the word.

"Who are you, the wish police? I can change it if I want to!"

"Why? What'd you wish for?"

"I'm not telling you, or it won't come true."

"Oh my God. You're, like, five years old. You wished for a new purse, didn't you?"

Ryan could be the poster jerk for childhood bullying, except at eighteen, he isn't really a child anymore. Not that I'd consider him an adult.

"Fine! I wished I were—" Chloe murmurs under her breath.

"Sorry. I didn't hear you."

"Rich and famous! God, Ryan, why do you always have

to bug like this? I wished that I were rich and famous."

"In Hazelton?" He laughs. "That's a joke."

"That's why I'm making a new wish." Chloe reaches into the box for the white crow, but it won't budge. It's as if the piece has become fused to the box. "Rachel, the crow won't come out. I think your game is broken."

I watch as Chloe pulls her hand away, her fingers grazing the lip of the box. It's like I'm seeing it in slow motion—but it can't be. Her fingers clear the edge of the spirit box, and without hesitation, the lid snaps shut.

Clack!

The momentum almost topples it off the coffee table. But the box just teeters there, rocking back and forth a few times, like one of those bottom-heavy blow-up dummies.

And that's my cue.

I back away, jumping onto the couch behind me like a scared child. A loud and almost involuntary "Holy shit!" comes out of my mouth. I stare at the box with wide eyes, pointing. "Did you guys see that? I knew we shouldn't have played with it!"

"Easy," Chloe says. "The lid is probably spring-loaded or something." I look down at Chloe and realize I'm the only one standing on the couch. Ryan is covering his mouth, hiding a laugh.

I'm so lame.

Keep it together. There's an explanation for this. The lid is spring-loaded.

"Come on. Sit," Mason says. "We'll open this thing back up and show you there's no boogeyman." He touches my foot and motions for me to sit beside him. For a guy who acts like a total child ninety percent of the time, he can be sort of nice—on occasion.

Taking a deep breath, I ease myself back down beside him. I reach for the box again. But it slides away from me, towards the center of the coffee table.

"Okay! You all had to have seen that! It just moved. This thing is creeping me out. Time to put it away."

"Chill. It's probably one of these jackasses bumping the table," Julie tries to reassure me, while Ryan and Mason shrug innocently. "Everyone, hands on the table where we can all see them. And no bumping."

Everyone places their hands on the edge of the coffee table.

You can do this, Rachel. Just pick up the box and see if the lid still works. Then you can put it away and forget we ever opened it.

The box stays put when I pick it up this time. It's just a box. Nothing weird going on here. I find the carved heart and give it a push to unlock the lid. Nothing. I try again, but it won't open. Picking at the lid doesn't work either.

"Great. I think it's broken."

No sooner do the words escape my mouth than there comes a piercing screech from inside the box. I don't think, I just react, dropping the box. As it falls from my hands, it hits the coffee table, bouncing off onto the shag carpet right between Julie and Chloe. They both shoot up, scrambling away from it.

Everyone's on their feet now. Julie, Mason, and I dart into the kitchen, crouching down in front of the sink. Chloe and Ryan run for cover behind Gram's favorite recliner.

The screeching subsides a notch only to make scratching and bumping noises. Something is trying to get out. It's like metal on metal. Scraping. Grinding. Every scrape, every thud, sends me deeper inside my head, burrowing into a place where I try to imagine this isn't happening.

My dark clouds are choking out the light.

The tiny nook in front of the kitchen sink is tight for all three of us. I'm pressed between Julie and Mason. We all stare as the box thrashes on the floor, bumping into the coffee table, then off the side of the couch.

Just as swiftly as it started, the box stops. Still and silent.

I look around, finding the pale faces of my friends. No one moves. No one says anything. Are they thinking that any little sound might set it off again? 'Cuz that's what I'm thinking.

Click.

It's the soft yet deafening sound of the wooden box unlocking. *Shit.* Our eyes whirl back to the spot where it landed. I don't want to look, but my morbid curiosity gets the better of me.

The lid slowly opens, letting out a gentle mist. It creeps without a sound along the shag carpet floor. The scent of wet earth and ferns after a rain fills the room. The cupboards under the sink creak as I press myself more tightly against them. The mist creeps towards us, crossing the division between living room shag and kitchen linoleum. It starts to fill the hallway, too, all the way to the bedrooms. The mist is everywhere. So much is pouring out that the box is overtaken by it, lost in the weeping tendrils from within.

Julie, Mason, and I stand up so our heads won't be swallowed by the mist. Three pale blue orbs rise from where the box sits invisible below the mist. The orbs emerge, drifting up like floating ash from a fire. I watch in awe, enchanted by their every move.

There's something strange about all this. Yes, the mist, and the orbs, everything is strange, but I'm not afraid. That's it. I'm not afraid. The feeling is cloudy and confusing, but that's it.

The pale orbs reach the ceiling and dissolve right through it. I'm lost in my own little world. *Focus on the spot. Where did they go?* A sharp gasp of air from Julie focuses my attention again—not on her, but on Mason.

Mason's face, just inches from mine, is dusted with a dark

purple glow. A fourth orb hovers inches in front of him. It's darker and larger than the other three, a swirling mass of dark purple. The wendigo? A lone, hot tear streaks down my face. Fear is creeping in. This is real.

What have I done? My heart is beating like I've run a marathon, but my breathing is unnaturally steady.

The orb hangs in mid-air, waiting. Then it shoots up, dissolving through the ceiling like the others. The room is silent. Looking back to the living room, I see that the mist has disapated. The wooden box lays open on the floor, fallen over on its side. The room is just as it was, except for the five pasty white people standing in silence.

"Mason, are you okay?" I reach over, touching his arm. "Mason?" His arm feels warm, really warm, like he's been sitting in front of a fire. Blinking slowly, he looks over at me.

"I'm okay. I'm better than okay, actually. I feel amazing." A confused yet genuine smile crosses his lips.

"What did that thing do to you?" I ask.

"Nothing. I just . . . feel great." I'm still gripping his arm a little too hard, but I don't let go. "I have to say, that was the most amazing thing I've ever seen. What the hell was that?"

"Um, I don't know." I look around at everyone, letting my hand slide from Mason's arm. "Is everyone okay?" They all seem so calm.

"I have to agree with Mason," Julie says. "I feel . . . good? Don't get me wrong, the way that box was screaming was putting me in need of a new pair of undies, but I'm okay. Maybe it was that mist." Julie takes a deep breath. "I can still smell it a little."

"Really? No one is freaked out?" I look around at their faces. Nobody says anything. *What is this, the twilight zone?* I glance at the box again. It looks just as it did before we started playing with it, except the carvings have all tumbled out onto the floor.

"Hey." Ryan raises his hand from the back of the recliner he and Chloe are still crouched behind. "I hate to be that guy, but I'm pretty fucking weirded out by this whole thing. So whoever is catching a ride with me is leaving now."

Weirded out. That's the understatement of the year. Jerk is right on, though. Ryan's keys jingle in his pocket as he stands up. He and Chloe head for the back door to get their jackets.

If ever there was a time I'd like the two of them to hang out longer, this is it.

I turn to Julie. "Are you leaving too?" *Please. Please. Please, don't leave me. I think we all just released some sort of ancient box ghost or something. Don't leave me here in this house alone.*

"Interesting after-party." Mason gives me one of his one-armed bear hugs again. "Don't be scared. I'll stay if you want." He gives me this sly little wink. *Yeah, that's not making me feel any better, but thanks, big man.*

"Go with Ryan," Julie says. "I'll stay with Rach. I don't have to be home for a while anyway. You can give me a ride home later, right?"

"Of course. Yes." My words come out rushed. "I have my mom's truck. Thanks." And that's why Julie is my best friend. Best friends don't leave friends alone in creepy, mist-filled houses.

The roar of Ryan's truck can be heard for blocks as he pulls away from the house. "I thought his dad bought him that truck brand new. Why does it sound like it has no muffler?" I ask as Julie digs for mugs in the cupboard.

"Boys and their toys. Ryan's money burns holes in his pocket. It's some custom job he had done to it. He's probably making up with *that* ride for the lack of what Chloe gets to ride."

I have to laugh at that, even if I have a million other things on my mind.

"I'm making us tea. Where does your grams keep the tea bags?"

"In the drawer right next to the sink. I'll have whatever."

I watch as Julie fills the mugs with water and puts them in the microwave. When they're done, she plunks a tea bag in each and brings them over to the kitchen table. Sitting with a huff, I plunk myself down on a chair. Wrapping my fingers around the steaming cup of tea, I breathe in deeply. Unfortunately, it doesn't have the same effect as that mist. My problems are all still here.

"Thanks, Julie."

"For the tea? No problem."

"No, for not leaving." I drown my tea bag with my spoon, pushing it to the bottom. "I just invited people over for some drinks and cards and . . . *that* happened!" I motion to the box laying open in the living room. "You guys are never going to want to hang out with me again."

"I wouldn't say that. Sure, this is probably the strangest thing any of us has ever seen, but we all like you. Hey." She gives my shoulder a little push. "Don't frown too much. You'll give yourself wrinkles. You're too pretty for wrinkles. On a different note, I guess we know that wishing box works. I can't wait for mine to come true. Could you imagine?"

"Why? What did you wish for?"

"For a new community center," she says. "One with a gym, and a games room, and a place to take classes and work out and stuff. I've been on the committee at school for it for, like, two years. It doesn't seem like it's ever going to happen."

I know the project she's talking about. My grams dragged me to a craft sale at the community center once. The building looks like it's made entirely out of school portables, like a patchwork quilt. The town has been raising funds for years to build a new one. It's just one of the many projects Julie gets involved in around here. That's why she's a lifer. She loves this town. She's never going to leave it.

Julie's watching me over the rim of her cup. "So what was your wish?"

I let the waiting air in my lungs huff out. "I wished that . . . that I knew what I wanted, and that I'd find it here in Hazelton." Saying it out loud doesn't sound as awesome as it did in my head. The look on her face makes me wonder if my best friend just found out what a nut bar I really am.

"I like it," she says finally. "I hope you find whatever it is you're looking for too." She sounds convincing. Thank God. I don't know what I'd do without my rock.

"Do you want me to call my mom and ask her if I can stay over? Or you could come stay at my place if you're too creeped out to stay here alone."

She knows what I'm thinking without me saying a word. "It's okay. I'll be fine." *I'll be no more screwed up than I already am.*

"Okay. I'll at least help you clean up a bit." She puts her mug in the sink before going to the living room. I see her hesitate for a second before bending down to sweep the carved animal pieces back into the box. "The wendigo piece isn't here."

"Don't worry about it. It's probably under the couch. I'll find it later." Maybe it's best if no one else but me touches the box from now on. "Do you want me to take you home?"

It takes only ten minutes to drive from my place to Julie's. Surprisingly, I feel relieved to be driving home alone. I hear my thoughts better this way, just me and the dark of the night. The moon is almost full, but its light barely touches the blackness out here.

Julie's place is a bit out of town, and on this road there aren't any streetlights—or houses. A heavy fog hugs the ground. It's hypnotic, swirling in my headlights as I drive. What happened tonight? There must be some explanation for those orb lights and those terrible sounds that came from the box.

The fog swirls on the road. The fog swirls in my mind.

I feel my body tense before I even know what I'm doing, and I see something ahead on the road. My knuckles turn white on the steering wheel. My foot hits the brake. I brace myself, but it's too late to stop before I hit it. I have two choices: either hit whatever's blocking my path head on—or hit the ditch.

The fog is thick. The road is slick. The tires are screeching.

I swerve. I miss it. And that's when I finally see its full outline. Standing in the middle of the road, silent and still, is a massive, snow white deer.

CHAPTER TWO

Tap tap tap.

A blunt pain in my forehead throbs. Crap. I hit the ditch. The hazy image of the truck's dashboard comes slowly into focus.

Tap tap.

I squint, as if that will help me hear the sound better. *Did I hit that deer? Was it really white?* I struggle to sort out the truth of what just happened.

Tap tap tap.

"Are you okay in there?" A muted voice comes from the other side of the mud-spattered truck window.

The truck has stopped. It's tilted at an unnatural angle and the seatbelt buckle is digging in to my right hip. My head is so foggy right now that I don't think my motor skills can regroup to unbuckle it. How long have I been here? Did I pass out or something?

Still breathing?

Check.

Heart beating?

Check.

Head hurting like a three-day hangover?

Check.

Still alive.

"Hey!" The voice from outside is yelling. "Are you okay in there?"

That person is still there. Still knocking on the window. It feels like they're knocking on my head.

A hand smears away the little specks of mud from the glass. I watch the whole scene like it isn't really happening to me. Two hands cup against the window and a face peers in. I stare back like a fish in a bowl, but it's too dark to see any features. I should say something. I want to say something, but the words keep swirling in my head without coming out.

The glow from the truck's dash, this person's incessant knocking, my splitting headache—it's all too much to process. It feels like everything's running on high speed except me. Closing my eyes only serves to make my head throb more. *Just stop for a minute, world, and let me catch up. I'm stuck in slow motion while you're whirling at warp speed.* A jarring noise from the door handle brings me back to the moment. The door won't open—it's locked.

"Can you unlock the door?" the muted voice asks.

My hand reaches towards the door lock, leaving a blurred trail as it moves. *Door open? Yeah . . . sure.* It occurs to me a split-second after I do it that I have no idea who's on the other side. A whoosh of cold night air hits me in the face as the door flings open. The sudden movement speeds my slow-motion world to normal.

"Whoa, I got ya." His voice is deep and kind. "I was driving behind you and I saw your taillights go into the ditch. Are you okay? What happened?"

"I . . ." The blood in my body can't decide where it wants to be, in my head or in my toes. With trembling fingers, I run my hand along my forehead to find a bump protruding, and groan.

"You hit your head?" I hear his voice but can't see his face. The darkness from outside and the glaring light from inside divides us. "Is it all right if I take a look?"

Bright lights, throbbing head, constricting seatbelt, total stranger leaning towards me—make it stop. My head is spinning. I can't breathe. *Remember to breathe, Rachel.* I shut my eyes tightly and shrink into my seat. I'm as far away from all this as I can be without actually going anywhere. *This night. My life. That deer. My head. This guy. Just leave me alone, world!*

It's too dark outside . . . I can't tell what the weather is like.

"Hey, sorry." His voice softens. "I didn't mean to freak you out. I was just trying to help." My eyes are shut but I can feel he's backed off a bit.

This isn't some horror movie. Get it together and say something. Open your eyes. I focus straight ahead, not turning to look his way. My hands are a splotchy pink and white from gripping the steering wheel. "My . . . dear. Um, no, I mean a deer. I think I almost hit a white deer—on the road." Good for me. Words—and they almost made a sentence.

"A white deer?" he says. "I've been around here a long time, and I've never seen a white one. Maybe it just looked white in your headlights." Without warning, he reaches across me and into the cab of the truck. What's he doing? Crawling in? My heart skips a beat.

"Easy. I'm just turning off the ignition." His voice is soft. "You're kind of jumpy, aren't you?"

I will my eyes to focus. *Just do it. Get a good look at this would-be axe murderer-slash-helper.* I look to the person filling the void left by the open truck door, and—he's not at all what I expected.

A perfectly angled, baby smooth, tanned jaw line greets me with the widest smile I've ever seen. *Wow.* He's holding out my truck keys for me. I watch them dangle from his fingers. His sleeve is rolled up, exposing a lean, toned forearm. My eyes keep drifting up, finding his deep brown eyes smiling at me. *Wow . . .*

Take the keys, Rachel!

"Thanks." I reach up to take them.

"Let's start over." I hear the laughter in his voice. "My name is Nathan Grey Hawk, but you can call me Nate."

I'm staring. I'm staring at him and I can't stop myself. He looks like a male model on the cover of a romance novel. He sweeps his long, black hair behind his ear when it falls forward onto his face. It seems to fall to the middle of his back. What I wouldn't give for hair that nice. He keeps on talking, and I just sit here like a zombie. *Tell him your name. Tell him anything.* I smile back at him, but I can't think. *Focus on something else.* He's wearing coveralls. They're kind of dirty. They smell faintly of gasoline.

"You smell like gas."

Holy fuck. What is wrong with me? If I don't die from obvious brain damage, I might just die of embarrassment. "No!" I spit out in a rush. "I'm sorry." The volume of my voice is way too loud. "I mean, my name is Rachel. Thank you for stopping. Thank you." My heart is pounding in my head.

Nate lets out a whole-hearted laugh. "I probably do smell like gas," he says, with a smirk. "My clothes are probably covered in it. I just came from work." He looks right at me with those brown eyes, and I have to look away.

"So, Rachel. Do you mind if I take a look at that bump on

your head? Just to see if I should be taking you to the hospital."
He stands patiently, waiting at the truck door for my okay.

I nod in reply, not wanting to speak for fear of releasing another idiotic comment.

He gently moves a loose strand of my hair away, tucking it behind my ear. I wince when he touches the bump on my forehead. "You're probably going to have a nasty headache in the morning, but I think you'll live. Although that's my non-medical opinion. As you may have noticed, I'm not a doctor—and I smell like gasoline."

"I—"

"I'm just teasing." Everybody's a joker in this town except me. "Come on. Let's get you out of here. That seatbelt cannot be comfortable. It looks like it's cutting you in half. Do you need help unbuckling it?"

"No," I say quickly. "I got it." As much as I'd like his gorgeous, gasoline-smelling, supermodel arm reaching over me, I'd rather do it myself.

I suck in my stomach muscles hard to provide just enough slack to unbuckle it. *Click.* The flood of relief is short-lived as I'm catapulted towards the passenger side of the truck. *Oh yeah, the truck's in a steep ditch.* Somehow that detail slipped my mind.

It's not quite an ass-over-teakettle tumble, but close. The

console dividing the front seats manages to slow me down so my head doesn't bounce off the passenger-side door. Unfortunately, though, my butt is now stuck up in the air for my helpful new friend to see.

What underwear did I put on today? Am I wearing big sail-sheet granny panties or some elastic string that passes as women's underwear? Dammed if I can remember, I think with horror. I'm pretty sure Nate has an excellent view of them right about now.

"Are you okay?" I feel the truck shift. He must be getting in the driver's seat.

"Yeah." That wasn't very convincing. My last shred of dignity sits sadly somewhere in the back of my mind, waving a white flag of defeat. "Just a sec, okay? I need to grab my bag."

My messenger bag has lost its contents all over the floor of the truck, and I figure I might as well get it while I'm down here. I stretch to reach my spilled things, which sends me sliding deeper in the foot well of the truck. I almost crumple in the bottom when I feel Nate's hand gripping the back of my jeans to stop me.

Oh my God. Hold on, jeans! Don't you dare slip down further.

Finding my cell phone hidden beneath a mini-pack of Kleenex, I click it on. Out of service. *Seriously?* I'm upside-down, half-shoved in the foot well of my truck, precariously hooked by the belt loop of my jeans to the hottest stranger I've ever met.

Maybe we're not really strangers anymore. He's probably memorized the exact colour and shape of my underwear by now.

"Um," I say, clearing my throat, "my cell has no bars." My voice echoes in the truck foot well. *Don't let it rain. One drop, two. You control your own weather.* "This night just keeps on getting better."

"Hey, don't worry about it." Nate hauls me out of the foot well by my hips, setting me back in the driver's seat as he moves back outside. "Reception can get spotty out here. You can try mine if you want. Maybe it's better." He pauses, like he's considering his words. "Or I could just give you a ride home or whatever."

Who am I going to call, anyway? Mom? Grams? This will just remind them how Eric died. I won't do that to them. I won't remind them how easy it is to lose someone. I can handle this. This is my fault—my problem.

"I guess I don't have much choice, do I?" I say, looking down at my phone. "A ride home would be great, thanks." His enormous smile is infectious, and I find myself letting just a small one cross my lips in response. "Or wait—do you think I could just drive the truck out of the ditch?"

He steps back from the truck, offering me his hand. "I'm not trying to judge here, but maybe you shouldn't drive anymore tonight." His smile twists, holding in a laugh. "Plus, the ditch is way too muddy and steep to drive your truck out."

My hope of hiding this from Mom and Grams is fading. "Great. How am I supposed to get it out of the ditch?" I cover my face with my hands. "My mom's never going to let me drive it again."

"It's your lucky night, then," he says. "I work at a garage in town and we have a tow truck. I can have it out for you by morning."

A smile warms my face. Maybe this will all work out.

I sling my bag over my shoulder and reach for his outstretched hand.

"Try to step close to where I am. It's pretty muddy out here," Nate says, guiding me out of the door. It's difficult to see the steepness of the ditch, but judging from the angle of the truck, it's not going to be an easy climb.

I inch myself off the driver's seat, trying to spot where to step. It's too dark. I can barely see the ground. Taking a tense, deep breath, I step out. My foot makes contact with the soft, damp earth and I know in that second what's going to happen. There's no time to react. My foot instantly plunges calf-deep into the boggy mud. As my leg sinks down, the force hurls the rest of me forward. Arms flailing, elbows pointing, body launching, I fly forward, ploughing hard in to Nate's chest. I think he tries to catch me. It's all a dark, muddy blur. With a slurping splat, the two of us slide to a stop. He's landed on his back with me on top, the pair of us a muddy, tangled mess. I'm sure from the sting in my elbow that I've hit him pretty hard somewhere.

"I'm so sorry! Did I hit you?" My hands pat around in the darkness, feeling his chest in front of me. Only when I shift a little does the light from the truck interior shine on him. He's squinting, one eye closed, holding his forehead.

"I guess we'll both have a headache in the morning," he says with a smile.

I should be embarrassed beyond repair. I should be apologizing again, but I'm not. I'm laughing. The kind of laugh that starts from your gut and moves through you, punctuated by the odd involuntary snort. I can't decide if it feels good or crazy, but I don't stop.

Letting out a deep sigh, I find my voice again. "I'm sorry to laugh, it's just—" I wipe away something close to my eye with my fingers, only to leave a wet trail down my face. I see now that my hands are covered in mud. I'm covered in mud. And I'm straddling Nate like a human mud-sled. "It's just kind of funny."

"Well, I've never been tackled by a beautiful girl in the mud before, and funny isn't the first word I'd use to describe this —but it's somewhere down the list."

The only words my teenage brain hears are *beautiful girl*, coming from the flawless lips of a mud-covered Adonis. The heat in my face rises but I don't look away. My mouth gapes a little. I should say something. *Boys don't call me beautiful.* My inner thought bubble bursts when it occurs to me that I'm straddling this guy and neither of us are doing anything about it. I should probably move. *Yep, any time now . . .*

"Um, we should probably go—or get up?" I say, finally acknowledging the intensely intimate nature of this position.

"Whenever you're ready," he says, moving his hands to rest under his head. "You kind of got me pinned here."

I'm on the edge of getting lost in his eyes. On the edge of forgetting what I just said to him. *Focus!*

I try rolling off to the right, but the truck door is in the way. My hands up on either side of his face, I do a sort of push-up. Pushing my hips down, I try to get leverage on my stuck leg by yanking on it as hard as I can. It seems like a good—and totally innocent—maneuver in the moment, until I realize what it must look like for the person lying under me. *I give up.* I rest my head down on Nate's chest, catching my breath. I can feel him trying to choke back a laugh.

"Oh, you think you can do better?" With my head pressed to his overalls, the words come out muddied and muffled. His breath catches, like he's going to say something but changes his mind.

"I can probably get your leg unstuck, if you'd like some help." I look up as he takes his hands out from behind his head and places them both on my hips. I'm suddenly very aware that a few of his fingers are touching my bare skin. "Bend your knees and put your hands around my neck."

I do as he says. He sits, lifting me a bit so he can move his hips higher up the sloped wall of the ditch. The result is not much different than the position we were in before, except now his face is just inches from mine. "And how is this better?" I ask.

"I can reach your ankle and get you unstuck." His hand moves down my leg, still half-buried in mud. He has to reach around me to grab my leg, which brings his mouth right up to my ear. I can feel him breathing. I'm not sure if I am.

With a heave and a loud slurp, my foot comes free of the boggy ditch. Minus my shoe. He lets go of my foot, sitting more upright. The crisp night air fills the tiny space between us. "I'll have to get your shoe when I come back for the truck. I think it's too dark to find it now." With both his hands on my hips, he lifts me up effortlessly and sets me beside him on the wet grass.

I watch while he climbs the steep bank. At the top, he offers me his hand to pull me up. The moment before my hand reaches his a wicked thought pops in my head. I could pull him back down in the mud.

But I don't. That's enough fearless Rachel for one night.

I sit quietly on the passenger side of Nate's truck as he drives me home. We don't say much. Mostly I just look out the window or fidget with my seatbelt. Every moment of silence between us is like coming down from some supernatural high.

My house is dark except for the single light outside. He pulls his truck into the driveway and shifts it into park.

"So," he says, like it's the first breath he's taken in a while, "here you are, safe and sound." He looks over at me, motioning to my forehead. "You know, you never really told me how bad that bump on your head is. I heard that if you have a concussion you're not supposed to go to sleep for at least two hours. Are you sure you don't want to go to the hospital? I could take you. I don't mind."

"I'll be okay. You've already done so much. And if it makes you feel any better, I don't think I'll be getting much sleep tonight. Today has been—something else." He waits for an explanation, but I don't say any more.

"Maybe you'll tell me about it sometime." He looks awkward somehow, crunching his face a little when he talks. "Oh wait, here's where I work." He digs around in one of the cubbies and hands me a business card. "I'll have your truck towed there in the morning. We open at nine, but stop by whenever."

"Thanks—Nathan." I read his full name off the business card. Owner and operator. *Impressive.* He looks too young to own a business.

"Call me Nate."

"Thanks, Nate." I open the passenger side door and slide out. "I'll see you tomorrow."

I watch him drive away after I reach the side door of the house. The slide and click of the lock seem to echo for miles. I've memorized how far it is to the left of the doorway before my fingers reach the light switch. I flick it and hear the familiar buzz and ping of the kitchen fluorescents coming to life. Everything is just as I left it. Standing in the silence of my gram's kitchen, I can't help but feel that something has been set in motion. It's a nagging thought that things will never be the same.

CHAPTER THREE

Ring ring ring ring.

Come on, Julie, pick up the phone. Please be up.

"Hello?" a groggy Julie answers.

"Hey, it's Rachel. Did I wake you up?"

"Yeah . . . What time is it?"

"It's about quarter to eight."

A deep sigh comes from her end of the phone. "It's Saturday. That time of day does not exist on weekends for people our age."

"I waited as long as I could before I called you. I need a ride somewhere—and I was hoping you could drive me." There's a long pause while her half-asleep brain processes the request.

"You're talking too fast. And why can't you just drive yourself?"

"I kind of crashed my mom's truck last night." Dead air hangs between us for a moment.

"Kind of? Holy shit, what happened?" Julie's awake now.

"It was just a few minutes after I dropped you off. I'm fine though. I almost hit a white deer, lost control, and hit the ditch."

"Why didn't you call me last night?"

"I don't know. I—"

"I'll be over as soon as I can."

"Thanks."

"Are you okay?"

No. I haven't been okay for a long time. "Yeah. Just come over, 'kay?"

About twenty minutes later, there's a knock at the back door. Before I can even say hello or open the door, Julie's inside. She crosses the few steps into the kitchen and gives me hug without saying a word. The chunky blue and purple highlights in her shoulder-length hair are a frazzled mess, which isn't like her. Julie's always ready for her close-up. She's also sporting what looks like yesterday's makeup.

"I'm here," she says, a little out of breath. "What

happened?" She untwines from me, holding my shoulders at arm's length. "From the beginning this time." It's more of a command than a request.

"I told you. After I dropped you off, I was driving home and almost hit a giant white deer standing in the middle of the road. I lost control and hit the ditch." Julie pulls out a chair at the kitchen table and sits down. I follow her lead and do the same.

"You're sure it was white?"

"Yes. Why doesn't anyone believe that the deer was white? Its whole body was white, like that little carving in the wooden box." I don't ask if she's thinking what I'm thinking.

She closes her eyes, rubbing her fingers underneath them. She smudges away her mascara shadows. "Maybe it was white. White bears have been around this area for years. Maybe there are white deer now too." The way she passes it off makes me wonder if I'm trying too hard to make this deer into something more than it is.

"So, how did you get home? I'm assuming your truck is still in the ditch, since it isn't in the driveway."

"Well, it might be out by now." I wince at the memory of the throbbing bump on my head.

"Oh my God. What happened to your head?" Julie brushes back a few strands of hair on my forehead.

"It's nothing. I must have hit my head when I went in the

ditch. I tried to cover it with makeup this morning. You still see it? I heard if you use green-coloured makeup it helps cover up bruises. Or maybe that's for zits. Anyway, I think I've made it look worse."

"Stop avoiding the question. How did you get home? And where's your mom's truck?"

"Okay, chill. I'm getting to that part." She lets my hair fall back over my ill-covered bump. "I banged my head on the steering wheel when I crashed. I think I might have blacked out for a few minutes, but I'm fine. That's how I got this." I point to my forehead. "I woke up to the sound of someone knocking on the truck window."

"You blacked out? Do you have a concussion?"

"I don't think so. It just looks bad. I'm hoping it shrinks so I can cover it before my mom gets back."

"You should probably tell your mom. She's not going to get mad at you. It was an accident."

An accident. That's what happened to my brother. *No, I can still fix this.*

"Just—trust me on this one. Don't tell my mom, okay?"

She quirks her lips into a frown, but agrees with a nod. "So, who was knocking on the truck window?"

I remember Nate's giant, white smile. "He said his name was Nathan—or Nate—Grey Hawk."

"Nathan Grey Hawk?"

"Yeah, Nate. Do you know him?"

"Son of Maren Grey Hawk?"

"I don't know, maybe. Who's that?"

"Maren Grey Hawk is on the town council. He's one of the most vocal members, always speaking about the evils of the oil and gas industry. He's a big reason why you don't see more projects going on around here."

Julie volunteers for virtually every community involvement group at school. I guess it's not a total surprise that she would know about what goes on at the town meetings too. She mentioned once that her mom goes to them all the time. Like mother, like daughter, I guess. This small-town mentality is still new to me.

"I've also heard," she goes on, "that Chloe's cousin hangs out with his sister . . . and they're always getting into serious bad shit."

"Serious bad shit?"

"Yeah."

"What's that supposed to mean?"

"It means that you probably shouldn't hang around with some people in this town. I'm just trying to help you out."

But you hang out with Chloe, whose cousin is into 'serious bad shit'? That's what I should say, but I don't. "Well, he seems nice to me. And I'm not hanging out with him, so just chill. He just took my truck back to his shop. That's why I need a ride, to go get it."

"You let him drive your truck—and take you home?"

"Yeah. He didn't drive it. He towed it. I think he owns that garage on the highway. Since you seem to know so much about him, have you ever actually met him?"

"I don't need to meet him to know that he's not the kind of person we hang out with."

"*We* hang out with?"

Julie fumbles with a loose thread on her hoodie. "Look, you're not from here. You don't know what it's like to grow up here. There are politics, even for people our age. You should just take my word for it that he's not part of our crowd." She finally breaks the thread on her hoodie and tucks in the loose end. "Let's just get your mom's truck back, okay?" She manages a half-hearted smile. I can tell there's a lot she's not saying, but I let it slide.

"Thanks. I'll get my bag." There'll be time to talk later. For now, I just need the truck back.

The ride there is short, which leaves me no time to think about what I'm going to say to Nate, even though I've been up all night thinking about it. There are no other vehicles in the gravel parking lot when we pull in, but I do see Nate's truck, along with another one parked around back. I realize I've been past this place every day for months now. The building is in slight disrepair, but it looks like someone's been fixing it up. The bright red paint on the bay doors is peeling, but the trim and some of the windows look brand new. There's a huge painted sign above the doors that reads *Grey Hawk's Automotive*. I guess if I'd grown up here the name *Grey Hawk* would have clicked when I heard it.

Julie shifts her car into park and turns off the ignition. "Do you want me to come in with you?" she asks.

It probably isn't the best idea for her to come in—she obviously doesn't like Nate or his family—but I don't want to go in alone. "Sure. If you want to?" *I'm such a chicken shit.*

A musty veil of engine oil and tires greets us as we walk through the door into the front office. There are some dusty chairs and a high counter, but not much else.

"Are you sure they're even open? It is Saturday," Julie says, shoving her hands in her pockets. She starts wandering around the tiny waiting area, looking at the car posters that plaster the walls.

"He said they opened at nine. Besides, the door would have been locked, right?"

"Well, is there a bell or something? It'd be nice to make this quick." Julie's not much of a morning person, but this grumpy attitude isn't like her.

I look around on the counter for a bell, but there's

nothing but an archaic computer and a cup filled with chewed-up pens.

"Good morning." A sing-song voice comes from an open doorway behind the counter. "I thought I heard someone come in." A dark-haired, late-thirties, Native man in navy blue coveralls comes through the door at the back of the office. "What can I do for you ladies this morning?"

"Hi. I'm looking for Nate. He said he'd tow my truck here for me."

"Oh, you must be Rachel." A smile brightens his face. *Oh God.* He totally knows about the mud and the ditch. I wonder how much Nate told him.

"He's got your truck up on the lift right now. Come on through." He motions us to follow him, and we head through the back door behind the counter and across two bays of the shop. I see my mom's truck up on a lift, caked in mud up to its side mirrors. "Nate," the man in coveralls yells over the shrill whine of some sort of power tool, "you have some visitors."

Nate emerges from behind the truck looking even more perfect than the night before, if that's even possible. He's not wearing coveralls this time. Instead he has on a fitted black T-shirt with faded jeans that hug every lean, sculpted inch of his godliness. I have to consciously reel in my gaze. *You are not here to drool. So he's good looking. Keep it together.*

"Thanks, Sam," Nate says, wiping his hands on a shop

rag.

Sam turns to Julie and me before leaving and gives us a nod. "You girls have a good day."

Nate makes his way to a sink on the back wall of the shop and starts washing his hands. "You're here early," he says to us over his shoulder. "I thought you might sleep in after last night." He dries his hands on a towel that hangs over the edge of the sink before turning to face us. "Hi, I'm Nate." He extends his hand to Julie.

For a brief moment, she hesitates. *Come on. Don't be an ass. Maybe I don't understand how things work around here, but—*

"Julie." She replies with one word as she shakes his hand.

"Nice to meet you." He lets go, seemingly unaware of her hesitation. "So"—he shoots me a smile that may have just stopped time—"your mom's truck has seen better days, but I think I can have it fixed for you in no time. Come with me, I'll show you." He keeps talking as he walks around to the other side of the truck. "When you hit the ditch, you couldn't have picked a boggier spot. It took Sam and me forty-five minutes to winch it out of there."

"Sorry. Thanks so much for getting it out, though."

"It's no problem. Sam said hearing about last night was payment enough."

I hesitate a step, causing Julie to bump into me from

behind. I guess I didn't tell him not to tell anyone. Julie clears her throat in a sort of choked-off cough and I start walking again.

Nate hasn't missed a beat. He keeps talking about what's damaged on the truck and how he can fix it. I'm listening, sort of. How can someone not be distracted by the way he looks in those jeans? I bet I could bounce a quarter off those cheeks. His long, black hair is tied back with a matching elastic and it flows halfway down his back. Not a split end in sight.

I'm walking close behind him when he stops. There's no time to react—I plough right into him. *Smooth move. Could I be anymore hopeless?* Turning quickly, he steadies me, catching me by my arms before I stumble into the pit under the truck.

"I, um, sorry. I'm not really with it today." I bite my bottom lip hard, trying to squeeze away the embarrassment written across my face.

His hands are warm on my bare arms. "You walk about as well as you drive," he says.

I can almost feel Julie rolling her eyes. Once I've steadied myself, Nate lets go with his hands—but not his eyes. I swear he watches to see my reaction, letting one finger trail down my arm as his hand returns to his side. *Did he actually just do that?* For a moment, Julie and the musty old garage disappear.

"So, as I was saying," Nate continues, "all I need to do is take off all the tires and pressure-wash the mud out of the rims, wheel wells, and disc brakes. Then I can put the tires back on and re-balance them. It should only take a few hours."

"Sounds good. My mom should be getting back from Vancouver at around six. Can you have it done before then?"

"No problem. I can have it ready for you by two."

"Great." A sigh escapes that I've been holding in for a while. I cringe at the thought of what I'm going to ask for next. Another favour from the guy who seems to keep rescuing me. "Um, I was wondering if I could make payments on this or something. It's just—I'm not sure if I can pay you all at once."

"Not a problem. In fact, don't worry about it. We're even —if you don't mind doing something for me." I hang on his every word. "There's a dance next Friday out on the reserve. Would you come with me?"

Every cell inside me just burst simultaneously, screaming YES. The sound of Julie's fake cough brings me back down from my own personal cloud nine.

I do a quick one-eighty to face her. "Hey," I say, a little too sweetly. "Do you know if I left my cell phone in your car? My mom said she'd call me when she was on her way back. She has a bad habit of coming home early. Can you go check if it's in there?"

"It's probably in your bag." She points to my messenger bag slung around my shoulder.

"Nope, I think I left it in the coin tray by that push-in

lighter thing." My eyes are begging. *Take a hint!*

"Okay." She breathes out the word. "I'll wait for you in the car." I mouth a thank-you before she leaves.

I turn back to Nate, finding him standing closer than before. "Sorry about that," I stutter, trying not to make direct eye contact. "I just thought about the last time she came back early from one of her trips. Don't want to go through all this trouble for nothing." I pause, catching my breath, and notice he's looking at me funny, quirking half a smile. "What? What did I say?"

"You ramble when you're nervous. It's kind of cute."

Wow. Forward much? "And you just say whatever is on your mind." I cover my mouth so nothing else escapes. "Sorry. I can't believe I just said that."

"Don't be." His deep brown eyes are locked on mine. "So, can I pick you up on Friday around seven?"

"That would be great. I guess you already know where I live, but here's my number just in case." I look away, fishing around in my bag for something to write on. Without thinking, I pull out my cell phone. "Or I could just put your number in my phone."

"Not in the car, eh?" he says with a giant grin on his face.

"No." What does he want, a confession? I sheepishly give him my cell to type in his number. "So I guess I'll be back around two to pick up my truck."

"It'll be ready." He hands back my cell after he's finished typing.

"Okay, thanks again. I'll see you later." I'm so flustered my legs barely work. I feel his eyes on me as I walk away. I make my way to the car where Julie is waiting. She doesn't give me a chance to even get my seatbelt on before she starts in on the twenty questions.

"You're going to that dance with him, aren't you? Wait." She stops me before I answer. "What am I even saying? Of course you are. He looks like a Spartan from the movie *300*. I need details. Tell me everything that happened last night, and don't leave anything out."

My mouth hangs open, but I'm just about to give her all the scandalous details when we both notice Nate running out of the side shop door. I roll down my window as he walks up to my side of the car.

"I'm glad I caught you. I almost forgot to give you this." He hands me my missing shoe through the car window. "I washed it off the best I could. Sam had to hold my ankles while I fished around in the mud for it. Anyway, thought you might want it back."

"Oh yeah. Thanks." Nate gives us both a wave before heading back into the shop.

The look on Julie's face is priceless. She must be trying to piece together what happened last night and how it could possibly involve me missing a shoe. I guess I owe her a good story.

"Come on, let's go for toast and waffles—on me. I'll fill you in on every sticky detail before your head explodes trying to figure it out."

CHAPTER FOUR

I got my mom's truck back from Nate well before Mom and Grams got home. Crisis averted. My mom commented on how clean it was. I hope she believed me when I told her I washed it for her "just because." I'm such a bad liar.

I didn't get any sleep again last night. I couldn't stop thinking about that wooden spirit box and what came out of it. It crossed my mind that I could ask Grams about it, but would she even believe me? Asking her would probably result in a call to the Weather Lady. I miss my therapist, but calling her would be admitting defeat, like I can't handle this new place. I can handle this.

I haven't heard from Mason since Friday night. Is he okay? How do you bring something like this up? "Hey, Mason, seen any wendigos lately?" Or maybe I'm overthinking it. This wouldn't be the first time I've blown things out of proportion.

Maybe I should just let this whole thing fade away. It was just a crazy game we played.

The dark clouds are clearing away. I can see the stars. It's going to be a beautiful night.

"Smells good, Ms. Barnes. Thanks for having me over for dinner," Julie says, hanging her coat on the wall hook near the back entry.

Julie sort of invited herself over for Sunday night dinner. It's cool. My mom's been bugging me forever to meet my friends. Since Julie's probably my best friend, it seems only right that they should meet. Julie has ulterior motives, though. She's here because she knows I'll bail on going out tonight if she doesn't personally escort me. I should probably go out—it would be good for me. It will give me something to think about other than Friday night.

"Oh, it's no trouble having you over. I'm happy to finally meet one of Rachel's friends. She should invite you all over sometime." My mom hands Julie a few plates to put on the table. Julie's expression doesn't waver.

"Yeah, that'd be great," Julie answers back. "I'll tell the others. Thanks, Ms. Barnes."

"Call me Marie. I changed my last name back to Stacey

after the divorce, but Ms. Stacey sounds too old."

Julie and I sit at the kitchen table while Mom finishes bringing over the steaming dishes: rosemary chicken, green beans, and fresh buns.

"Wow, looks fancy," Julie says. "What's the occasion?"

"Just thought I'd make something nice. I've been so busy with work and things, the only time I get to cook is on the weekend. Plus, I'm pretty sure this is the only sit-down meal I'll get with Rachel this week. Thought I'd make her favorite since she'll probably want to spend her birthday with you guys this year." She had to mention my birthday. She doesn't even look at me when she says it.

"You didn't tell me your birthday is coming up. I'll make sure she has fun, Ms.—Marie. An eighteenth birthday needs to be celebrated," Julie says, glancing up at me while piling her plate with more green beans.

"Yeah, it's next Saturday." *Gee, thanks, Mom.* Julie has no idea how much I hate that date. Birthday dinners, birthday parties—I used to look forward to those things. Now they just mark the day that everything changed.

"I know Eric died on your birthday," my mom would say, "but we don't have to be sad for the rest of our lives. We should celebrate your birthday, be happy." I get this speech from her every year.

A silent nod of agreement is always my reply. I never say what I really think: "Sure, Mom, let's celebrate. Another year of remembering that I'm still alive and my brother isn't."

A lot of people think traumatic events eventually heal with time. I wonder how much time they mean, because there never seems to be enough.

"You know what," Mom interjects before Julie can say any more, "maybe we'll just barbecue here before you all go out for the night. I know how Rachel likes to keep it low-key." She looks right at me, her eyes offering a silent apology for bringing it up in the first place.

"Yeah. Sure. Where's Grandma? Aren't we going to wait for her?" I ask, trying to change the subject to anything else.

"She's out at a friend's place for dinner tonight. She said she has to be at work early tomorrow, though, so I don't think she'll be late."

My mom lifts the lid off the roaster. The smell of roasted chicken and rosemary wafts up in billows of steam from the pan. For as long as I can remember, my grams has always kept wild and unruly rosemary plants growing in every sunny corner of this house. Nothing reminds me more of my grandma than the smell of rosemary.

"So, what are you girls up to tonight?" Mom asks.

"We're going out to Ross Lake for a bonfire." Julie's quick

to speak before I can say anything. "Once the weather starts getting warm, we all go to the lake for a fire. It's kind of a spring tradition out here."

"Okay, but don't be out too late. It's Sunday, and you guys have school tomorrow."

"Um, no." Julie keeps on talking and eating. "We have a few PD days this week, mixed with some sort of teachers' conference, so we have the whole week off."

"Oh. Must be nice," Mom answers. I'm not surprised she didn't know about it. I've always been the kid that my parents don't worry about. The one to take care rather than be taken care of. Even after Eric died, it was my idea to see a shrink. "Well, be back by midnight, then."

"Midnight?" Julie keeps the conversation going. "My mom's letting me stay out till one. I have my car. I could bring Rachel home when I come home. Would that be okay?"

It's her first time meeting my mom and she's already renegotiating my curfew. I don't even feel like going out.

"All right." She agrees so quickly I wonder if she has her own plans tonight. "One. But remember, it's a small town, and I'll eventually hear about all the bad stuff you girls get into."

Julie backs her 2000-something Toyota Camry out of the long driveway at my grams' house. The gears are a little stiff and it sounds like a pullback racer toy when she backs it up. Her car was a hand-me-down from her parents, for her and her sister to share. Lucky for Julie her sister is still too young to drive, so there isn't much sharing going on.

"So," Julie starts, "I'm guessing she didn't notice anything about her truck."

"No. She did mention how clean it looked. Nate did a good job of putting it all back together."

"*Naaate.*" She says his name like she's tasting it. "I'm going to be seeing a lot more of him, aren't I?"

"Maybe. We'll see."

"Well, if he's going to be hanging around, don't forget to ask if he's got any other Spartan-looking friends for me." This is more like the Julie I know. I was hoping she'd come around.

"So why the change of heart?"

"About what?"

"About Nate. I know he's fantastically good looking, but that can't be all of it."

"I don't know." She shifts the car into drive and starts towards the highway, not even glancing my way as she speaks. "Maybe I'm just a little tired of small-town politics." Whatever the reason, I'm not getting into it. I'm just happy she likes him. It'll be easier to have him around.

"So, are we picking up anyone else?"

"Nah. Chloe and Ryan are sort of back together again—

he's picking her up. I think Mason is catching a ride with them too."

"All righty then." I relax a little deeper into my seat. "So how long does it take to get to Ross Lake?"

"About fifteen minutes."

I love the fact that it takes only minutes to get anywhere in this town. Although there aren't many places to go, its smallness, simplicity, and predictability are growing on me. This could be the kind of place where things aren't complicated. I look out the window and watch the endless miles of trees go by. Only a few driveways and road signs divide up the forested wall. Julie switches on the car radio. Having no other music options in this car, it's always set to the only rock station Hazelton gets.

"I hope you're all having a fantastic weekend," the evening radio host blares with way too much energy. Just a reminder to all of you who may be enjoying the parks and wooded areas around town—it's springtime! And you know what that means: less snow and more bears. So be smart out there and don't forget your bear safety."

"Bear safety?" I ask.

"Yeah, I wouldn't worry too much about it," Julie answers. "I've lived here my entire life and I've only seen a bear, like, twice."

"Oh." Bear safety hasn't crossed my mind, having spent

my whole life in a big city. "So what do I do if I see one?"

Julie laughs a little as she puts on her turn signal. "Just don't look tasty, I guess."

"Thanks, I'll keep that in mind."

The parking lot for Ross Lake is a little ways off the road. It's only when we stop that the seclusion of this place really hits me. You'd never think it was just off the highway.

"Are we early?" There's only one other car in the parking lot.

"Yeah, I told Chloe we'd get here early and get a good spot for a fire."

"Okay." I fish around the empty Kleenex boxes and random articles of clothing in the backseat of Julie's car for my backpack. "I put a blanket in my pack in case we get cold," I say, swinging my bag over one shoulder. "Were you able to get any coolers?"

"Yep, I got my cousin to boot for us. He got us ciders and Long Islands." The bottles clink around in a cooler as she takes them out of the trunk.

"Awesome. I owe you one."

We've barely crossed from the gravel to the grass when we spot Ryan's unmistakable truck peeling into the parking lot. Ryan drives a brand new, shiny, black Ford. Julie told me it was an eighteenth-birthday gift from his dad.

Julie runs over to Chloe as soon as Ryan parks. It's like they haven't seen each other in months. Even though they definitely saw each other on Friday, probably yesterday, and maybe even today. Chloe jumps out of the truck, giving Julie a big hug that proceeds to jumping up and down, screaming, and carrying on about how drunk they're going to get. Part of me thinks this whole charade is stupid. The other half wonders what it's like to have a friend like that.

"What? Not going to get in on all that schoolgirl hugging and screaming?" Ryan's standing beside me. "I've always hoped it might turn into kissing one of these times."

I've always hoped that money doesn't make people jerks. Ryan confirms it for me, because I'm almost positive he'd be a jerk even if he wasn't rich. "Thanks, but I'm good. Hey, I thought Mason came with you guys."

"Nah. I tried calling him to see if he was coming, but there was no answer. Maybe his cell's dead."

The girly giggle-fest has stopped and Julie and Chloe walk up beside us. "Why don't you two run over to Mason's place and see if he's coming? Chloe and I'll find a good spot to set up. Besides," Julie winks, "I have to fill Chloe in on all the current events."

"What's that all about?" Ryan asks, looking at me.

Does everyone need to know about what happened? "I got in a little accident Friday night and drove my mom's truck into a ditch. But it's all good, my mom suspects nothing—I think." I'm so not telling Ryan about Nate. It's bad enough that Chloe gets to hear about it.

"You suck at telling stories," Julie says with a smug little smile. "I'll fill Chloe in on all the juicy bits. Why don't you and Ryan go get Mason? Don't be too long, 'kay?" she says, mostly to Ryan. "Rachel has to keep up with us drink for drink." Drink for drink with the two of them? I think my liver just cringed.

"I need to go to his place anyway," Ryan says. "I'm pretty sure I left my sunglasses there last week." Ryan walks around to the driver's side of his truck. "You coming?"

Julie and Chloe have already started to haul their stuff down the beach. I guess I'm going with Ryan. Julie's always making decisions like this for me. It was nice when I first moved here not to think about things too much, but now it's getting to be a bit much.

"Yeah, sure." Going anywhere with Ryan is extremely low on my list of things to do. He drives the way any eighteen-year-old boy with a brand-new truck would: fast and borderline criminal. I thought his driving looked bad as a spectator, but from the inside of his truck, it's a whole new experience. It crosses my mind that holding on to the holy shit handle the entire way to Mason's place isn't very cool, but I don't really care. I know he notices. What an ass! I can see his stupid grin out of the corner of my eye.

He finally slows the truck and turns into the narrow driveway of an acreage. I see Mason's truck parked to the side of a large ranch house.

"You go inside and get Mason. I need to chuck a whiz."

My lip curls in disgust. Wow. *Such class, Ryan.* "There are bathrooms inside. I'm sure—"

"It's a guy thing, just go," he says, interrupting me. "I'll be, like, a minute." I hear the zipper of his jeans descend as he steps out of the truck—and that's my cue to leave.

Mason's house has one of those doorbells that goes on forever. *Ding-dong, ding-dong, ding ding dong dong.* I stand on the front porch, mentally burning all images of Ryan peeing in the yard out of my mind. No answer at the door. I knock. Still no answer. I try the door, and it's not locked.

"Helloooo," I call as I poke my head in. "Mason?"

I can see across to the living room, where a socked foot hangs over the end of the couch. I shut the front door behind me as I walk in. Mason's sprawled out on his back on the living room couch. His face and clothes are filthy. He even has bits of grass and leaves in his hair. He must be passed out. No one could sleep through that doorbell.

There's a small unoccupied spot of cushion left beside him on the couch, so I sit. I lean in closer, whispering in his ear, trying to wake him gently. "Maaasooon."

"I heard Ryan drive up and you ring the doorbell and call my name." He inhales deeply, but doesn't open his eyes. "I'm awake." The corners of his mouth rise up.

"Okay." This feels awkward all of a sudden. I sit up straight. "Then why didn't you answer the door?"

He opens his eyes and looks right at me. He lies on the couch like the sprawled-out position couldn't be more natural. "'Cuz I've never had anyone try to wake me with a kiss before."

I feel the flush rise in my face. "And you thought that's what I was doing?"

He props himself up to a half-sitting position, smiling widely but not answering.

"W-well," I stutter, "I wasn't. That's not what I was doing." He's still staring, just taking me in. I can't decide if I'm shocked or flattered. "If I wanted to kiss you, I would have," I blurt out, looking right into his eyes when I say it. His smile only gets bigger.

I want to get up from the couch. I want to stop analyzing every smudged, dirty detail of his face, but I don't. And then I see something. A flash, a sheen, glazes over his eyes then disappears. My whole body tenses and I know he notices. Something primitive inside me goes from flirty to fearful, and I want to run, but where would I go? I'm about to say something, but I'm interrupted by an obviously fake cough coming from the direction of the front door.

"Hey, guys. I don't mean to interrupt your conversation over there, but—"

Ryan is inside the house, standing not ten feet from me.

"Are you coming out to the lake, Mason?" Ryan walks a little further into the living room, grabbing his sunglasses from the side table. "Whoa—buddy. What the hell happened to you? You look like shit."

"Do I?" Mason runs his fingers through his hair, picking out a leaf and a few blades of grass. I stand up so he can sit up straight without fumbling around me. He stretches and stands up from the couch in one fluid motion. "Yeah, I'm still coming."

Ryan's already fidgeting with the keys in his pocket. "I take it you'll need to have a shower and change," he says, giving Mason a once-over.

"Yeah, I guess. You guys go ahead. I'll take my truck and meet you out there." Mason rubs his temples, and a few more bits of debris float to the floor.

"Cool." Ryan's already at the front door, holding it open. "Saddle up, Rach. We're leaving."

I cringe at the thought of spending one more second in Ryan's truck. *Jerk who pees on front lawns, or dirty guy who blatantly hits on me. These are my choices.* "I'll catch a ride with Mason, if that's okay." The lesser of two evils.

"Suit yourself." Ryan raises an eyebrow. "Hope you

decide where you want to kiss him," he says as the front door slams shut behind him.

That's not what I said.

"Ryan's driving a little too much for you?" Mason's standing directly behind me. I can feel his closeness even though he's not touching me.

"Yeah, I guess you could say that." I turn around and almost bump into him. "Whoa, I didn't realize you were right there." I put up my hand for balance, touching his chest.

Being alone like this, with a guy who talks and looks at me like this, should be putting my nerves through the roof. But it doesn't. I feel—something different. I still get butterflies. I'm still touching his chest, staring at the folds of his T-shirt. Even though Mason is always dressed in jeans and a T-shirt, he always looks like rugged meets fashion meets perfection. Today it's a tentree shirt; the little number is stitched into its single front pocket. Maybe I should let go before he thinks something of it. I pull my hand back, like I finally figured out how to get it unstuck.

"Sorry." *Just say something else so we can get back to the lake.* "Which way is your bedroom?" My graceless social skills never cease to amaze me.

"Sorry, what?" Yeah—even I'm dumbfounded by that last comment.

"No, it's not like that. What I meant was, you go shower

and I'll pick you out something to wear. So we can get out of here faster."

"You want to pick me out something to wear?" He gives me another confused look. A leaf falls to the floor as he runs his fingers through his hair.

"Yeah." Is that a weird thing to say? Julie picks out my clothes all the time. Shit, maybe it's a girlfriend thing. "Or maybe that's just my lame excuse to snoop through your stuff. Come on, I want to get back out there before Julie and Chloe drink all my Long Islands."

He slowly pivots away from me and starts up the stairs. I follow close behind. "First door on the right is my room. First door on the left is the shower." He stops in the doorway to the bathroom and watches me go into his room.

I can feel his eyes on me. "What?" I turn back to look at him.

"You surprise me." A second feels like an hour as the wheels in my head turn, trying to decode what he's really trying to say.

"Go shower. Ryan wasn't kidding when he said you needed one." He turns and shuts the bathroom door. A second later I hear the shower turn on, and I'm glad to be alone.

What am I doing? Trying to stir up another romance? I still need to talk to him about Friday night, and all I seem to be doing is . . . I don't even know what I'm doing. But first things first: clothes. I hope it's still okay to pick those out.

Mason's bedroom is massive. There's a neatly made queen-size bed with an oh-so-comfy-looking navy blue comforter on it, two bedside tables, and a large dresser against one wall. Along the other wall sits a large, wooden study desk. Everything on the desk is neat except for a scattered pile of papers. I brush my fingers over them as I pass, noting that they're university applications. Five or six of them. And what looks like a few acceptance letters. I guess he's not planning on staying in Hazelton forever. It's not a big surprise, but I've never heard him mention it. There isn't one stitch of dirty clothes anywhere in his room.

I open the bifold doors to his closet, which to my surprise is a walk-in. My inner clotheshorse lets out an envious sigh. There are slanted shelves up to the ceiling for shoes, multi-level racks with drawers, and hangers for everything else.

I quickly pick out a neatly folded pair of jeans and a simple black T-shirt. He can get his own socks and underwear. Stepping out of his closet with the clothes I set the outfit on his bed. To the left of his bed is a large picture window that overlooks a clearing in the trees. You can see the mountains too. Along the windowsill are four framed pictures, each with the same two people in them: a younger-looking Mason and a slightly older-looking girl I don't recognize. I pick up one of the frames to take a closer look.

"That's my sister and me. My dad took that picture two summers ago on a camping trip. It was the last picture he ever took of her."

My heart skips a beat. He's right behind me again. "Oh my God." I grip the picture to my chest, spinning around to face him. "I didn't hear you come in. How long have you been standing there?"

"Not long," he says, looking at me and standing a little too close for comfort. His dark brown hair is wet and slicked back, yet as always, few strands find their way to the front. Dark brown hair and bright blue eyes. What are the odds of getting that combination?

"And you're dressed."

"Yep. Would you rather I not be?" He cocks one eyebrow.

I close my eyes tight. *How long was he in the shower? How did I not hear him come in and get dressed?* I back up a step, holding the picture against my chest like it's a shield. "Stop it, Mason." I open my eyes to find him a little closer than he was before.

A playful smile sweeps across his face. "Stop what?"

"You're—" I take a deep breath in. "You talk to me like I don't have two brain cells to rub together. I'm not anybody special, but I'm not an idiot. Don't talk to me like I'm cheap."

"I'm sorry." His face softens as his hand reaches out to

me, asking for me to give him the picture frame. Our fingers brush as I hand it back to him. I can't help but notice how much my hands are shaking. "I act like someone I'm not a lot of the time, and—I'm sorry."

"It's just easier that way sometimes." Mason flips the frame over in his hands, tracing the face of the girl in the picture. "It's easier to act like she's still alive and everything's normal. This is my sister, Angie. She was hit by a drunk driver two years ago." He blinks a few times and swallows hard. "So," he murmurs, fumbling a moment with the picture, "should we get back to the lake? They'll be wondering where we are."

CHAPTER FIVE

The parking lot at Ross Lake is almost full by the time we get there. I guess Julie was right to come early. I see a few fires near the water, already blazing.

"Do you know where the others might be?" I ask, as Mason trolls the lot for one of the last spots. "They didn't really say where they were going to set up."

"They're probably at the north end of the lake." He parks his truck at the end of a row, half gravel, half grass. Not really a parking spot, but I'm guessing no one's going to care around here. "It's a little more sheltered over there." Mason reaches for my bag in the backseat before I can. Stepping out of the truck, he swings the bag over his shoulder and walks around to my side.

"I can carry that," I say, getting out of the truck.

"I got it." He stops beside me, shutting the truck door and offering me his hand. "Come on, let's go."

I look at it, not taking it right away, but he doesn't waver. "Come on," he says, taking my hand anyway. "I don't bite. That costs extra."

I want to say something, but it's kind of nice.

We go north, up the beach along the water's edge. Though it's called a beach, there is little in the way of sand, the shoreline instead filled with pebbles and grit. It is thirty feet wide at the broadest parts, bordered by tall pines and a grassy area. Looks like most of our graduating class is out here tonight, maybe one hundred people. It's not long before Mason and I see Julie, Chloe, and Ryan through the gathering crowd. They've piled wood into a tepee shape but haven't gotten their fire going yet.

Julie shouts over the din of mingling people as she walks towards us. "Hey, that was fast. Ryan only beat you guys by fifteen minutes."

I'd tell her why we got here so fast, but commenting on how fast a person can get dressed is sure to bring up other questions. Holding Mason's hand all the way across the beach is probably stirring up questions too. I make a move to zip up my hoodie as an excuse to let go. If Mason thinks anything of it, he doesn't let on.

"You guys said to hurry up. Maybe I drive as fast as Ryan."

Julie and I find a spot to sit on a weathered beach log. "It's cold out here," I say. "I thought you guys would have had a fire going."

"Ryan and some other guys have been trying everything to light it, but I think the wood is too wet. Someone's gone to get gas or something. I can totally see eyebrows being lost on this one." Julie rubs her arms. I huddle a little closer.

"I heard about your night." Chloe comes to sit on the other side of me. "So when are we going to get to meet this Nate?"

I'm surprised Chloe cares enough to ask about him. "I told him I'd go out with him to a dance this Friday. I'll see how that goes before I bring him around." I zip up my hoodie as far as it will go, tucking my nose into the collar. It's getting cool fast. The sun hasn't gone down yet, but it will soon.

"Okay. Well, let me know if you get bored of him. He sounds . . . fun." And there it is. I don't even technically have a boyfriend yet, and she's trying to steal him. *Bitch.* She's the only one of us who ever has a guy, and when I get even a sniff of one, she has to try to stake a claim. My tightly zipped hoodie gags my words before they come out.

"Hey," I say to Julie, my voice muffled through the fabric. "The guys look like they're going to be a while with the fire. I've got that blanket in my backpack." I barely finish the sentence when I feel Mason wrapping all three of us in the blanket I brought. "Thanks." He doesn't say anything, just smiles at me as he walks back over to Ryan.

"What was that?" Julie asks.

"What?" I ask.

"That look. The blanket."

"He carried my bag from the truck. I guess he heard me say I wanted it." Even as the words leave my mouth, I wonder how that could be true.

"Uh-huh." Julie squints at me, as if trying to squeeze out more details. "Two guys liking you at the same time. I'm impressed."

"It's not like that." I'm interrupted again by Mason standing in front of us. He's holding three opened coolers.

"Two ciders for you guys," he says, handing the bottles to Chloe and Julie, "and a Long Island for you." I take the drink from him, trying my hardest not to blush. "Do you girls need anything else? I'm going to go help Ryan with the fire." He's not asking them, just me.

Courteous, attentive, not an asshole. These are not words usually associated with Mason Allen. And they aren't helping my he's-not-into-me case. "I'm good, thanks," I say, and turtle a bit more into my hoodie. Julie doesn't comment. She just nudges me as he walks away.

"Two guys." Julie raises her bottle to toast. "Cheers to that." They both giggle and laugh, but not me. I wouldn't know what to do with one guy, let alone two.

The three of us huddle together under the blanket, watching the boys try to start the fire. They've stopped asking me questions about boys, and I've stopped stuttering out answers. I take another drink of my Long Island and realize it's almost gone. There's only a bit left in the bottom. I can feel a slight buzz already, and I'm glad.

Ryan comes over in a huff and starts packing up his stuff. "We're moving, girls. The wood is too wet to light, even with lighter fluid. It must have rained all last night." He stands up, slinging his backpack over his shoulder, not waiting for any of us before he starts walking down the beach. "There're a few fires going down the beach. Maybe we can join one of them."

Chloe doesn't say anything, but I can tell she's fuming. Ryan didn't carry her stuff, help her up, or even wait for her. Not that she needs help. No wonder they're forever breaking up. It's the getting back together I don't get. The three of us stand up together, not wanting to lose the warmth of the blanket. Waddling like three penguins, we follow Ryan and a few others down the beach towards the closest bonfire.

Crap. I've left my backpack behind. "Hold up a sec. I forgot my bag." Trying to get the three of us to turn and not lose the blanket isn't going to be easy. I duck out underneath and wave them on instead. "You guys go ahead. I'll just be a minute." Chloe and Julie shuffle off without argument.

Turning back, I see Mason. He's still standing there,

alone, by the pile of rain-soaked firewood. Everyone else is gone from this end of the beach but us. I stop about twenty feet away and watch him. His back is to me, but I can see he has something in his hand. Whatever it is, it's glowing blue. But the sun's getting low, casting long shadows, and maybe it's playing tricks with my eyes. The glowing blue light he's holding is still there.

With a puff of air from his lips, he blows the glowing light from his hand and watches it float lightly towards the firewood. The light is beautiful. I never want to look away.

The instant the light touches the wood, flame roars towards the sky, flames that I swear burn a bright blue, if only for a second. The heat from the flames, even at this distance, singes the air in my lungs. I can't breathe. Taking another breath in is almost impossible. It's like drowning in an ocean of burning air.

Oh my God, Mason! My grip loosens from the neck of my drink. It slides from my hand and I don't try to stop it. I need to help him.

I do nothing but choke. My world stalls and stutters in slow-motion flashes. The flames. The falling bottle. The burning heat. And then it stops. The air around me cools.

Mason's standing in front of me, one hand on my shoulder, the other holding my drink. I swallow hard and my throat burns. But he's not burned. He looks fine. He's caught my drink before it hit the ground, and crossed twenty feet to do it. I just stare at him, and he stares back.

"Just breathe," he whispers to me.

So I do, and the air hits the back of my lungs like a sack of flour.

"Hey, you got the fire going!" It's Ryan, somewhere behind me, yelling from down the beach. "Woo hoo! Still got your eyebrows, buddy? How'd you get it started?"

Mason takes my dangling, limp hand from my side and wraps my fingers around my drink. He leans in and whispers, "Don't say anything. Just trust me." I notice him swallow the lump in his throat. "Please."

I hear the approaching feet behind me.

"I'm going to let you go. Don't fall over, okay?" I didn't notice he was holding me up until he let the hand steadying me slip from my shoulder. I tip a bit, finding my balance.

Mason's voice changes from a whisper to a shout when he answers Ryan. "Hey, man, I guess I'm just a better Boy Scout than you." He's lying. He's trying to cover this up, whatever this is.

Julie and Chloe resume their spots on the log, patting the space between them for me to sit. I appreciated the warmth of being between them before, but now it seems suffocating. They didn't even notice what Mason just did. I need some air. I jolt to life from my mannequin-stiff state and announce far too loudly, "I'm going for a walk!" No explanation, just that.

"But we just got the fire going. Aren't you cold?" Julie asks with a puzzled look on her face.

Before I can say anything, I feel Mason's arm around my waist. "I'll give her the tour so she doesn't get lost," he says, pulling me in closer. "Or cold."

I hear their giggles and whispers as we walk down the beach towards the trees. As soon as I think we're out of their sight, I duck out from his arm. I have no idea where I want to go, just away from here. I veer off towards the woods.

"Hey, where are you going?"

"For a walk. Alone."

"Slow down. You can't just go tramping through the woods all by yourself."

I stop abruptly and turn and face him. "And why not?"

"Because there's scary stuff in the woods."

"Scarier than you?" *There, I said it.*

He cocks a half smile and offers me his hand. I bat it away. "Come on. Walk with me."

"I don't want your hand or your arm." A heat inside me rises. I stutter to get out the words. "Don't touch me." I look up at his taunting smile. "Tell me what's going on." He rolls his eyes like I'm crazy for asking. "Screw you." I turn a one-eighty and start walking away.

Bam. I walk right into his chest. I push away from him

with both hands. "What are you? Get away from me."

"Hey, I'm just kidding around. Settle down."

"Kidding around? You're scaring the shit out of me." I take another step back. "Something happened Friday night. Didn't it? Tell me what's going on, or I'll go back there and ask them." I point in the direction of the beach.

"Do you honestly think you could get away from me?"

What?

My world stops dead.

There are no clouds in my sky, no sun, no moon, no stars, no wind and no weather.

He stares right through me as if he sees something else, something only he can see. "Stop it, Mason. This isn't funny." I stare right back. There's a standoff between us, and I'm not even sure what we're fighting about.

"I'm sorry," he stutters, blinking his eyes. "Please, let me walk with you. We should talk. About what happened back there and Friday night." *Friday night.* I guess I'm not making this up after all.

He steps aside and gestures for me to walk beside him. I move onto the path leading into the shadowed forest.

I let the air escape my lungs, filling them back up with the coolness of the forest. "How—" I whisper until I find the words. "How are you so quick? I didn't see you move, and then you were in front of me. You're silent when you want to be, at least. And that blue light thing. What the hell was that? I saw you start the fire with it, and it didn't burn you. I barely have eyelashes left, and the heat didn't touch you!" I'm on a roll now. "Your friends ask you how you started the fire and why you looked so dirty at your place. And you brushed them off. Maybe they didn't notice. I did"

"Hey—" he starts.

"I'm not done yet." I stop and turn to face him. "Look at me." I stare in to his crystal blue eyes, waiting. Waiting to see what I saw before.

"What are you doing?"

"I saw your eyes turn silver before. I know what I saw." They're still blue. *Change, damn it!*

"Do you want me to answer all those questions? Some of them were more like statements."

I throw my hands up and storm down the path. "This is stupid," I mumble under my breath. How could I think I could open up to someone and not have them think I'm nuts? *The Weather Lady knew you were off, but at least she got paid for it.* Mason's probably going to go back and tell the others what I just said. Great. Guess I'll be hanging out with me, myself, and I for a while. I yell back at Mason, not bothering to look. "Are you ever serious, Mason Allen?"

I blink once, twice. I'm losing it.

Mason's not behind me. He's sitting on a rock ten feet in front of me, waiting like he's been there for hours. Hot tears well behind my eyes. "Stop it! You're freaking me out. I'm asking you what's going on and all you're doing is showing off."

Something happened to him Friday night. *Something wendigo.*

"I'm not showing off, Rachel." His tone is flat and level. "I'm showing *you.*"

"I'm not imagining this? Someone didn't slip some freak drug in my drink?"

"No." A single word from him and my reality explodes. "Pretty cool, eh? Want to see what else I can do?"

He's just sitting there on that rock. "I don't know if I do, actually." I can't think straight. I need to sit. Right here, right now. I don't go over to the dry rock he's sitting on. I just plunk down in the middle of the damp forest path.

"This happened Friday night?" I find my voice. It hid away there for a bit, but I found it. "I saw a white deer, and you've seen a wendigo?"

"So have you," he says, cocking his head to the side like some bird of prey.

I look up to see Mason's eyes glaze silver and then turn back to blue. Every cell inside me stills. I want to run but know I wouldn't even make the first step. My mouth opens but no words come out.

"It's still me, Rach."

Mason's a wendigo? From the story he told on Friday night, it sounds like a monster. A monster who kills people. Is that why we're out here in the woods?

"I see things a little different now, but it's still me." He stands up, offering me his hand, and I shrink back. "Would it be cheesy to say that this wendigo will never hurt you?" He stands firm, hand still extended for me to take.

I reach out and take his hand. *This isn't something you get to run away from.*

The night is dark. The thick clouds veil the moon, but it is still there, trying to shine.

I'm up. He's in front of me, holding my arms to steady me. Warmth radiates from him, and if I didn't know better, I'd feel safe.

"Walk with me." His voice is softer, not demanding. "And I'll try to explain." He takes my hand in his. "Don't try to run, okay? I'll only catch you and—" He pauses like he's finding the right words. "Well, it sounds like your heart is going to beat right out of your chest. So just don't. Just walk. I'll talk, and you can just . . . breathe."

So we walk. And I make my feet move, one foot in front

of the other. And I listen.

"After I left your place on Friday night, it found me." His voice is like one of those books on tape, telling a story. "Ryan dropped me off at my place and peeled out of the driveway as usual. It found me before I even got into the house. Not that four walls would have stopped it. You won't believe what I can do now, the powers I have. That spirit box is real. This is real—and it changes everything."

Without hesitation he takes the hand that isn't holding mine and raises it out in front of us. A blue light emerges from his fingertips like curling smoke. It's beautiful. Scary beautiful. My feet stop moving.

"What is that?"

"It's what connects us to everything. It's what gives us power—and what takes it." He speaks almost reverently. "This is life."

I want to touch it, hold it, and keep it for my own. "Will it hurt me?"

"Not like this, no. It surrounds you every moment of every day. It's in you, around you. It's everywhere. You just don't see it." He brings his hand closer and I am drawn to it. I run my hand through it, twice. There's no heat, just a slight tingle. I want to giggle but I keep it in.

A thought pops into my head, ruining the beautiful

moment. "Why are you showing me this and hiding it from everyone else?"

He snuffs out the smoky light by curling the flames back into his hand. "There's a lot to explain about being a wendigo, and I don't think the others will understand."

"And what makes you think I'll understand?" I look right at him.

"Maybe I'm just hoping that you will."

This is my fault. This is happening to him because of me. I have to find a way to fix this.

"Okay," I say, and nod my head. "I'll try and understand." *I can fix this.* "It's getting dark, Mason." There's no chiding comment about being afraid of the dark, like the other night. Without a word, the blue light springs from his hand again, casting a glow on the path in front of us.

"Thank you. For trying." He squeezes my hand. I'm still holding his.

We start back the way we came while I replay Mason's story about wendigos in my head. He said they kill people. Does he kill people? Our strides along the path aren't rushed. We walk side by side, matching each other's pace.

Is he a monster?

"You need to promise me something," I say. My voice is strong. "You're going to let me fix this. This happened to you because of me, and—"

"On two conditions." He butts in like it's an everyday conversation, not missing a step. "Don't tell anyone about this. And understand what it is you're trying to fix."

"I do understand. Or, I understand enough."

"No you don't. It'll take much longer than just one night to explain it. Trust me to explain it, and I'll trust you to fix what it is you need to fix."

"How can you be so sure about all this? Why am I the only one freaking out?"

"Can you just trust me on this? It's complicated."

I walk in silence beside him for a few more strides before I speak again. "Why can't I tell anyone?"

"Do you think anyone would believe you?" I hate it when people answer questions with questions, but he's right.

"What about Julie, Chloe, and Ryan? They might believe me."

"And if they did, how do you think they'd react?" He answers his own question. "When people get scared, they do stupid things."

"Okay, fine. I won't tell." He gives my hand a squeeze. It feels like I've spent the whole day holding it.

The last few beams of daylight are dipping below the mountains. I can barely see the path in front of us, even with the blue light. I'm guessing we're only a minute or two from the beach when he stops. He goes stone still, pushing me behind him a step or two.

"What's wrong?" I whisper. The blue light absorbs back in to his hand. I'm momentarily blind while my eyes adjust. Mason says nothing, but I get my answer. The sound of thrashing branches and tumbling rocks come from the trail up ahead. I can't make out what it is, but its low, throaty growl rolls deep from its throat. I'm frozen behind him, waiting for whatever it is on the trail to charge at us. Every nerve in me wants to run, but my legs won't take me.

I finally see it. A grizzly. At least I think it's a grizzly. It's immense, towering above both of us as it stands on its back legs. Mason gently lets go of my hand, taking a step towards the bear. *Holy fuck!* He's lost his mind. Just because he can scare the shit out of me doesn't mean he can take on bears. *What did Julie say about bears? Think. Think.* "Just try not to look too tasty." Great. I'll have to tell her how much that helped, if I survive this.

At the last moment before the bear charges, something about Mason changes. Time begins to slow down and Mason stands his ground, unafraid. He stares intently at the bear, not backing down. His body seems to move by instinct, not thought, as he positions himself for a fight. The Mason I know is not there anymore. He's been replaced with an exact duplicate, but it's not him. I'm understanding a little more now: this is the wendigo.

It's when I hear a sound that shouldn't exist in this world that time speeds back up. As if released from the darkest of places, a scolding hiss erupts from Mason's lips. The bear stops mid-run, throwing its head back in confusion. A standoff. Mason darts to the side, rebounding off a tree and crashing into the side of the grizzly, knocking it over. It's like an episode of *Wild Kingdom* on steroids—and meth. I hear the bear yelp as it tumbles onto its side. Mason is back standing in front of me again, his movements almost too fast to follow.

I curl my hands around the back of my neck, locking my fingers together. I can't watch anymore. Is this real? I step back to regain my balance and snap a twig under my heel. The bear fumbles to its feet and whines. It turns slowly to walk away when I hear another, lower hiss come from Mason. It takes off into the trees with a staggered gait.

That bear has just discovered a new link above it on the food chain. Maybe we both have. It's all just too much. A showdown with a bear, and Mason wins. Where's my blinking red reset button, the one I can press when things get a little too surreal?

I take a deep breath, putting my hand against a tree beside me. It has a big crack in it, like it's been hit by lightning.

"Mason, are you okay?" I reach out to touch his shoulder with my other hand but before I do, he growls low and deep. My hand flies back like I touched a hot pan. I step back onto another dry twig. The snap echoes in the silence of the woods. He turns his head slightly back towards me. I only see one eye, glazed silver, looking not at me but at the ground.

I keep backing up, trying to remember which way it is to the beach. My steps are fumbled and hurried. I turn and start to run. People's voices. I can hear them now. I'm almost there. The trees start to thin. The grasses blend into the rough gravel and sand beach. I'm not far from Julie and the rest of them. I can hear their voices. A cold sweat shivers through me. I stop running. He's not chasing me. He let me go. I turn and stare back at the black woods. It's raining. I hadn't noticed till now, but I'm starting to get cold. By the time I get back to the bonfire, my hair is stringy and plastered to my face. I sit next to Julie without a word and cuddle in close.

"You guys were gone a while," Julie says. "We almost left without you. No one wants to stay because it's raining. Do you want a ride home with me, or is Mason going to drive you?" She doesn't wait for me to answer. She just keeps on talking. Which is fine. "Where is he, anyway? Did he meet up with Cory and Mike down the beach?"

"Yeah." I just agree with her. It's easier than the truth. "I'll catch a ride with you." Lying is easier than it should be. I feel bad not telling Julie the truth, but what am I supposed to say? "No, Mason is off fighting bears in the woods with his new wendigo powers."

"Here's your backpack." Julie hands me my bag stuffed with the blanket. "Don't worry, we'll get tons more chances to come back to the lake this summer."

I'm not sure how to feel about that.

The ride back to my place is quiet. Julie chimes in a few times about Chloe and Ryan getting back together and how they might break up again after tonight. I respond with a few head nods and an *uh-huh* or two, but mostly I just look out the car window watching the raindrops join together to form little rivers down the glass.

Driving up to my house, I see the kitchen lights and the glow from the living room TV. My mom and grandma are probably still up watching one of their favorite reality shows.

"Hey, is everything okay? You're pretty quiet tonight," Julie asks as she puts the car in park.

"I'm okay." *I'm not okay. Not sure I'll ever be.* "It's been a long weekend, Jules. I'm just tired."

"Yeah, I guess." She doesn't look convinced, but hopefully she'll let it slide. "Go get some sleep. Chloe invited us over to her place tomorrow to hang out. I'll come pick you up around noon."

"Okay." It's easier just to agree right now. "Thanks for the ride home."

"No problem."

I make my way to the side door of the house, giving Julie a wave as she drives away.

No one ever uses the front entrance. I remember my grams telling me once that "family and friends use the side door; the front door is reserved for the uninvited." Julie's taillights disappear around the corner and down the main road. I fumble for my keys inside my backpack.

When I look up, I find Mason sitting on the steps not ten feet in front of me. I grab my keys so hard they almost break skin.

"I could ask how you got here," I say, not seeing his truck anywhere, "but I think I can guess." I release the death grip on my keys and sit down beside him. "Are you okay? I'm sorry I took off. I didn't know what to do back there." He sits beside me in silence, looking at the ground, kicking around a rock with his shoe. "You growled at me, and—"

"I know." He cuts me off. "I'm sorry. I just needed a little time to regroup."

"I'm going to help you fix this. I can figure this out. You're going to be fine." I put my hand on his knee, leaning into him. He covers my hand with his, lacing his fingers between mine. The warmth of his hand envelops mine.

"Rach?"

"Yeah?"

"I'm sorry if I was a jerk tonight, at my house. And at the

lake."

"You were a jerk." I'm holding his hand again and calling him a jerk. This isn't how I pictured the night going.

"I deserve that."

"But you also saved me from being eaten by a bear. So, I'd say we're even."

"Yeah, I did." He lets a big breath out, smiling. "That was kind of cool."

CHAPTER SIX

"I don't want to take them." I push the bottle of pills across the glass coffee table towards the Weather Lady. "Here, take them back or something."

She looks at the bottle but doesn't pick it up. "It's totally up to you whether or not you take them. I prescribed them only for occasional use. For when your skies get a little too cloudy, and you need a little help clearing things up." She glances down and writes a note in her book. "Think of them as your own personal bottle of sunshine and rainbows."

Yeah, that's just it. Rainbows only show up after a rain and then fade away like an illusion. That's what these rainbows are—just a brief reprieve from the rain.

My bottle of sunshine and rainbows stares back at me from the inside shelf of the medicine cabinet. It's been three years, and the bottle is still one hundred percent full. My brother, Eric, had a drug problem. Not prescription drugs, the illegal kind. After my parents figured it out, they sent him to rehab. There, they gave him different drugs, the prescription kind. Neither kind solved my brother's problems. I figure they won't solve mine either. I'm not sure why I keep the bottle.

I grab a hair elastic from the medicine cabinet shelf before shutting its mirrored door. Raking my messy bedhead into a ponytail, I take a long look at the reflection staring back at me. I screwed up. I should have told them all to put the spirit box away. Now look what's happened to Mason. *It's all my fault he's like this. Am I going to be afraid of this problem because it seems too big to handle? Who's going to fix this?*

"I am," I whisper to the reflection. I try to believe it. I try to believe I am strong enough to fix things this time.

I hear the jingle of keys and the side door in the kitchen slamming shut. My grams and mom should be at work already. Poking my head out of the bathroom, I say, "Hello?"

"Hey." Grams looks over at me. "Did you just crawl out of bed? You look like crap." She's digging through a pile of papers in the kitchen, only half paying attention. "And aren't you supposed to be at school?"

"There are a few PD days and a teachers' conference this week, so I have no school." I walk into the kitchen, letting my sock feet skim over the yellowed linoleum. Cracking open the fridge, I reach in for what's left of the six-pack of Pepsi. Feeling one of the cool blue cylinders in my hand, I crack it open and take a long swig. The harsh bubbles burn down my throat. From the moment I've been able to buy it myself, I've drunk a Pepsi every morning.

"How do you drink that crap first thing?" She doesn't look up from her searching. "You're going to have no teeth by the time you're thirty."

"Like coffee's any better." My words come out garbled through a mouthful of pop. I gulp it down and stifle a burp. "So, why are you home? I heard Mom say you had to be at work early."

"I was at work. I came home to pick up some papers I forgot. Which reminds me, you need to come by the office and fill out paperwork for the summer student job. It's just a technicality. You've already got it. We just need to send some forms off to the government."

Got to love small-town nepotism. Grams got me a summer student job at the town municipal office, filing papers or something, which is great, because I have no plans after graduation. I should be making plans . . .

"I'm going over to Chloe's house around noon, but I can come by after that." I re-adjust the ever-creeping gym-shorts-slash-pyjama-bottoms I'm wearing. I bet I look as gross as I feel.

"Okay. Come around two thirty if you can. I should be done my stuff by then and I can help you with the forms." She gathers her papers and heads for the side door. Just before leaving, she stops. "One more thing. I noticed you unpacked the spirit box I gave you. It's been sitting out on the living room coffee table for a few days. I put it back in your room on your shelf." She pauses for a moment, not looking directly at me when she speaks. "I'm really glad you're starting to unpack things, honey."

"Yeah." *Please don't talk about unpacking things.* "I was just showing it to some friends. Sorry. I forgot to put it back."

"Oh. You had friends over?" The jubilant surprise in her voice is a little insulting.

"Just a few people. It wasn't a party or anything." Unpacking, friends, and Eric. These are the three "no-fly zone" topics that make my hands go clammy and my stomach do flips.

"It's fine you had people over. That's great." Her smile fades to a more serious look as she moves again to head out the side kitchen door. "Just be careful with that spirit box. It's not a toy to be left out. I'll see you around two thirty." The screen door slaps shut behind her as she leaves with an armful of papers.

I drop the can of Pepsi into the kitchen sink. The shock of it hitting the basin sends foam spewing out of the top. *Shit.* Did she open the spirit box? Does she know we've been playing with it? Does she know what it really is? I use my T-shirt to wipe the few droplets of projectile Pepsi from my hands. Striding down the hallway, I stop in the doorway to my bedroom. It feels different in here now, yet it hasn't changed any since I got out of bed. The spirit box is on my bookshelf, exactly where she said she'd put it. I must not have noticed it. It looks so normal, sitting there like a trinket on a shelf.

I want this all to be a dream, but it's not. The reality of my life, packaged in one tiny bedroom, stares back at me: cardboard boxes left unpacked and stacked shoulder-high—and the spirit box. The one thing I finally let see the light of day. I breathe deeply, convincing myself to step inside. It's the exact same room I slept in last night, and the night before, but it confronts me now with a reality I don't want to face. My footsteps don't make a sound as I step onto the compressed shag carpet in my room.

Lifting the spirit box as if not to disturb it, I set in on my bed. The wooden lid creaks in quiet complaint as I open it. There lay the three white animal carvings, strewn about in the box. Taking each piece out one by one, I place them softly on my comforter. I hold the knob that opens the false bottom. Would Grams have checked and put the wendigo piece back? I open the false bottom. It's not in there. I'm not sure if I expected it to be back in its spot or not, but there's a pang of disappointment when it isn't. Grams didn't put it back. She must not have checked. It must still be in the living room somewhere. If the wendigo piece was back where it should be, maybe this all wouldn't feel so real. But it is real.

Carrying the empty spirit box to the living room, I put it on the coffee table. Both the couch and the loveseat have a pleated velour dust ruffle that skirts the floor. I check under the loveseat first. Nothing but a lost spoon and thirty-five cents. I lift the ruffle on the couch and look under. There it is. All the way at the back, leaning up against the baseboard. Lying flat on my stomach, I stretch as far as I can to reach it. But the little voice of reason inside me whispers, *Whoa. Maybe you shouldn't touch it. What if it does the same thing to you as it did to Mason?* My hand recoils before I finish the thought. I need protection. Something I can use to pick it up.

Going to the kitchen, I fling open the cupboard door next to the stove. There, on a hook, are my Grandma's favorite hot pink oven mitts. Putting them on, I mutter a promise to myself that I'll wash them after this—twice. It's ridiculous to think that these can protect me from anything more than burns from a hot casserole, but the layer of quilted cotton has me feeling fearless.

Back in the living room, dressed in my "hungry bum" shorts, stained T-shirt and hot pink oven mitts, I'm ready to dive under the couch again. Face deep in the living room shag, I feel the wendigo carving in my grip. Reeling in my catch, I open my hand. Maybe it was the drinks we had on Friday night, or the fact it was late, but the wendigo now looks just like a carved trinket, something you'd see on an old lady's windowsill. How could something so innocent cause such trouble?

It's not going to answer your question just by staring at it. Put it away, Rachel. My quilted, pink hand hovers over the spirit box, ready to lock it up and forget it, when a thought crosses my mind. Giving the wendigo the blame for all this would give away the power to fix it. *This is your problem, Rachel. Yours to fix.*

"Hey." Julie is standing in the middle of the kitchen with a confused look on her face. "I knocked, but obviously you didn't hear me. Um, what are you doing?"

Oh, just chillin' in my grubbies on the living room floor. And you? "I'm looking for that lost wendigo piece from Friday night." I hold up the piece with my gloved hand and crack a smile. "Found it!"

"Why are you wearing oven mitts?"

"'Cuz I don't want to touch it." It doesn't feel right to put it away in the spirit box just yet. "I think it might be broken, maybe?"

Julie walks over to me and sits on the edge of the couch. "What's going on with you? You've been acting off since Friday night." She looks at me, searching for an answer with her brown eyes.

"I'm still really freaked out by this thing." I gesture towards the spirit box on the coffee table. "The lights, the fog, that white deer."

"Yeah, it was pretty foggy that night, but—"

"That's not what I meant. I meant the fog in my living room." She looks at me like I'm someone who likes to self-medicate.

Taking a quick glance around the room, she says, "What fog?"

She's serious. Her questioning look tells me she thinks I'm losing it. Sliding off the couch, she sits cross-legged beside me on the floor.

"Hey, listen." Her nose scrunches like she's trying to remember something. "I thought Friday night was a bit weird too, but I think we remember it differently." Her reassuring smile seems distant somehow. "And you're not the only one who's seemed off since Friday. Mason is too. I ran into him this morning before I came over here." Her eyes drift out of focus a little. "There's something different about him lately." Huffing out a breath, she blinks, then continues. "Anyway." She looks at me again, shaking off the thought. "We got talking about Friday night and that spirit box." She gestures towards it. "It's just a carved box with figurines in it. If any wishes come true, it'll be pure coincidence." Her voice sounds canned. Why would she say that? She was there Friday. She saw what happened.

"What about the white deer I saw? That was real."

Julie shuffles closer and puts her arm around my shoulders. "It could have just been a regular deer. I'm not saying that white ones don't exist, but maybe it just looked white in your headlights. And it definitely doesn't have anything to do with that box." She gives my shoulders a squeeze. "Feel better? That box is just a box. Anything else you think that spirit box has done that's creeping you out?"

Yeah, Mason is a wendigo now, and I'm guessing he has the ability to make you think what he wants. Why else would you be acting like none of this is strange?

"What about the orbs of light that came out of the spirit box?" Judging by her look, she thinks I've gone mad.

"Orbs?"

"You know what," I answer quickly, before she can say anything else, "I haven't been sleeping well. Maybe I dreamt it or something." I wish I had.

I stand up, leaving her sitting on the living room floor. I take the spirit box back to my room, replace the three white pieces, and put it back on the shelf. I'll think of a better spot for it later. Somewhere I don't have to look at it. Still holding the wendigo piece in my pink, protective mitts, I mumble, "I'll get to fixing this later." And I put it in my jewelry box on the shelf.

"So, did you forget I was coming over to pick you up? Or are you going over to Chloe's dressed like that?" Julie's followed me, hovering in the doorway to my room.

"I'm coming." Smoothing out the wrinkles does nothing to improve my outfit. "Can you give me twenty minutes for a shower? I'll try to be quick."

"No prob." She flops down on my bed, where the carvings had been only moments ago, and takes out her cell phone. I shiver at the thought of lying there without a care. "I'll text Chloe and tell her we'll be late."

"Yeah, thanks." Realizing I'm still wearing the oven mitts, I pull them off and set them on the shelf beside the spirit box. The light from her cell phone shines on her face in a pale glow. She might not remember what happened Friday night, but I'll never forget.

I've been to Chloe's house a few times. It's similar to mine, a typical 1960s bungalow. I think most of the houses in this town were built around the same time. Her place is a sandy beige with concrete steps out front that lead to its sky blue front door. A giant pine tree towers over the house in the middle of the front yard, browning out what's left of the grass beneath it. Covering the rest of the lawn is a mix of crabgrass and yellow dandelion heads.

I follow Julie up the front steps. It's odd that we don't go around to the side door. It feels as if we're door-to-door salespeople, marketing something you never knew you needed. She knocks hard twice and walks right in. I guess this front door isn't always for the uninvited. *If ye be friend, knock hard and enter.* The unwritten rule of entry in this town still baffles me. I'm not sure I'll ever get used to it.

"Hey, you made it. Nice to see you finally got out of bed, Rach." *Rach* doesn't faze me when anyone else says it, but when Chloe shortens my name, the sincerity of friendship is nowhere to be found.

"Yeah, sorry. I slept in." I guess that's what Julie told her. Better that than what I was really doing.

Julie takes off her jacket and throws it over the back of the living room couch. I keep mine on, but take off my shoes. Following Julie, we both head to the kitchen.

"I'm just teasing." Chloe walks into the kitchen carrying a box piled high with clothes. "I sleep till noon every chance I get." She plunks the box down on the floor, next to some pet food bowls that look like they've never been washed. "I went through my clothes and found the stuff you lent me. I put a few of my shirts in there too. I know you've been eyeing them up. Just give them back whenever."

A muffled "thanks" from Julie comes from behind the

open fridge door. Kicking the door shut with her foot, she emerges with three 7Ups. "Do you still have that bracelet of mine with the butterflies on it? Can I get it back?" She sets the cans of pop on the kitchen table.

"Yeah, sure. It's in my purse. I'll go get it." Chloe ducks around the corner for a moment to fetch her purse. In that brief moment, I feel slightly less like the third wheel on a gimpy bike. Julie and Chloe have been friends since daycare, or maybe birth. I get that Chloe probably thinks I cramp her bestie mojo with Julie, but I'm not trying to steal anyone's best friend. It's just nice not to be alone all the time. Sitting down at the kitchen table, I take a pop and open it. "You guys share clothes?"

Julie thumbs through a newspaper on the table as she answers back. "Yep. The nearest decent mall is super far away, so it's lucky that we're the same size. Saves us from suffering the same outfits all the time." Julie's a pixie for fashion. It actually might kill her to wear the same outfit twice.

Chloe plunks her oversized purse on the kitchen table, dumping out the contents. Receipts, wrappers, and change go everywhere. I save a few things from spilling over the edge of the table. "I really need to organize this thing," she says, but probably doesn't mean it. Picking through the mess, she finds the bracelet Julie was asking for and gives it back.

"I could help you sort this, if you want," I say, and instantly regret it. I might as well say, "I'll dig through the personal stuff in your purse." She probably thinks I'm weird. I start neatly sorting the little papers into piles. "You have a lot of lottery tickets."

"Yeah, my mom and I buy two tickets every week, mostly out of habit. I just let them pile up in there. We're never going to win anyway."

"My mom says lottery tickets are taxes for people who can't do math." *Oh my God. What's wrong with me?* Julie snorts a laugh from across the table, which nearly results in pop shooting from her nose.

"You finally got a good one in." Julie gives me a playful, open-handed slap on the back.

"But really, what would you do if you won?" I say, pressing on. "I'd buy myself a car." I look over at Julie, giving her a nudge. "I do enjoy my personal chauffeur here, but having my own wheels would be nice."

Chloe doesn't pause the rhythm of shoving her things back in her purse as she speaks. "I'd leave. Just go—somewhere, you know? Away from here. Travel the world. Do all those things you only see in magazines." She slows down a breath, putting the last bit of loose change back in her purse. "Yeah, but don't worry, it'll never happen. You guys are stuck with me forever."

Julie clasps the delicate butterfly bracelet around her wrist. "I would love to sit and chat all day about what I would do with millions of dollars, but I came here to hear the juicy details about Chloe and Ryan getting back together." She takes another swig of her 7Up and smacks her lips. "So dish, Chloe."

I try to pay attention, but my interest wanes as the two of them analyze every syllable spoken between Chloe and Ryan the night they got back together. It's like watching a play-by-play of some sporting event I don't understand. *Really, girls? Is this what we are predestined to be like? Swooning at any male who feigns interest in us?* Then again, I guess I'm just as pathetic with Nate.

I've never really dated anyone before. Well, nothing serious at least. There was a guy once, back in Vancouver. I was in grade nine. He told everyone in our class that I was his girlfriend. So I guess that means I've had a boyfriend. We went out a few times, to the movies, and hanging out with his friends. He was kind of sweet. He would open doors for me and hold my hand. I guess he lost interest after a while. Within two weeks, he'd sent me a note in English class, dumping me. It's not that I had any serious feelings for him, but I went home and cried that night. Rejection sucks, I guess.

"So, did you have make-up sex?" Julie asks Chloe.

I realize that I've been reminiscing about holding hands while they're talking about make-up sex. I look up from the entertainment section of the paper I've been pretending to read. "You slept with him?"

Chloe's cheeks flush red. "We didn't do much sleeping." Both she and Julie giggle. "Hey, don't knock it till you've tried it,"

Chloe says, looking right at me.

I huff out a breath I've been holding in too long. "I'm good, thanks." I look back down at the newspaper, trying to hide my . . . embarrassment? Anger?

"So you've never had make-up sex—or sex in general?" Julie asks.

"No. Yes. I mean—no." Suddenly I feel like the oldest virgin on the planet. My cheeks are burning.

"Oh," Julie answers. It's amazing how so much judgment can come from a word with only two letters.

"Yes, *oh*." I fire back.

"Hey, don't get mad. It's cool if you haven't. We were just talkin'," Chloe chimes in.

I smirk a fake smile. I don't want to talk about this. Time to change the topic. "Hey, the lotto numbers for this week are in the paper." I gesture to the newspaper I'm still clinging to. "Give me your tickets and I'll check them for you."

Chloe hands me the pile of lotto tickets I so neatly sorted for her. "You'll have to find which ones are for this week."

"So, do you love him?" I mumble my question, wanting to ask but knowing I shouldn't.

"Love who? Ryan?" Her voice hitches like I caught her in a lie. "No. I don't think so. It's not always like that, you know?" Chloe doesn't look at me. The kitchen is quiet for a moment, before the two of them go back to picking apart the details of Chloe's on-again-off-again romance. I'll sit out this round of questioning.

This week's tickets are on the top of the pile Chloe handed me. I smooth them out on the table: Lotto 6/49 and LottoMax. Lotto 6/49's top prize is three million dollars this week and LottoMax is forty-two million.

I read the winning numbers from the newspaper and then check the tickets. I have a pen ready to circle the numbers if I find any matches. I circle. I keep circling. I keep checking, over and over again. Every number matches—on both tickets. I check again.

Every number matches on both tickets.

My eyes feel glazed, but my mind is whisked back to Friday night. Chloe's voice echoes in my head: *I wish I were rich and famous.*

It's coming true. This is real.

"The numbers match," I stifle to speak. The words barely come out.

"Cool. How many?" I have Chloe's attention first. "Did I win anything?" She stretches her hand out for the tickets.

"All the numbers. Forty-five million dollars," I croak out.

"Ha! Very funny. You're just full of jokes today. Let me see." Chloe steals the newspaper and tickets away from me.

"Holy shit!" She turns the page and tickets to Julie. "I fucking won—both. Forty-five million dollars. Every single number!" By this point, she's screaming and jumping up and down, and so is Julie. I would still be sitting in my chair if they hadn't pulled me into a group hug. She wished for this from the spirit box.

Bang!

The sound sends a shattering boom through the small kitchen. What the hell was that? We all stop, out of breath, looking at the front door where the noise came from.

"What was that?" Julie's hold on our group hug loosens.

"Just the paperboy, maybe? He really hurls it some days," Chloe answers.

"Today's paper is on the table. It's what I used to look up the lotto numbers."

"Right." Chloe takes a step back, hands on her hips, catching her breath. "Well, open it and see."

Chloe and Julie follow behind as I cross from the kitchen, to the living room, to the front door. Reaching for the doorknob, I hear a fluttering, rustling sound that grows louder as I inch the door open. My stomach is in my throat. I slowly turn the knob, inching the door open towards me.

Crows. Everywhere. There must be hundreds. Thousands, maybe. They're on the roofs of neighbouring houses, on cars, on trees, on telephone lines, even on the railing leading up the steps to Chloe's front door. Black feathers and beady eyes decorate every available perch. Other than the odd flap of wings, they don't make a sound. Their eerie silence sends a rush of cold through me.

I'm entranced by the spectacle. I've never seen anything like it before. Chloe and Julie have crept over to the picture window in the living room, opening the blinds for a better look.

"Holy crap." My voice is hushed. "I've never seen crows flocked together like this before. Why are they all watching your house, Chloe?"

"It's not a flock," Julie whispers. "It's called a murder."

I look over at Julie, one eyebrow cocked. "They're here to murder us?"

"No!" Julie speaks in a whisper, not taking her eyes off the birds. "A group of crows is called a murder. Hey," she says, annoyed. "There isn't a lot to do around here. I've gotten kind of addicted to the nature channel. This looks like a crow funeral."

"What? You're making this up," Chloe cuts in.

"It's true. Google it. When a crow dies, other crows from miles around will gather around the dead one. Some people think it's to grieve the dead crow. Like paying their last respects or something."

"Cool," Chloe answers. "So where's the dead one?"

I inch the door open a little further to get a better look. Black eyes flit towards me and then away. The birds don't seem bothered much by my presence, and only the ones closest to me adjust their perches.

A few crows in a nearby tree start to croon a low, chortling noise, and I look up. Their sound starts the rest of the birds in the same strange chorus. The chortling hum of that many birds is an amazing sound, yet somehow very sad.

Opening the front door to its fullest, the chorus stops almost immediately. But the birds don't move. My eyes try to find what the birds are looking at. Me? No. The thought of thousands of crows swooping down on me crosses my mind. I step forward anyway, bringing my foot to the threshold of the door where it bumps something. Looking down at my feet, I see what the birds have come to grieve. Its downy white feathers ruffle slightly in the breeze. Lying dead, on the front steps of Chloe's house, is a snowy white crow.

This is happening. Wishes are coming true. The wendigo, the white deer, the white crow.

Both Chloe and Julie have come to stand behind me again. We all simply stare until Chloe breaks the silence. "It must have flown into the door and broken its neck. I've heard of sparrows doing that." Kneeling down, I pull the sleeve of my hoodie over my hand and reach out to touch it. "Whoa! What are you doing?"

"I'm checking if it's dead." I give the bird a nudge with my covered hand. The other birds watch me in silence.

"It looks pretty dead to me. Should we put it in a garbage bag or something?" asks Julie.

"I don't know." I cautiously look up at the thousands of shiny black eyes staring back at me. "I don't think we should move it until the other birds are gone." I slowly inch back in to the house and stand up, leaving the front door wide open.

The three of us stand there, looking at each other in awkward silence. The winning tickets, the white crow, the spirit box. This isn't coincidence. They'll believe me when I say the spirit box is real. They'll have to.

"Somebody say something," I whisper.

"Okay." Chloe's the first to break the silence. "Enough *Wild Kingdom*. Shut the door so the dirty birds don't get in. I've got to call my mom and tell her she can quit her job, 'cuz we in the money!"

"But . . ." My voice sounds weak. "Don't you guys see? It's the white crow from the spirit box." I turn to face them, letting the door close a little but not all the way.

"Oh, yeah," says Chloe, "there was a white crow in that box. Cool. Too bad it's dead."

Cool? How about *oh my God, this is really happening*? I turn to close the door, checking to make sure I don't close it on any birds. "Guys, where's the white one?" It's gone from the porch.

We all turn in unison as we hear the caw of a single crow coming from inside the house.

It's the white crow, perched on back of Chloe's hideous, green velour, floral-patterned couch. I guess it only knocked itself out flying into the door. It hops from the back of the couch to the floor right at our feet. We all back away, giving it room to go out the door. It looks at us, tilting its head and chattering before it hops out the still-open door and flies away. Almost in unison, all the crows take flight. From the trees, the power lines, the cars, they all lift off, cawing loudly, filling the sky with black wings.

I swat at the front door, slamming it shut. Silence fills the room. "This is all from making wishes on the spirit box. You guys see that, right? She wished to be rich and famous and—"

Chloe throws a confused glance at Julie. "It's a coincidence, I guess." She chokes back a giggle.

What? Chloe was there, too, when the fog and lights came out of the box. "When was the last time you saw Mason?" My voice is too sharp, but I'm past caring.

"This morning, I guess. He came to drop off my English notes he'd borrowed. Are you okay? You—"

"Yeah, I'm fine. Listen, I've got to go." I bend down and grab my shoes, taking a quick inventory to see if I've forgotten anything. "You should call your mom, Chloe." I try my best to produce a genuine smile. "Tell her the news. I have to get to the municipal office and sign some paperwork for my summer job. I told my grandma I'd be there by two thirty." I open the front door to find the yard free of birds. Everything looks as it should.

"Wait, I can give you a ride there." Julie turns to look for her jacket and car keys.

"It's okay," I say, putting on my shoes. "I could use some fresh air, and it's not far to walk." I check again to make sure I have everything in my pockets. Anything to distract from their questioning looks. "I'll see you guys later, okay? And congratulations, Chloe—you're rich." I feel their eyes on me as I walk away.

I need to get out of here. *Before my dark clouds turn to thunder storms.*

CHAPTER SEVEN

Plif, plif, scuff. The soft soles of my Toms pad against the sidewalk. I'm walking to the municipal office, I think. I have a slight clue on how to get there—but not really.

Nothing ever happens the way I imagine it. I shouldn't be in this town. I should be in Vancouver, looking forward to graduation instead of dreading it. I should be sorting through art school acceptance letters with Eric instead of trying to ignore the fact that, come fall, I'll have no purpose.

I stop at the corner where the sidewalk ends. *Left? Right? Straight ahead?* I'm walking blind with my eyes wide open.

I fill my lungs deep with damp afternoon air. It feels like I haven't taken a breath in weeks. I look back to where I came from. I can't see Chloe's house anymore.

My cell phone is nestled in the back left pocket of my jeans. I instinctively reach for it. I could call someone. They could come pick me up. *No. You can figure this out.* It doesn't help that I can't find the street signs.

Beside me, a long, metal pole juts up from the ground. It looks like it once held a street sign, but not anymore. No signs, no directions. I guess left.

I don't recognize this street at all. I've been in this town for over four months, and I don't know where the hell I am! My hand still hasn't left my back pocket, my fingers still touching my cell phone.

Grams and Mom are busy at work. Chloe and Julie are just a few blocks away. Julie offered to drive me. *But Julie thinks you've lost it.* I feel like my brain has used up its last bit of sanity watching that white crow and Chloe winning two lotteries.

I hear her voice from Friday night on repeat in my head. *Rich and famous* . . . I wish I were rich and famous. I guess she got her wish.

The loud buzz of my cell phone brings me back to the here and now. I answer instantly, almost dropping the phone in a puddle.

"Hello?" I don't look to see who is calling.

"Hey, it's me." Julie's voice ties knots inside of me. "You sound out of breath. You okay?"

"I'm—fine. Just a little turned around is all."

"I can still drive you if you want. It's not a big deal.

Really."

I hear Chloe's excited squeals in the background. A shiver of my surreal reality runs over me. "It's okay. I can walk. I'm almost there anyway."

The air hangs limp between us. "Are you okay?" Her concern seems genuine, but I don't want it. Not right now.

"Yeah."

"You left in kind of a hurry, and—"

"Yeah, I know. Sorry. I just have to get to that appointment. And it wouldn't look great if I was late."

"Okay. But if you want to talk, I'm here. Give me a call later, 'kay?" I hear Chloe in the background prodding Julie to hurry up.

"Sure." My mind is already a hundred miles away. "We'll talk soon. You'd better go, Chloe sounds like she's going to explode." I put the phone back in my pocket and start walking again.

I come to another intersection and stop. It's not a main road, just another side street with no street sign and rows of houses. I should've let Julie pick me up. I could call Mason. I want to talk to him anyway. I could ask him what he said to Chloe and Julie this morning. Ask why they think all this is just a coincidence.

There's a large puddle spanning almost half the street. I

can't cross without getting my shoes soaked. Something must be blocking the drain. This happened all the time in front of my old house in Vancouver. I'd go out with a shovel and clear the storm drain when it got clogged with leaves and branches. It must have rained heavily last night.

Unlike Vancouver, I don't have a shovel, but there's a broken tree limb on the sidewalk that will work just as well. Walking over to pick it up, I notice a squirrel beside it on the ground. Its tiny, furry body is curled up in the fetal position, matted and wet from the rain. It doesn't move an inch when I get close. It's obviously dead. As I bend down to pick up the branch, however, I think twice. Will it come to life like the white crow?

I wonder how it might have died. Maybe it fell from the tree when the limb broke? Somehow, that doesn't seem likely. I've seen squirrels do some crazy acrobatics and never fall. I look up to see where it came from. The tree towers at least forty feet above my head, swaying gently in the breeze. A better question might be, what broke the branch?

Putting my foot on the tree limb for balance, I snap off a more manageable piece. I use it to move the squirrel from the sidewalk to the grass. It just doesn't seem right to leave it on the path.

Dragging the piece of branch back to the stagnant drain, I wedge it under the obstruction that's causing the water to back up. I push as hard as I can, but whatever's clogging the storm drain is really stuck. The look of it reminds me of wet dryer lint, all matted up and dirty. I feel it start to give way. With a slurp it comes free and water starts to rush down the drain.

Squatting down to have a closer look, my heart sinks. The water has receded enough to make out what's in the gutter. Its little hand-like paws, the black mask around its eyes, its black-and-white ringed tail. It's a racoon, and something else . . . Its orange fur sticks up in spikes where it isn't covered by leaves and dirt. The smell of them both hits me and I teeter back, gagging.

A cat and a raccoon.

I stand. And the quiet tree-lined street, without warning, turns strange. I cringe at the too-bright rays coming from the sun. Looking across the street, I notice another broken tree limb. It's more like half a tree, actually. Something feels off about this. There's something lying heaped beside it: a dog—no, it's bigger. A deer. I make out a set of antlers that first looked like branches from the tree.

What's going on here? A dead squirrel, a cat, a racoon, and a deer? I bolted from the bizarro scene at Chloe's place only to find another one out on the street. I need to go. This isn't right.

Turning in the direction I saw the branch, I start to move, walking at first, then faster, now running. No birds chirp, no dogs bark. There are no sounds at all but me and the echoes in my head. Not slowing, I jerk back to look behind me. No one's there.

Dooonng.

My face collides with a street sign. Metallic sounds ripple behind my eyes as my head starts to spin. Before I know it, I'm sinking to my knees, the soft grass beneath me. I roll to a sit. The irony of running away and smacking into the very thing I was looking for is not lost on me.

I try to slow my spinning brain by putting my hands to my temples. The pain isn't as bad as it sounded, but I definitely jostled something. At least no one saw it. I peek an eye open and scan the area around me, but there's just me, sitting alone near the curb.

Then I see it, across the street: my white deer. Was it his eyes I felt watching me? I blink hard. The deer stands at attention, unmoving, staring back at me. His coat is snow white, his eyes a soft, dark brown. A set of new velvet antlers crowns his head. Stunning. Before all the craziness of today, I might have convinced myself that the deer I saw Friday night only appeared white in my headlights. But this deer is no illusion.

From across the street, kitty-corner to me, he lowers his head to get a better look at me. I stare back, our gazes locking. The logical part of me questions if I should back away, but I don't move. I'm not afraid. The white deer makes no attempt to come any closer, and neither do I. Maybe it's wondering if I'm okay? *I'm wondering if I'm okay too, deer.*

I'm entranced by our silent conversation. Then his ears twitch and he raises his head. He bounds off behind a long row of overgrown lilac bushes and is gone. *Don't go, deer! I didn't get my wish: to know what I want and to find what I'm looking for.*

I don't hear the truck pull up or him get out.

"Rachel? Are you okay?" It's Nate—always finding me on the side of a road somewhere.

I crane my neck to see his towering frame shadowing over me. My calm state jolts into overdrive. Did he see the white deer? Oh God, did he see me slam into the street sign? I'd never live that one down. I shield my eyes from the sun with one hand and steady myself with the other.

"Hey," I say as nonchalantly as possible. "When did you get here? This must look kinda strange. Me sitting in a ditch— again."

His head bobs in agreement and his lips purse into a smile. "Yeah, a bit. We really should stop meeting this way."

"I agree, yes!" My voice is too eager. "No more ditches." Although . . . the last time I was in a ditch with Nate, it wasn't all bad. The memory floods back in a flush of rose to my cheeks. I teeter and stumble as I get up, bumping into him. His strong arms catch mine.

"I don't see your mom's truck. How'd you end up here this time?"

"You didn't see the deer?"

He looks at me as if we're having two different

conversations, and we are. "What deer?" He glances over my head. "I just saw you sitting here, so I stopped."

I open my mouth to tell him about the white deer but change my mind. He won't believe me anyway. I settle for telling him half of the story. "There's a dead deer back there," I say, pointing the way I came. "And a racoon, and a cat, and a squirrel. They're all dead." I search his face, trying to judge his reaction. "I didn't kill them."

"The thought that you killed them never crossed my mind, but okay." I feel his hand slip from my arm, but he doesn't completely let go.

"I'm sorry." I let out a breath I've been holding for a while. "I . . . You . . ." I close my eyes and try to straighten out the words in my head. "These last couple of days have felt like a rollercoaster riding a tornado." I look up at his eyes and find them looking back at me. "Honestly, I want to tell you every detail, but I can't." I keep going before I lose my nerve. "It baffles my mind that a guy like you would even take the time say hi to me. And it makes me say the dumbest things. Maybe I can tell you my long story about today sometime, but I can't right now." I think that's the most and least I've ever said to anyone.

His perfect forehead creases a bit between his eyes. "You're the strangest girl I've ever met. I'll take a rain check on your long rollercoaster story." The spot where his hand once held my arm goes cold as he sweeps a loose hair behind my ear.

"How's your head, by the way? You're making me second guess not taking you to a doctor the other night." He smells like the outdoors and fresh laundry. *Mmm.*

"The bump on my head from Friday night is almost gone." The bump on my head from two minutes ago, however . . . "It feels a lot better, actually." The look on his face says he's not convinced. "No, seriously, I'm fine. I'm just . . ." The little hamster that runs the wheel in my head must be dead too. I got nothing.

Nate's mouth tightens a bit at the corners. "You don't have to say anything."

My eyes flit to the ground, but he lifts my chin back up to meet his gaze. "Can I ask where you were going before you mysteriously had to sit on the side of the road?"

Shit. I'm going to be late. "I'm going to the municipal office. I need to fill out some paperwork."

His smile widens ear to ear. "Can I give you a ride? It just so happens I need to stop by the municipal office too."

"Do you really have to go there, or are you just saying that?" I'm staring again. He notices. *Damn it.*

He pauses for a second before answering. "Does it matter?" Touché, Nathan Grey Hawk. "Come on, get in." He leads me to the passenger side of his truck, opening the door for me.

"Thanks," I say as I climb in, trying not to look too long

at his lean form as he runs around to the other side and hops in.

"It's a good thing I found you. The office is on the other side of town. You were totally headed in the wrong direction."

That sounds about right. Lost in the metropolis of Hazelton.

By the time we reach the municipal office, it's raining. Nate finds a close spot to park and we both race for the front door. He beats me and holds the door open, getting soaked in the process. After wiping my feet on the dark, industrial doormat, the loud squeak of my shoes announces my arrival to everyone.

Grams is in the back near the copy machine. By the look on her face, she's having some trouble with it, and using some choice words, too. A delicate lady Grams is not. Nate and I take a seat in the small, dusty waiting room, which consists of four chairs and a well-used coffee table covered with outdated car and fishing magazines.

Other than Nate and me, there's only one person in the waiting area. He looks impatient, as if he's been there for a while. I recognize the logo on his jacket: *Allen Drilling*. Mason's dad's company.

"Dave," my grandma calls out from the back of the office, "I have your paperwork."

The man in the waiting area gets up and makes his way to the front counter. "Thanks, Ellen."

"Oh, don't thank me yet. Harry had more concerns about your site locations. He didn't approve your proposal again."

Dave mumbles a curse under his breath. "Seriously? What's wrong with it now? Is he here? Can I just sit down and talk with him?"

"Sorry, he's out of town for a few days. But he left you a note." She reaches into the thick, brown envelope on the counter and pulls out a few pieces of paper. "He says"—she licks her finger and thumbs through the pages—"your first site location is too close to a road allowance, and the second is too close to the nesting area of a known indigenous species." She sounds out every syllable to get her point across. She stuffs the papers back in the envelope and hands them over to Dave. "There's more, but you can read it yourself."

"Every time I submit this thing, he finds something else wrong with it. I give up, Ellen." His hands go up in defeat. "I don't know what to do. What am I supposed to do about this?"

"Well, if you ask real nice, Nathan over there might help you out." Nate glances up from the twelve-month-old car magazine he's been flipping through. "Nathan's been running a guiding service in this area for years. He knows this place better than anyone."

Nate stands up and shakes Dave's hand. "Hi, call me Nate. Why don't you come over to my shop sometime and we'll see if I can help you out." Nate fishes a business card out of his wallet and hands it to Dave.

"Sure, thanks. You'll probably hear from me later this week, after I talk to my boss." Dave gathers all his papers and stuffs the business card in his pocket. "Thanks, Ellen, you have a good rest of your day. Talk to you soon, Nate." Grams gives Dave a dismissive wave as he heads out the door.

"Sorry if I put you on the spot there, Nathan. I kind of feel bad for the guy. If it isn't the band councils shooting down the oil and gas projects, it's the municipal district."

"No, problem, Ellen. I don't mind. It's early in the season and I'm not booked up yet."

Ellen? My grandma has a first name, but I didn't expect Nate to use it.

"So what brings you in here today? It feels like forever since I've seen you. When did you get back from college?" She comes around the counter and gives Nate a hug.

"Oh, I've been back for a while, almost a year already. I've just been working a lot. It's probably why we haven't run into each other sooner."

"Oh, good. Where at?" Typical Grams, always probing for more gossip.

"Actually, I bought a share of my uncle's garage. He's semi-retiring from being a grease monkey. That's why I'm here, actually. I got a notice that my business license is up for renewal. I thought I'd stop by and take care of it."

"Okay. You're not in a hurry, are you? Do you mind if I get my granddaughter started on some paperwork before I get you yours? It's a probably going to take her a while to fill it out, and it's just me in here today."

"No problem, you go ahead and help Rachel. I'm in no hurry." If Grams' ears could turn and point forward like on one of those hunting dogs, I think they just did.

"You know Rachel?" Her voice is lilting, her head tilting ever so slightly. I see the gears turning now.

"Yeah, we met a while ago. One of her friends brought their car in for a tune-up. Julie, was it?" *Aw.* He covered for me, and I didn't even have to ask. Smooth.

"Um, yeah," I answer. *Was that convincing?*

"Oh, okay."

I can hear it in her voice. She wants to roll out the twenty questions. Every time my mom and Grams come within a five-mile radius of an eligible young male around my age, their date-ability meter goes off. *Please don't embarrass me, Grams.*

"Have a seat, Nathan. I'll just get Rachel started on her paperwork."

Nathan goes back to his dusty car magazine while I go up to the counter. My eyes are down, looking through my wallet for my ID, when a small stack of papers slides towards me. Attached to the papers is my grandma's hand, and not much farther behind that is her face.

"So, you've known each other for a few weeks, eh?" she whispers, low enough that only I can hear.

I put my hand on the papers and try to slide them out from under her grip. "Yep." But she holds tight.

"Is that all I get? *Yep*?"

"Can we talk about this later, please?" I know she's not going to let up, but maybe I can postpone her bombardment until Nate is out of earshot.

"I get off work at five. I want all the details before nine. Deal?"

"All the details about what?" I make one last-ditch effort to get out of twenty-question night.

But her raised eyebrow tells me it's game on. "Or I could start spouting random embarrassing stories about you. You know, my mind isn't what it used to be. I'm getting old. I might just start rambling uncontrollably." She smirks.

"So, it's going to be like that? You wouldn't."

"Hey, Nathan," Grams motions with her free hand for Nate to come over, still holding the stack of papers firmly with the other.

There's no way I'm getting out of this. I'm going to have to dish something. I have to get a lot better at making up stories, or she's going to stir up the most embarrassing thing she can think of and blab it to the hottest guy I've ever met. *Think! Quick!*

Nate comes and stands beside me, brushing his hand against me as he settles it on the counter. Busted. There's no way Grams didn't catch that. She knows we didn't just meet once at some car garage.

"Hey, Grandma?" My voice is rushed. "I'm going straight home after this. Do you need me to pick up anything for supper?" I give the stack of papers another tug, and she finally lets go. "I thought I'd cook tonight." I've never made supper in my life. Anyone who knows me knows this.

"I went shopping yesterday, hon. There should be something in the fridge to make." I can see the glint in her eyes— she knows she's won this round. "Can't wait to see what you cook up."

I break my stare, defeated, and look down at the stack of paperwork.

She turns and smiles at Nate. "I just need your signature on a form and a cheque for the balance. Then we'll have you on your way."

I watch as she walks to the back of the office and pulls hard on a large file cabinet drawer to open it.

Nate bumps me with his elbow, glancing down at the employment forms I'm filling out. "When do you start working here?"

"Not for a couple of weeks. As soon as I finish my exams."

"Cool." He looks up for a second, I assume to see if my grandma is in earshot. "So, can I give you a ride home? It's still raining pretty hard out there."

"That would be nice. Thanks."

It's nice for once . . . not to feel the rain.

I listen to Nate talk about his day as he drives me back to my place. He tells me that his grandma and mine are good friends. I'm surprised, but I shouldn't be. This town is small, and everybody knows everybody. I've only been here a few months, and even I know everyone within a couple of houses of me.

Vancouver isn't friendly like that. It's not that the people are rude, 'cuz they're not. It's just different. In Vancouver, I lived in the same house until my parents got divorced, and the neighbourhood didn't have any other kids my age. I mostly hung out with my brother. My parents weren't friends with the neighbours, who were pretty much strangers to us. In Vancouver, nobody ever checked on our house when we went on vacation or came to tend our garden when we were away. We just set our alarm and left. Not like here. The sense of community in Hazelton is growing on me.

Nate pulls into the long driveway in front of my place

and puts the truck in park.

"Thanks again for the ride," I say.

"Didn't want you to end up in some ditch without me." He casts me a look I'm not sure how to take.

I reach for the door handle, trying to hide the blush crossing my face, when I feel his hand brush over mine.

"Hey," he says, as I let the half-open truck door linger in my hand. "You sure you're doing okay?"

I'm tired of lying and telling half-truths. Besides, I can't come up with anything believable right now. "No, not really." I look back at him.

"I was going to head out to my grandpa's place after this, but I don't need to go right away. If you want to hang out."

It's kind of sweet that he wants to talk, but—no. "Don't worry about me too much." A shy smile touches my lips. "People say I'm tougher than I look." I push the truck door open and step out.

The rain has slowed to a drizzle.

"Are we still on for Friday?"

"Yeah, of course."

"Awesome. I'll pick you up at seven."

Even after he's left, I smile like an idiot for at least twenty minutes.

This rainbow was worth the rain.

CHAPTER EIGHT

The slap of the screen door slamming shut startles me. I check the little clock on my laptop: 5:18 p.m. Grams must be home. I said I'd make supper. Hope she didn't take me seriously on that.

The glow of my computer screen has fried my eyeballs. Maybe it's time to take a break. Google doesn't seem to have the answers I need about Mason's predicament anyways. I've found folklore about wendigos, most of which looks a little too Hollywood. And there is nothing about spirit boxes that looks like any help. If the information I need isn't on the Internet, where is it? *Think.* I refuse to believe my generation doesn't have the ability to think beyond what's directly in front of them. I click to a different screen when I hear a soft knock at my bedroom door.

"Can I come in?"

"Yeah. Just surfing the Net, Grams." I swivel my computer chair towards my bedroom door, tucking in my legs in to avoid all the cardboard boxes.

"I thought I was coming home to a three-course meal."

"Seriously? You know I can't cook." I stand up and push my chair back under my desk. "Well, I guess I could make mac and cheese with hot dogs. That'll count as three courses if I make it super runny. Soup and side dish, with hotdogs as the main course."

"Mmm. Sounds disgusting. How about I cook and you keep me company?"

I use the wall for balance as I avoid the stacked boxes on the way out of my room.

"I don't mean to push, honey," Grams butts in before I can leave, "but are you ever going to unpack? You like it here, don't you?"

"I like it here. I'll get to it, don't worry." I know she's asking because she cares, but I wish people would just let it go. I'll do it when I'm ready.

"Okay." She reaches over and gives me a one-armed bear hug. "Cheer up, kid. You look like you just lost your best friend. You make some tea and I'll see what I can scrounge up for supper."

"I don't really want tea, but I'll make you some."

"Oh, come on." She talks as she heads to the kitchen. "I'm going to cook and you're going to talk. You'd be surprised at how many of life's important conversations occur over hot beverages."

By the time I'm finished making tea, my mom walks in the door from work. She works at a place called Mountain Data Services. I don't know if she got the job before we moved here or not, but she started within a few days of our arrival. It's all she ever talks about. Part of me is happy that she's happy—at work and in this town—but the other half is kind of pissed. Has she forgotten why we ended up here? The event that changed everything forever? Sometimes I think she wants to forget and live in this fake Norman Rockwell version of our lives. Before she even finishes taking off her coat, words are spilling out of her mouth. "So, I hear you have a boyfriend?" The way she sing-songs *boyfriend* makes an involuntary flush rise on my checks.

"He's not my boyfriend, Mom."

"I saw that eye roll. He must be something."

Mom vision can spot an eye roll a hundred yards out. "He's just a friend. He—"

"Drove her home today from the municipal office, and they've known each other for a little while now," Grams chimes in.

"Are you two going to let me speak, or are you just going to talk amongst yourselves? 'Cuz I'm good with either."

"I don't think so." Grams pulls out a kitchen chair and motions for me to plant my butt. "Sit."

"There's not much to say," I mumble as I sit down.

"Wait, wait! Let me get a cup of tea before you start." Grams brings two cups to the table and hands one to my mother before they both take a seat.

"You too with the tea, Mom?"

"Of course. Important conversations happen over tea." She gives me a puzzled look as if I should know this. I have to admit, it's kind of cute. The two of them huddled over their steaming cups, looking at me like two old biddies eyeing the last lemon square at a social.

I glaze over a few half-truths about Nate and me, leaving out the part where I crashed Mom's truck. I also tell them about Chloe and her mom winning the lottery, but not the part about the birds. I should be writing down who I tell what these days. Who would believe the truth, anyway? I barely do.

It's Thursday, and I'm happy to report that the last few days have been uneventful. Mostly I've been hanging out at home, helping Grams get her garden ready for planting. She won't be able to plant anything for another couple weeks, but there's still lots of yard work to be done and I like helping her outside. There's something to be said for working with dirt. Maybe it's the simplicity of making something grow. Whatever it is, it's good for the soul. I take another two bags of potting soil from the shed and throw them in the wheelbarrow. The ground is wet, and the wheel sinks into the dirt as I make my way to the front of the house.

Mason finally called me back last night after I left him three messages. He sounded normal, if that term even applies to him anymore. I didn't bring up his conversations with Julie and Chloe and how they don't remember things the way I do. I chickened out, I guess. I didn't want him to react the same way the girls did—with wilful ignorance.

I told Mason about what I'd found on the Internet about wendigos. His lack of concern irked me, but he did agree to come over tomorrow to look at what I'd found. He tells me things are going fine with him. For now, I'll believe him.

Julie has been hard to get a hold of since Chloe's big lottery win. I can't entirely blame her. She's sent a few text messages informing me what mall they're currently blowing tons of money at. It's hard to imagine that the lottery people have already given Chloe her money. So they must be racking up some pretty serious credit card debt. I'm a bit envious. Who wouldn't be?

Julie said she'd make it up to me for being gone all week. She's coming over tomorrow to do my hair and makeup before my date with Nate, which is awesome. I'm so useless doing girly things like that, so I appreciate the offer. I proved my lack of prowess once when I thought it would be nice to give myself highlights. I used straight bleach on my hair. Let's just say it took a long time for my "highlights" to grow back after I burnt them off.

I rip open the last bag of potting soil and dump it into the planter by the front door. The air fills with the smell of wet peat moss and topsoil. I think I'll call it quits after this, maybe go back on my computer and see if I can get something new to come up in my search engine about wendigos. Sitting back on the front steps for a minute, admiring my work, I see my mom's truck pull into the driveway.

"Hey," I call out as she parks the truck and rolls down the window. "What are you doing home so early?"

"I'm not staying. Just thought I'd pop by and see if you wanted to go out for lunch."

"Sure, where to?"

"There's a little diner near my office. I thought we could try it out."

I stand up and dust my hands off on my jeans. "Should I change?" I gesture towards my old, ripped jeans and my 1996 *Camp Crazy Horse* T-shirt.

"Nah, you look fine. Besides, it's a diner in Hazelton.

Who are you going to see?"

"Fine, I'll just grab my phone." I run into the house and grab my keys, wallet, and phone. No new messages. That's good. Life is normal. Last weekend was crazy, but it's nothing I can't handle.

News vans and cars line the street, so we park two blocks away from the diner. "Busy day today," Mom says on the walk over. "I bet they're all here to interview Chloe and her mom." I nod in agreement as she opens the door to the diner.

We wait by the front till beside a small, handwritten sign that says *Please wait to be seated.* The diner is so tiny it doesn't strike me as the sort of place to have formalities, and judging by the frazzled wait staff, I'm guessing the policy is new. They've probably never seen this kind of business.

After a minute, a tired but smiling waitress comes over and seats us in a small booth next to the windows. It's cozy here, decorated in a rustic, West Coast fashion. The open, lofty ceiling has exposed, knotted beams decorated with old snow shoes, animal traps, and an overturned canoe. The walls are a cluster of faded old pictures. I assume they're from around the area.

"So, do you know what you want?" Mom says, not looking up from her menu.

"Grilled cheese with ham and an iced tea."

"You always get that."

"It's a classic. I know what I like." I put down my menu and glance around the place while my mom reads every selection on the menu, trying to compose the perfect meal.

Seated across from us are three guys. They don't look like they're from around here. Their designer clothes and haircuts give them away. They're probably reporters or journalists. Another guy hurries into the diner and finds a seat at the fourth chair at their table. I can't help but smirk. Maybe I'm fitting into this town better than I thought. I actually find myself wondering what these "outsiders" are talking about. Ironic . . . an outsider like me suspicious of other outsiders. I'm not exactly eavesdropping, but I'm not tuning them out either. At least that's what I tell myself.

"So, we've got an interview with the girl and her mother about the lottery tickets at four. I'd also like to talk to a friend of the family or something. Maybe expand on the story a bit, if we can."

Our waitress comes back to take our order. I spit mine out quickly, hoping to catch the last bit of the guys' conversation.

"If there's time, maybe we can get another story while we're here. There's talk around town about rare white animal sightings. I think Indigenous people call them spirit animals."

There have been sightings? Other than what I've seen?

My heart starts to race a little. Nobody in a million years would put it together that the white animals have anything to do with the spirit box. Not even Julie and Chloe think so—thanks to Mason, probably.

"Rachel."

"Hmm . . . yeah?" I look back at my Mom.

"I called your name twice—and you're twisting your napkin in your hand like it owes you money. Something wrong?"

"No. Nothing."

"Okay." She's fidgeting with the little sugar packets on the table. Like mother, like daughter—fidgeting when we're nervous. She either has bad news or awkward questions. "I have a bit of an ulterior motive for taking you out for lunch." *And here it is.* "But first I want to make sure you're doing okay."

"I already told you, I'm okay. What do you want to ask me?" My words are clipped.

"Okay. I've noticed that it's been almost five months since we got here, and you haven't unpacked your room yet."

"Do we have to talk about it here?" I don't mean to sound so harsh. I can't help but feel a little trapped. She brought me to a public place so . . . what? So I wouldn't make a scene? Whatever she wants to say must be pretty bad.

"I know with the divorce, and all the moving, and your

brother's death—"

"*Eric*, Mom," I snap. "He has a name."

"Eric's death has been hard on you, but I want you to give this place a chance. This is home for me. It's where I grew up. It's not perfect, but if you give it a chance, it'll grow on you too." She's stopped fidgeting with the sugars. I try to push down my angry feelings over the way things turned out. It's hard to do sometimes.

"I'm really happy to see that you've made some friends at school. What are their names again? Julie, Chloe, Ryan, and Matthew?"

"Mason, not Matthew."

"Okay, well—good. Have them over sometime. In fact, did you invite them over for your birthday barbecue on Saturday? I promise to not make it a big deal. I get it if you don't want to hang out with the old folks for long, but since it's your eighteenth, your dad and I got you something special."

"A barbecue sounds great, Mom. I'll invite them over." The Weather Lady said I should try to enjoy my birthday. I guess this year I'll take her advice.

"And your boyfriend, too?"

"Maybe. And he's not my boyfriend." Our waitress sets down our drinks. She mumbles as she hurries away that she'll be right back with our food. I thankfully take a sip of my iced tea.

Having uncomfortable conversations with your mother can really dry out your mouth.

"One more thing I wanted to mention."

There's more? The "I'm worried about you" speech wasn't it?

"I also wanted to tell you that your dad is going to come visit for the weekend. He'll be here on Saturday."

"Okay. He can have my room, and I'll sleep on the couch." Whew, all that drama for nothing. It's been a few weeks since I've spoken to him, and we haven't seen each other since we moved out here. It'll be good to see him.

"He's not staying with us this time. He's staying at the hotel with—" My mom trails off as the waitress comes back with two steaming plates.

"Who has the grilled cheese with ham?"

"That's me." I munch on the fries while I wait for the waitress to leave so I can reach the ketchup. Mmm. Grilled cheese with ham. My happy place.

The waitress turns to leave and I see him out of the corner of my eye. Nate. He's standing at the counter paying for what looks like takeout. And he sees me, too. Me, in my dirty, ripped jeans and *Camp Crazy Horse* T-shirt. *Crap.* He's coming this way. Of course he is. This guy has some kind of radar for when I'm at my worst.

"Hey, Rachel. Thought I'd come over and say hi." He extends his hand to shake my mom's. "Hi, I'm Nate."

"Nate, nice to meet you. I've heard all about you." *Really, Mom? 'All about you'?* What's left of my coolness just shriveled up and died. I can tell he's trying to hold back an even bigger smile than the one already on his face.

"Hey, I can't stay. I've got to get back to work. I just stopped by to pick up lunch. So, I'll see you around."

"Sure, see ya." Just as I'm enjoying the slow-motion replay of him turning around, my mom breaks the silence.

"Oh Nate?" I glare at her like a judge at a death row criminal, wondering what last words she might have. "We're having a barbecue on Saturday for Rachel's birthday. We're going to eat around six-ish if you'd like to come over."

"I didn't know Saturday's your birthday." I try for something a little more intellectual than "uh-huh," but I'm a puddle. "I'll have to get you a present, then." He says it like it's a secret, and I resist the urge to fan my face to cool off. I've got to rein in the ol' hormones, especially in front of my mother. "But I'm sorry." He looks back at my mom. "I don't think I can make it to the barbecue."

"That's all right. Some other time then," Mom replies.

"Sure. I'll see you around, Rachel."

In a voice an octave higher than my own, I answer back,

"See ya."

"Well," Mom says after Nate is out of earshot, "I guess you don't have to worry about inviting him to the barbecue. He can't make it."

"Yeah. Thanks for the heads-up on that, Mom. God, you're worse than Grandma."

"What? You looked like a baby fawn over there, as doe-eyed as a Disney character. I didn't think *you* were going to ask him, and I thought he should come."

I sigh, but can't help smiling. Mom and Grams, they just put it all out there. It's a quality both admirable and annoying.

About a block from the house, I see there's a truck parked in our driveway. From here, it looks like a police vehicle. My chest tightens. The last time the police were at our house, they were delivering the news about my brother. But when we get closer, I can see there's a large *Fish and Wildlife* decal on its side door. We roll to a stop beside the truck. Mom opens her door and waves to the wildlife officer knocking on the front door of the house.

"Steve," she calls out as she bounds up the front steps to meet him. I can't hear what she's saying. Climbing out of the truck, I join the two of them at the bottom of the steps.

"Rachel, this is Steve. He works for the Fish and Wildlife office. Steve and I have known each other since we were little." There's a strangeness about how she introduces him. I slough it off and shake his hand.

"Nice to meet you, Steve. What brings you here?"

"All the officers are going around today dropping off notices." He hands me a bright yellow flyer from the stack he's carrying. "There's been a rash of animal deaths in the area over the past few days. We're hoping some of the residents might be able to help us figure out what's been killing them."

"Oh? I saw a dead racoon, cat, and squirrel the other day —and maybe a deer. Sorry, am I supposed to report that kind of stuff to you guys?"

"Normally people don't report small animal deaths. And unless you hit the deer, don't worry about it. We've had thirty-eight individual reports in the last three days of large animal deaths. Many of the reports coming in are of deer and elk. Which made us think there might be a large predator in the area. But we've had four reports of dead cougars and bears as well, which has thrown us for a loop."

"Maybe there's a poacher in the area?" my mom says, as she reads the flyer.

"Maybe. But we can't figure out why a poacher would kill animals and leave the entire carcass untouched."

"Maybe they're using them for target practice." Just saying it leaves a bad taste in my mouth. Who would do that?

"That question came up, too. But from what we've found so far, none of the animals have bullet wounds."

"So how are they dying?" I ask.

"That's what we're trying to find out. We've sent a few of the animals off to be tested for cause of death. We should know what happened soon. But if you have any information you think might be helpful to us, the number for our office is at the bottom of the flyer."

Steve seems uneasy, standing on the front step of our house. With stilted movements, he touches my mom's shoulder, reconsiders, and lets his hand slide off. "I'll see you around, Marie. And nice to meet you, Rachel." Out of the corner of my eye, I see a lingering look pass between him and my mom as he leaves.

"I'll see you later, too. I have to get back to work," Mom says, as she gets back in her truck. And with that, I'm left standing alone, yellow flyer in hand, as they both drive away.

CHAPTER NINE

I watch in disbelief as the tiny polished rocks that decorate the flowerpot on my desk start to move. They trail over the lip of the pot and across my desk in a line, like cartoon ants marching in formation. I lift my laptop up so the tiny rock army can pass under it. They do a tour of the top of my desk. Then they return back up the side of the flowerpot, arranging themselves much like they were before.

"Uh . . ." There have obviously been new developments with Mason that I didn't know about. I can't decide if I should be looking at him or the rocks. One thing's for sure, gaping my mouth open like I'm trying to catch flies isn't helping. I take stock of him, leisurely sitting on my bed. He looks like he's seen rocks move by themselves a hundred times before. He doesn't even seem to be concentrating, but he moved them. I know he did. "That was . . . How?" I shift uncomfortably in my computer chair.

My eyes feel like saucers. "You can move things with your mind? What's that called—telekinesis?"

"Telekinesis is the ability to move things with your mind, yes. But that's not exactly what I did. This all just started happening yesterday." He's quiet for a few seconds. Perhaps I'm not the only one searching for words. "I don't want you to think I'm crazy."

An involuntary snort escapes me. "Crazy? Oh, I think we passed crazy a few miles back, somewhere between the glowing blue orbs and you fighting grizzlies with your bare hands. I'm pretty sure whatever you have to say won't make me think any differently of you." This is by far the strangest conversation I've ever had.

A shy smile turns up the corners of his mouth. "Okay. Well, you're the only one I can talk to about this. So here goes."

Wait. I'm the only one he can talk to about this? When did we go from strangers to telling each other things we wouldn't dare tell our best friends? I don't know how I grew so comfortable talking to a guy as unpredictably crass and magnetically attractive as Mason Allen.

"I just knew I could do it," he says.

"Do what? Move things with your mind?" I analyze every shoulder shrug, every cautious look.

"Yeah, but it's more like . . . I can tell things what to do."

"So you told the rocks in my flowerpot to march across my desk?"

"Exactly." He nods matter-of-factly.

"And you knew you could do this *how*?"

His mouth twists a little. Does he know how unbelievably distracting that is to the opposite sex?

"It's like I've always known *how* to do it but didn't occur to me that I *could* until yesterday."

I blink a few times. "Gee, that explains everything."

He sits up taller on my bed, his eyes wandering around my bedroom. "Okay, so I suck at explaining things. Let's try this again." His gaze stops on a glass of water left overnight on my desk. "For example"—he pauses to make sure I'm looking at the glass—"if you wanted to pick up this glass, you'd just do it. No one has to show you. You just know how."

"This is your idea of an explanation? I don't get it. I would pick the glass up with my hand, Mason, not my mind." His brow furrows. Is he as frustrated as I am? "Sorry. I'm trying to get it. You talk. I'll just listen."

He crosses his legs on the bed, fluffs a few pillows behind his back, and looks so deeply in to my eyes I think the image of him might be branded in my memory forever. "This wendigo thing—it's like it's unlocked some secret door in my brain. It's like all this knowledge was always there, but only it had the key."

The look on his face is something close to pure bliss. "It's the most amazing thing. I'm more connected to everything. I suddenly have the knowledge of a thousand people, and a whole new understanding of how things work." He stops talking and his eyes glass over. He blinks a few times and returns his focus to me. "Now do you think I'm crazy?" He huffs.

"No, I'm just . . . processing." I drag my fingertips over the rocks in the flowerpot. I still don't get it.

"Let me show you something else." Taking the flowerpot from the desk, he touches the half-dead gerbera daisy in it. Some of the plant's dry leaves spring back to life. Others fall off, and new ones sprout in their place. I'm in awe again. It's like watching a time-lapse film that captures weeks of a plant's growth in a matter of seconds. By the time he's done, the plant is twice the size it was before with double the blooming flowers.

"See? I told it what to do. I took my energy and connected with its energy." A smile crosses his face, like he's remembering something. He puts the plant back on my desk. My hand immediately goes to it. I can't help but touch it to see if it's real. I want to understand what he's trying to show me, but somehow I think I'm just not equipped to understand this.

"Yesterday," he continues, "my mom asked me if I could water her herb garden for her. She keeps it on the windowsill behind the kitchen sink."

He continues his story, relaxing back against the pillows

on my bed. He looks good, lounging there. I mean really good. This wendigo has changed him, not just with powers, but his whole being. He has a presence now that makes you take notice. His voice sounds the same, but with a little more age. Everything about him is flawless. I can't help but be entranced by the movement of his lips over his teeth when he talks.

"So I just told her herbs to grow, and they did. She asked me this morning where I got full-grown herb plants. I just said I must have a greener thumb than her. Rach? Are you okay?"

He brings me out of my little trance. "I'm fine. Your story about the herbs is sweet. And strange. Your powers are . . . cool. I guess."

He smirks and holds back a laugh. "So since yesterday, I've been trying my new abilities out on everything. I've found it works on some things and not on others. How do I explain it? Most everything has an energy that is connected to this giant web. The whole planet is living and breathing. All I have to do is plug in and I can change things the way I want."

"So your powers aren't just good on plants and rocks? They work on anything? Like animals and people? You can control them, too?" I can't believe I just asked that. What kind of bizarre reality am I living in?

"Animals and people are a lot more difficult than plants and rocks, but yeah." He sits up and readjusts himself on my bed. "Animals and people have a mind of their own. So it's more like the art of persuasion."

"Oh." My voice sounds flat in a way I don't mean it to.

"So *now* you think I'm nuts?"

"Yes, but I think I'm in the same boat." Why is he smiling?

"Okay, well . . ." He rolls his shoulders back, stretching out the tension in his back. "I shared the crazies in my head. How about you give it a go?"

"About what?"

He gestures to the piles of sealed boxes stacked around my room.

"You want to know about the boxes?"

"Everyone wants to know about the boxes. They're just too polite to ask."

"And you're not?"

He shrugs his shoulders, half-apologizing, but says nothing.

"Where do I start?" I have to think back. Dust off a few cobwebs. Re-open files I thought I'd locked up forever. I get up from my computer chair and sit across from him, cross-legged on my bed. Even after years with the Weather Lady, I never thought I'd actually be talking about this with someone. *Deep breath. You can do this.*

"All this didn't just happen overnight. I mean, I didn't

just pack up my things one day and decide never to open them again." A lump is welling up in my throat. My mind reels backs to that day. "I remember every detail. It was May fifth, four years ago."

"You remember the exact day you lost your mind? That's messed up."

Screw this. The first time I ever talk about it without having a therapist present, and he's teasing? Why did I think he might understand what I went through?

"Do you want me to tell you or not?" I don't look at him when I say it. "I'm only telling you this because I feel like I owe you something. Since I've pretty much screwed up your life."

"Hey, you haven't screwed up my life. It's gotten a whole lot better from my point of view. But enough about me. Go on. I'm listening."

I straighten up and try to get more comfortable. As comfortable as one can get when talking about such things. My bedroom feels smaller. My throat's tight, but I can do this. *Deep breath.* "I remember the date because it was my fourteenth birthday—and the day my brother died." There's a reason I don't talk about this. My chest hurts like a car just crashed in to it. I can't breathe. "Can I have one of those pillows?" I gesture with my hand without looking up.

He reaches behind and hands me one of the many pillows propping him up. I bury my face in it. It smells like rosemary and laundry soap. Like Grams' house. It's funny. When you know something's going to hurt, it helps somehow to hold on to something safe. I need a minute here, away from life, safe in the confines of my pillow. I try to go to my place where nothing hurts, but it's not there. I feel his hand touch my knee. He's probably wondering if I'm okay, just like everybody else.

"I just need a sec," I mumble, still breathing in the scent of my pillow. His hand hasn't moved from my knee. I don't care. It feels nice. It feels warm—peaceful, even. The calm consumes me. It flows over me like warm water and I'm taken away. Away from . . . *What was I so bothered about?* I look up from my pillow. Mason's sitting cross-legged on my bed, about a foot in front of me.

"Feel better?" he asks, taking his hand back.

"What did you just do?" I touch the spot where his hand once was.

"It doesn't take a genius to see that you're hurting. I just —helped you feel better."

"You were in my head? I thought you said you couldn't control people." I blink hard, trying to gather my thoughts.

"More like you were in mine." *What?* I'm trying to keep up, but this conversation just keeps getting weirder. "I let you see my memories, transferring a feeling onto you. Basically, I distracted you."

Distracted. I think back to the countless hours I spent with the Weather Lady and the multiple prescriptions she gave me to help "deal" with the pain of Eric's death, none of which helped much. Yet in one fleeting moment, he's taken it all away through distraction.

And in that moment, my whole world doesn't hurt so much.

I reach across and put his hand back on my knee. "I'll tell you about the boxes . . . with a little distraction." He doesn't say anything. He doesn't have to. The same feeling of calm passes through me as before.

"My brother, Eric, was seventeen when he moved out of my parents' house. Eric and my parents didn't get along. They constantly fought about everything. School, friends, staying out . . . They couldn't find any common ground."

I think back to Eric's apartment, dingy and decrepit. Apartment 12B. I hear only really shitty apartments get letters after the numbers, like a way of marking the truly disgusting ones. Even the door to his place was beat up. It had scratches on both sides like something was trying to get in—or out.

"He moved into an apartment that he shared with three other roommates. They lived on top of each other like rats. One roommate didn't even have a bedroom. He just slept on the couch in the living room. I remember Eric telling me that rent was expensive and the place was only temporary." Just thinking about his apartment brought back the smell. It was the kind of scent you could taste, thick and sticky like syrup. If crushed dreams were a smell, that would have been it. "I guess it wasn't as temporary as he thought, because six months later he was still there."

When I think about what happens next, I know the feelings that come with it. They're still there, not completely numb, but somehow bearable with Mason's help. I feel lighter, as if he's carrying all the pain for me. My fingers brush Mason's hand to make sure it's still there before I go on.

"For my birthday, Eric promised to take me to a movie. We went to the late show because he had to work until eight that night. He was working two jobs and taking classes to finish his GED. After the movie, he drove me home in his beat-up Honda Civic. That thing was so loud." I smile at the memory. "He could've fixed it if he wanted to, but I think he liked the fact that it drove our parents crazy."

His loud car fades from my mind and I'm left with the burned-in memory of the last time I saw him. It rolls through my head on repeat. "After the movie, he dropped me off at our parents' house. He waited in the driveway until I was inside." In my head I hear the sound of the door clicking shut, his car driving away, and the silence that followed. I swallow hard at the thought of what comes next.

"I'd gone to bed, but wasn't quite asleep when I heard a knock at the front door. I hid at the top of the stairs. I didn't want them to know I was listening. Two cops stood talking to my parents. I heard every word the two officers said, but my brain refused to believe it. They mentioned Eric's name, and an accident a few blocks away. It wasn't until their last words that I lost it: "Identify his body." The words rang in my ears—I couldn't turn them off." Mason's fingers move slightly on my knee. "That's when I ran. I ran out the back door. I don't know if my parents or the cops noticed. I didn't care. I knew the route Eric would have taken driving home. So I just ran."

I relive that night in my head. The cold Vancouver rain pelting my face. My bare feet so frozen and raw from running on the wet pavement that they're burning. I don't care how much it hurts. I think maybe, if I get there in time . . . But I'm wrong.

"I saw red-and-white lights flashing up ahead, but the ambulance drove away before I could get there. I yelled for them to stop, but they didn't hear me. There were only cop cars left when I got there. Their flashing lights were blinding." I squint at the memory as if I'm still there.

"I ran past them to a twisted, broken guardrail that divided the road from a deep ravine." In my head, I'm there. I'm overlooking the rail into the ravine. It's dark. I can't make out shapes, but I can see the glowing taillights of his Civic.

"Some cops came up behind me and grabbed my arms. Their hands were so cold. They held me back from the edge.

"They didn't know it was all a bad dream to me. They

pulled me back. I screamed louder. I don't know what I said. It felt like the whole world couldn't hear me." I see in my mind the last glimpse of the ravine. The taillights on Eric's car flicker and die, and my whole world goes dark.

I sniff and wipe away a tear. Mason's hand hasn't left my knee. "I don't remember if it was my parents or the police who told me what actually happened, but I was told Eric fell asleep at the wheel and drove through the guardrail into the ravine."

I shake my head. "He was always so tired from school and work. Maybe if we hadn't gone to the movies that night, he would have gone home to sleep. If he'd listened to me, and didn't fight all the time with my parents, and moved back in with Mom and Dad, this wouldn't have happened. He wouldn't have had to work two jobs. He wouldn't have been so tired."

"It's not your fault." Mason's eyes look pained. "Sometimes things happen that we have no control over. I get it, though. I lost my sister to a drunk driver a few years back. I tortured myself with what-ifs for a long time. But eventually, I found a way to deal with it."

We both sit in silence on my bed. I remember the picture in Mason's room. He said it was the last one his dad ever took of her. How did he deal with losing a sibling? Maybe that's a question for another day.

Mason draws his hand back from my knee. It instantly feels cold, like someone has stolen my security blanket.

"So is that why you have all this stuff in boxes? Was it your brother's stuff?"

"No. It's hard to explain." I twist my face in an effort to find the words. "After Eric's death, my semi-normal, happily dysfunctional family just . . . stopped."

"Stopped what?"

"Stopped everything." The memories come faster now. "First, my Mom stopped going to work. She took a leave to sort out my brother's funeral arrangements and stuff. But other than that, she just sat on the couch in her pyjamas. Sometimes she wouldn't shower for days. She lost a lot of weight. She was still eating a bit, because I'd find dishes of half-eaten food on the coffee table in the living room. They'd sit there for days. Everyone was too lazy to clean up.

"This went on for months. Some part of me wanted her to get up, carry on, but I never said anything. Every day, before I left for school, I'd put hot buttered toast and coffee beside her on the couch and give her a kiss. And every day when I came home she'd be exactly where I left her."

"Where was your dad in all this?"

I pause for a moment, sorting through the dusty files in my head. I haven't had to think about them in a long while.

"He wasn't around much after Eric died. I'm pretty sure he went back to work after a week or so. He started coming home late. Maybe he felt guilty seeing my mom like she was. Maybe he felt like it was his fault somehow.

"About eight months after Eric died, my parents sat me down and told me they were getting a divorce." The words taste stale in my mouth. "Our house went up for sale. My mom and dad got places on opposite ends of the city. I changed schools and lost touch with most of my friends. Not that I had that many.

"I went to live with my mom. I thought she needed me. But it turned out that getting a divorce and moving away from everything gave her some kind of new zest for life. Our first day in our new place, I went into the kitchen to get her toast and there she was, dressed in a skirt and dress shirt, hair done, makeup on. And she had breakfast ready for me."

"That's good, right?"

"You might think so. But it was like she snapped back too far. Every time we moved, which was a lot, she would buy all new stuff for the place. Practically everything we owned was new. It was like she didn't want anything around that would remind her of the past. She'd replaced almost everything that we'd originally brought with us. The longest we ever stayed in a place was about six months. I got used to packing things up and moving."

Mason has a puzzled look on his face. "Then why do you have a room full of boxes? After moving so many times, you must have packed and unpacked these things a million times. Right?"

"At first I did. It wasn't until the second or third move that I started boxing things up and keeping them that way. It might seem strange to box up random things, but I was saving it from my mother. Every time she'd buy something new, she'd throw out the old stuff." My pulse picks up. "That old stuff—it's what my life used to be, before it got—" I say the last word almost too quietly to be heard. "Broken. Part of me thinks that if I keep everything all boxed up, maybe some part of my normal life is still in there."

I take a deep breath to compose myself. I climb off the bed and sit back at my computer desk. "I think that's enough show and share for today." I feel a thousand times lighter having told someone about the boxes and my brother, but I'm done with the emotional marathon. And maybe he is too. I only know what he tells me about his powers, but his usually olive color seems a bit drained from his face. "I still have the wendigo stuff on my computer, if you want to see."

He sits up, letting his legs hang over the side of the bed. "Okay, let's see what you got."

I open up the folder marked *Wendigo* on my laptop and start with the first website. It opens to pictures of twirling crystals and wolves howling at the moon. I look over at Mason to see him arch one eyebrow in suspicion. "What?" I ask.

"This is your reliable research? It looks like a site for Madame Scam-ya's psychic readings."

"Be patient. It was hard to find anything on wendigos except for Native folklore and some creepy sci-fi stuff." I click away at the site until I find the page I'm looking for. "Here." I point to the screen. "One thing that everyone agrees on is that wendigos either eat people or take their souls."

The silence in the room is deafening.

"You think I'm eating people or stealing their souls?" I can't tell if he's being sarcastic or genuine.

"No, I'm just reading what it says on the website. You have to admit, though, it's doing strange things to you. From what you've told me, you can control things with your mind, you're ridiculously fast, you can see in the dark, and your strength is off the charts. Who's to say if we don't figure out how to get this thing out of you that you might—"

"Eat people."

"Yeah. Maybe."

He looks me straight in the eyes with a stare that's borderline hypnotic. "I'm not going to eat people. That's disgusting."

I break his gaze and look down at my keyboard, trying to gain some composure. I click on another site that I've saved. It opens up to a picture of a wolfman-meets-swamp-monster. "One thing that no one seems to agree on is what a wendigo actually looks like." Mason leans over to look at the screen. His closeness sends every hair on my neck standing straight up.

"Yikes, that's supposed to be a wendigo? Glad I still look the same."

"Yeah, you look pretty much the same."

"What do you mean, 'pretty much?' I looked in the mirror this morning and thought I looked fairly non-monster-like today."

This is awkward. *Just say it.* "It's your eyes. They're different. And some other stuff."

"Different how? Have they changed colour or something?"

Crap, he's looking at me again, and every thought in my head flutters out. "Not right now, but I've seen them turn silver."

He blinks a few times, as if he's taken aback by what I said. "Oh. Well, I'll start wearing sunglasses if it'll make you feel better." He grabs my huge, girly sunglasses off my desk and puts them on. They look ridiculous on him.

"Come on, be serious."

"Okay, sorry. Just trying to lighten things up. You need to smile a little more."

One corner of my mouth creeps up.

"Aw, was that a smile? Don't smile. Don't smile."

And of course, I can't help but smile. "Cut it out. I'm trying to show you important stuff here." I shove his shoulder playfully. *Holy crap.* He's like a rock. When did he get so ripped?

"There's one more thing I found that might help." I open the last site. "This mentions a ceremony used to remove wendigo spirits from people."

He sits up on my bed, closing the gap between us a few more inches. The air between us radiates. "You want to use witchy hoo-doo powers to rid me of this thing?"

I'm taken aback by his closeness. There's something about this guy that I just can't shake. Oh, right—the crazy ancient spirits currently camping out inside his body.

"I don't have witchy hoo-doo powers." I push my chair back to put more space between us and look at my computer instead of his eyes. "The site's not very specific about how the ceremony works. It just talks about it. I thought we could—"

"Ask someone about it?" he interrupts me.

"Yeah."

"Like who?"

"I don't know. I—"

"I don't think it would be wise."

"Why not?"

His face tightens slightly as he stares at me. "Just give me a little longer, okay? We can figure this out." I want to trust him.

"Fine. You can have another week of playing with plants and rocks. After that, we're getting this thing out of you." My small smile turns into what could be a perma-frown.

He reaches over to take my hands in his. "Thanks. Hey, you know if you keep frowning like that, your face is going to stay that way forever." My eyebrows lift a little. I don't want to give in to his silliness.

"I've got just the thing to make you smile." He lets go of my hands and sits up taller on the bed. He looks as if he's concentrating.

"What are you doing?" He's staring at my chest.

"Shh. I'm not very good at this yet."

"What are you doing, Mason?" I feel the fibers of my sweater tighten around me. Then it starts hiking up around my neck, like it's being pulled upwards by an invisible string. "Hey! What's wrong with you?" I cross my arms tight, holding down my top. "In-ap-pro-pri-ate, Mason. I thought you said you had something to make me smile."

"Well, it made me smile."

My cell phone buzzes across my desk, breaking the increasingly awkward moment.

Sorry running late. Be there in five.

It's from Julie. I almost forgot, she's coming over to help me get ready for my date with Nate—and Mason is still here. How am I going to explain this? A guy and girl can hang out without it being anything, right? This is a problem I never thought I'd have to deal with.

"Hey," I say, staring down at my phone.

"What?"

"That was Julie texting me. She's coming over here in five minutes. Is your truck parked in the driveway?"

"Yeah, why?"

"'Cuz it would be kind of weird if you were still here when she got here." My voice is getting all high and squeaky. It annoys even me.

"Okay. Why?"

He's going to stand there until I tell him.

"I think she thinks there's something going on between us."

"Well, there is, kind of."

"Right—well, I just don't want her thinking we're dating or something." I can tell I'm blushing. My cheeks feel warm.

He's quiet for a moment. "Why would you be concerned if she thought that?" He pauses for another second. "What's she coming over here for?"

"What's with the third degree?" I run my fingers through my hair and don't meet his eyes. "She's coming over here to do my hair and makeup. I have a date tonight." My voice is small and quiet.

"Oh. How did I not know you have a boyfriend? That

whole sweater thing . . . Sorry."

"I don't have a boyfriend. I have a date." You could cut the silence with a knife. I grab his hand to lead him towards the front door. "Please, just go. I'll see everybody tomorrow at my birthday barbecue, and you can ask me all the questions you want then."

He stops just short of the door and turns to face me. "Okay, fine. I just have one question."

Don't look at his eyes. Don't look at his eyes. "Fine. What?" I say, my eyes half closed.

"Who do you have a date with?"

"Nate Grey Hawk. He's taking me to some sort of dance out on the reserve."

"Nathan Grey Hawk! Isn't he like twenty-one or something? He's too old for you, Rachel."

"It's not exactly up for discussion. Come on, Mason, Julie's going to be here any second. Unless you want to tell her what we've really been up to, I suggest you go," I say, pulling him to the door.

"I don't feel good about you going onto the reserve at night all by yourself."

"I won't be by myself. I'll be with Nate."

"That doesn't make me feel any better."

He isn't budging. He's blocking the open doorway in the

kitchen. I hear the crunch of gravel as Julie's car pulls into the driveway. *Great.* She bounds up the front steps to the door with her usual enthusiasm.

"Hey, Mason. What are you doin' here?" I hear an accusing tone in her voice.

"Just dropping off Rachel's sunglasses." He slips my girly sunglasses off his head and hands them to me. "She forgot them in my truck the other night, when we all went to Ross Lake."

"Thanks." I take my sunglasses as he hands them to me.

"I'll see you girls tomorrow. What time is everyone getting here?"

"Around six," Julie says.

"Great. See you then." He turns and walks to his truck, flashing us both a smile.

Julie squeezes her way past me and into the kitchen. I let the kitchen door slide from my hand and close. She's already unpacking hot rollers and makeup on the kitchen table. It'll be nice to get done up, I think. I hope I still look like me by the end of this.

CHAPTER TEN

I'll never get used to how dark it is out here. In Vancouver, I got used to the perma-glow of city life. It might annoy some, or keep them up at night, but that glow chased away my fears. We've driven for miles without seeing the luminous glow of even one streetlight. Out here, the inky darkness mingles too closely with the shadows I try to hide from.

Nate is driving. We're on some gravel road headed out of town. We passed what seems to be the last lonely house a few kilometers back. I can't tell the direction we're going. Without my concrete jungle of street signs and tall buildings, I'm lost.

The passenger side is fogging up. Even the truck window knows I'm nervous. I try to breathe less, if that's even possible. Using my sleeve as a squeegee, I clear a small circle in the fog. But I can't see much out my makeshift porthole except the silhouettes of lodge-pole pines lining the road, lit dimly by the passing headlights of the truck.

"You look really nice. You did your hair different?"

"Thanks. Julie did it for me. I'm not good at hair and makeup stuff." A nervous scoff escapes my tight-lipped smile. Julie's passion in life, other than planning her own fashion ensemble, is dressing up her friends. Which is why I'm wearing a dress that's more like a long shirt. At least she let me cover up my shoulders with a jean jacket.

I sweep a loose curl behind my ear and glance towards Nate in the driver's seat. He's wearing this soft, green, patterned dress shirt with the sleeves rolled up. It has snaps, not buttons, and he's wearing a tight white V-neck T-shirt underneath. *What is it about rolling up the sleeves on a shirt that makes it so . . . Whew.* I find myself counting the snaps he's left open at the top: three. Well, this is a first. I think I'm envious of his shirt and its close proximity to the radiant heat of Nathan Grey Hawk's chest. His chest rises and falls with the steady rhythm of a tide. How is he so calm? I'm so nervous that the butterflies in my stomach are threatening to revolt. Another sighing breath escapes me.

"You look really nice too," I say. It's lame, but at least I'm returning the compliment.

I wipe away a few more drips from the window with my sleeve. Julie would kill me if she knew I was using her favorite vintage jean jacket like this. The view out of my porthole is still the same; nothing but the dimly lit shadows of the endless pine trees.

"We're almost there, if you're wondering," Nate says, but he doesn't look over at me. "The hall is hidden by all the trees; it's only a few more kilometers." A smile, like he's holding back a laugh, crosses his lips. "You know, just in case you're thinking I was taking you out to the middle of nowhere."

The middle of nowhere. It crossed my mind, not that I'd admit it. "No"—my voice is an octave too high to be believable —"I'm just looking out the window at the . . . scenery. Not that there's much to see. It's so dark. People who live out here, they must be like owls or something." *Really, owls? Just stop talking!* "'Cuz you all must be able to see in the dark really well."

Nate chokes back a cough-laugh. "Nervous?"

"What? Why?"

"You're rambling. It's kind of cute."

"Cute, eh?" Nate thinks I'm cute. My mind dissects every letter of the word. C-U-T-E. I shift my weight to regain a more comfortable position—which now seems impossible. The leather truck seats creak with my every move.

Nate slows the truck and turns off the never-ending dark road. We pull into a gravel parking lot flooded in the yellow glow from a towering yard light. The parking lot is filled with vehicles, mostly pickups, but a few cars here and there. Civilization! I can feel the music coming from inside the hall even before Nate turns off the truck. We find a spot to park on one side of the massive, timber-framed community hall. I tell myself I can do this. I'm virtually an adult. Going on a date shouldn't turn me into a complete train wreck or babbling girl puddle.

The click of his seatbelt sparks my attention. "Hey. I'm really glad you came with me tonight. It's been forever since I've been to one of these things."

Without even trying, Nate exudes a quiet confidence. The way he's looking at me, I wonder what he sees. A girl made up to be someone else, with clothes and makeup that aren't even hers? Or *me*?

My worries about the crowds of strangers and loud music outside the truck fade to a dull hush. I notice his eyelashes, how they sweep over his dark brown eyes. I notice his unblemished skin, smooth like he's never shaved a day in his life. And his lips, drawing me in.

No concrete jungle. No street signs. I'm lost in this moment.

Slap. Squeeeaaakkk. A sweaty hand streaks down the driver's side window.

And—moment gone.

"Well," Nate says, a momentary flash of frustration crossing his face. "I think we've been discovered. Come on, let me introduce you to my *idiot* friend, Finn."

He steps out of the truck and is immediately greeted with a sloppy bear hug from who I suspect is a drunk Finn. I slide out on my side and walk around the hood—and their voices hush. They're talking about me, and it couldn't be more obvious. Of course they are. Nate, this superior example of maleness, has just brought me, plain Jane, to a party. Finn's eyes scan over me like I'm a barcode on a package of cheap deli meat.

"Hey, nice to meet you. I'm Finn." He extends his hand for me to shake, but not before wiping it on his jeans first. Finn's long, dark hair is pulled back in a ponytail like Nate's. He also has perfect, baby-soft skin with not a whisker on it, boasting a smile almost too big for his face.

"Hi, I'm Rachel." We loosely shake hands, and I wonder whose are clammier.

"I know. I've heard all about you." I bite my bottom lip to stop from blushing. He told his friends about me. *Wait.* I flash back to the chilly night in the muddy ditch. Right. Of course that night would be a good story. "Nate told me you were pretty, but . . ." His voice lingers just a little too long on that last word. "I wasn't expecting this." Finn's still holding my hand, looking right at me, as if trying to find some detail he's missed.

"Okay, Finn, that's enough." Nate gives him a playful shove and wraps his arm around my shoulders. Nate's to-die-for-scent floats across me, and I'm back to my happy place. "So who else is here?"

"I saw Mark and Darrin a while back," says Finn. "Oh, and Jamey is in there too. She looks exceptionally hot tonight, by the way."

"Dude, don't tell me my sister looks hot. How drunk are you?"

"Drunk enough to tell you your sister's hot." They stare at each other stone-faced for three seconds before they break into wide smiles and laugh. Their joking looks like it comes from years of friendship.

I think back to the friends I had in Vancouver. I'm not drawing a total blank, but there was definitely a gaping void in the best friend department. Thinking back further, I'm not sure I ever had one. And I never missed it until I began to notice it everywhere else. Julie and Chloe, Nate and Finn, Mason and Ryan, but who do I have? Julie? Mason?

Nate and I make our way over to the front doors of the hall, Finn following close behind. When the large wooden doors open, I'm greeted with a shocking hammering of music. I can barely see through the crowd clustered by the doors. Nate takes my hand and weaves us through the sea of people. From what I can make out between the packed bodies and flashing strobe lights, the hall is beautiful. Almost every square inch of it is made of exposed wood, from the floors to the open rafter ceiling. Even with so many people, I can still smell the crisp, fresh scent of cedar. We stop in front of a canteen window that leads to the hall's kitchen-slash-makeshift bar.

"Can I get you a drink?" Nate yells to me over the music. "No worries about drinking age, just get what you want."

No worries, eh? Should I be a good girl and get a Pepsi— or something else? "I'll have a gin and seven if they have it." The look on his face is funny, his mouth slightly open like he wants to say something. Did I say something wrong?

He leans over the counter and talks to the guy on the other side of the window. A few seconds later, he hands me a red plastic cup. "You're in luck. They have gin."

"Thanks." He takes my hand again and leads me over to the far wall. I see Finn standing there with a few others. They don't exactly stop talking when we arrive, but something feels off. Maybe it's me. Crowds make me uneasy. I take a sip of my drink. It's strong. However, it's deliciously dulling my edges.

"Nate!" a few guys chime in together, arms and drinks raised. A tall guy with a slim build comes over and gives him a pat on the shoulder, hard enough that it looks like it hurts.

"Buddy, you made it. I thought you'd weasel out of coming. Give us some lame excuse like you had to work or something." He pats Nate's shoulder again, this time giving it a squeeze. "So who's this you've brought with you?" I feel the heat in my cheeks, a combination of the gin and the fact everyone is staring at me. I feel like I'm on parade all of a sudden, the only blonde head in an ocean of black and brown.

"This is Rachel. She's Ellen Stacy's granddaughter. She and her mom just moved back to town."

Obviously these guys know my grandma, so I know what they're thinking: *Ellen Stacy is full-blood, but this girl has blonde hair and blue eyes.* I see that same confused look every time someone refers to the Native side of my family.

I take a mouthful of my drink and gulp it down. Its warmth flows through me like a welcome haze, while Nate and his friends carry on a conversation I have no intention of joining. Nate takes our jackets and hangs them over a chair. I wish I didn't give him mine. I feel exposed without it.

The pounding beat slows as the song changes. You know how some songs sing to your soul? This is mine. I breathe it in and listen deeply. For a moment, I'm not standing in a roomful of strangers. I'm just me. For a moment, life isn't so loud.

"Would you like to dance?" Nate asks.

I take one last gulp of liquid courage before setting it down, and my world slows. I try not to think about who's watching, or if I might step on his feet. He takes my hand and we find our way onto the dance floor. For a brief second I'm thirteen, awkward and clumsy like I'm at my first junior dance, but the feeling is fleeting. I'm saved by his hands guiding mine, both up and around his shoulders. He's much taller than I am. My eyes line up with his collarbone and the small divot between them. His hands trace down my spine and settle in the small of my back.

"My friends can be a little intense sometimes. I thought we could slip in a dance before they start with the questions about me bringing a date."

"Your friends like to grill you about your choice in dates, too? I guess we have that in common."

"What do your friends say?"

"My friends say I don't know what it's like to grow up here, but they also think you're gorgeous, and wonder if there are any more like you." I just said that. And I think I made him blush.

"And what do you think?"

Oh God. He's looking right at me, dancing so close. "I think I . . . love this song. I'm happy I came here tonight."

"Good. I was worried you might change your mind and cancel." He curls me in a little closer. I'm surrounded by the warmth that radiates from him. I'm losing track of my song. If he wasn't holding me, I might float away.

"When someone like you asks a girl like me out, you go." There's my nervous laugh again. He holds me back a few inches, creating a gap of cool air between us. His dark eyes consume me and I gaze back.

"You know what makes you so awesome?" He doesn't wait for me to answer. "The fact that you don't even know that you are."

My mouth opens to say something, but the gap between

us fades. Is he going to kiss me in front of all these people? Oh God. This would be amazing, if I knew what I was doing. I can't do this in front of all these people. *Do something! Dive, dive!* I bury my face in his chest, biting my lip.

I'm such an idiot. He was going to kiss me, and I deked out. The slow beat of the music picks up again. Another perfect moment lost and added to my collection. His smile has lost its usual vibrancy. Taking my hand from his neck, he leads me back to his friends. We're almost back to the group when a tall, slim girl darts from the crowd towards us.

"Hey, I've been looking for you. Where's your jacket?" Before Nate can even get anything out, she mows down his words. "Janice and Amy just went outside for a smoke, and my jacket's somewhere back in the coat check room. Can I borrow yours?"

"And get it smelling like cigarettes? Go get your own," Nate says.

"Ah, come on, Nate. Don't be like that. You wouldn't want to look like a jerk in front of your date." They look at each other as if they're waiting for the other to cave, but neither is budging.

"Rachel, this is my sister, Jamey." He sighs and tips his head towards Mark. "Jacket is on the back of Mark's chair."

"Thank you," she says in a singsong voice and gives him a peck on the cheek. She grabs the jacket and rushes past. "Nice to finally meet you," she yells over her shoulder.

"Nice to *finally* meet me?" I repeat to Nate. "Seems like a few people know all about me. Been telling stories?"

A giant smile spreads across his face. "Oh, come on. You're not mad, are you?" He gives me a playful nudge. "How often do you get to tell a story about mud wrestling in a ditch with a hot girl at midnight—and have it be true?"

I can't help but smile back. "Yeah, I guess." The heat in my cheeks rises up.

"Sorry. Didn't mean to embarrass you."

Instead of going back to his friends, Nate finds an empty table tucked against the back wall and pulls out two chairs. I sit and adjust my minidress for the thousandth time tonight. My tights are not cooperating, and it feels like my butt is hanging out the back. "You look hot," Julie said. "Nate will love it." I sit perfectly still so my hemline stays where I put it. I want my comfy jeans back.

Nate turns his chair around and straddles it, facing me. "I was stoked you said yes to going out with me tonight. So I told a few people. First, that you were coming to the dance, and second, how we met." He has a mischievous yet sincere expression on his face. How could I possibly be upset with him? That look should be illegal.

"Don't worry about it. It's cool." I look down and fidget

with the edge of my skirt—again.

This is nice. We're talking, but I don't know what to say. What are you supposed to talk about on a date? I could ask him what he does. But I already know that. I'm overanalyzing this. *Just be cool. Oh God, he's leaning in again. What's he doing?*

"Hey." He's so close he only has to whisper in my ear. "You look like you're holding your breath." I feel his soft breath against my cheek and huff out a nervous giggle. "Tell me something about yourself." He leans back a touch, but stays close. The suspended reality ebbs away.

"What do you want to know?"

"Start with something easy. Your favorite colour."

"Blue."

"Okay. What about things you like? Do you have a hobby?"

"I'm in the photography club at school. I was in one back in Vancouver, too, but here it counts for credits. Not so cool, eh?"

"Photography, huh. What do you like to take pictures of?"

"Back home, I took some amazing shots of downtown and the seaports, but here I haven't really found my muse."

"Your muse?" His mouth twists up a bit at the corner.

My hand goes up to hide my nervous smile. "Yeah, I don't know. Isn't that what artists say? I need to find my muse."

He reaches up with his hand, touching mine.

"Your smile is beautiful. Don't cover it up." His voice is soft, but I can still hear it over the music. His hand slides off mine as he leans back. "I know some amazing spots to take pictures around here. Maybe I could take you out sometime."

"That'd be great." I clear my throat. "Thanks. Hey, I noticed when we came in that there are totem poles outside. I'm doing this project at school where we're supposed to take a picture of something that represents our family and write about it. Since my grandma is from here, I thought maybe one of the poles might represent her family. You could take me there to take pictures sometime."

"Sure, let's go."

"Right now? I don't have my camera. Besides, don't you want to stay in here with your friends?"

"They'll be fine without me—and it would be nice not to have to yell over this music."

Nate gets my jacket and we cross the dance floor towards a side exit. The cool night air hits me as he opens it.

Away from the swirling crowds of the hall . . . Into the blanketed darkness of the night.

CHAPTER ELEVEN

The heavy metal door slams behind us, shutting away most of the pounding music. There's a light above the door. It casts strange shadows over us and the stairs we're standing on. Holding on to the railing, I take in the dark field. It's edged by even darker trees, that surround the hall and the two of us. I'm not sure if coming out here is much better than staying in there.

Hey, Nate, there's something I should tell you. I have this bizarre, totally childish fear of the dark that stems from an intense incident that happened years ago. It's silly, really, but I'm on the verge of curling up in the fetal position right now . . .

Nate leads the way without hesitation down the slick, metal stairs. They tremor with every step. I follow slowly, hesitating at the edge where the overhead light stops. The air feels heavy and wet. If I didn't know better, I'd say the humidity was 110 percent. Yet, it's not raining. Tiny drops of water hang in the night air, dampening everything they touch with a misty, white fog. The stairs creak with my shifting weight. *Just go! He's right here with you.* Looking down at my shoes, I notice dew forming, like sweat.

Other than the light above me, a faint, ambient glow comes from the lights in the front parking lot. It sends a pale, eerie radiance over the barely visible totem poles, creating solitary shadows that protrude from the mossy earth. I blink, willing my eyes to adjust to the dim light, the only light for miles.

"You know what?" I look at Nate, who has stopped in front of me. "I think it's going to rain—and you don't have your jacket. Maybe we should go back in." I let one foot creep a step backwards.

"I'll be fine." He smiles that oh-so-Nate smile. The one that reminds me why I'm here, considering a walk in this inky blackness. "Besides, my sister is out here somewhere. I can steal my jacket back. If we can find her." His hand stretches out towards me. I want to take it. I don't want to stand here like an idiot, but that's exactly what I'm doing.

"Okay," I say, but I'm frozen. My feet are planted as if they've grown roots.

"Something wrong?" *You can do this. The building is right here. You should be able to see it if you need to go back.* I bring both feet to stand on the last step again, but as much as I want to, I can't move forward.

He comes back to where I am, standing so close I can't help but count the unbuttoned snaps on his shirt again. *Three.* Because I'm one step off the ground, we're almost eye to eye—another moment with kissing potential.

Does he realize my brain is like a record spinning too fast right now? I'm doing everything I can to avoid direct eye contact. Admitting you're afraid of the dark at any age isn't exactly cool, but it must be obvious that I'm death-gripping the handrail. He waits patiently for me to look up, and when I do, I'm greeted by a look that shows no hint of judgment.

"See that pole in the middle out there?" He points behind him, into the misty field. "Just past those other ones. It's like eight, maybe nine poles from here." It's hard to make out, but I see it. "That one is really cool and super old." His hand slides over mine on the railing. The warmth of it softens my grip a little. "Come on, let me show you."

God, this is uncomfortable. I peer past him into the night. There's nothing out there but shadows. *You can always turn back towards the light in the parking lot. You can see it from here.* "Okay."

The air is thick—not the slightest breeze blows. It feels as if the night is waiting to pounce. But it's all in my head, it's just the dark . . . just light with more shadows. My hand in his, I step over the edge.

Every step he takes feels like one and a half of mine, but I don't say anything. I shouldn't have let Julie put me in this outfit.

Navigating this uneven ground in these tiny shoes is proving difficult, and my foot catches on something. I know I'm going down into the knee-deep, swirling fog. My eyes are closed, my face is clenched. But Nate catches me with speed and grace, like rescuing pathetic girls is his day job.

"Whoa. There are some big rocks out here. We can slow down if you want. I've been out here so many times I guess I know where I'm going."

I hold onto his arm like a kitten clinging to a rope in one of those "Hang in There" posters. "Thanks. These shoes aren't made for walking." That sounded dumb. "Your arm is freezing." That isn't much better.

"I'm fine, really." He hoists me back to my feet, setting me down gently. "We're almost there. I'll walk slower."

I glance back the way we came. The community hall is just a silhouette now, haloed by the pale glow of the parking lot light. He keeps on talking. We keep on walking. With every step we take, the shadows get longer and the glow gets farther away.

"When I was a kid, my parents would drop my sister and me off with my grandparents every Sunday. Jamey would spend most of her time with my grandma, painting and stuff. I would be out here my grandfather. Watch your step." He pulls me towards him, my feet narrowly missing a mound of dirt. "If he wasn't here telling me the stories of the totems, we were out hiking the trails. I bet he's told me a story for every totem pole here."

"Each one has a story?" I ask, glad for the distraction.

"Each one *is* a story, actually. Totems are how the people recorded histories back then."

Finally slowing, we stop at the foot of a wide totem pole. In the dim light, the fog clings to it like soft Spanish moss hanging from an old growth tree, making it look older than I am, older than I'll ever be.

"My grandfather told me that he helped raise this one."

"Really? It looks so old. How old was he when they put it up?" I crouch down, careful not to kneel on the wet grass. Running my fingers over the smooth wood, I feel damp moss covering half of the face carved into the bottom.

"He didn't say how old he was, and I'm not sure if I believed him, either, when he said he helped raise it. He's old but not that old. He likes to tell stories."

I stand up, making the fog swirl around me. "Do you know what animal this is?" I point to the bottom carving on the totem.

"That's a frog."

"A frog? Really?" I see now how the carving resembles a frog, with its large eyes and wide mouth. "I've heard a few stories about totem animals before. I thought they were supposed to be powerful or mysterious. A frog doesn't sound very impressive."

"Sure it is. In this totem's story, the frog can live between two worlds. Frogs are hatched in the water and grow into tadpoles with gills. They evolve, lose their gills and tails, grow arms and legs, and become frogs, living on the land." Nate gets right into explaining it, like he's teaching an elementary school class.

I lean in and give him a playful shove. "Right. I took biology, Nate. They can live in water and on land."

My joking comment doesn't faze him a bit. "Yeah, but in this story, frogs are much more than that. They have the ability to change themselves to survive. They can survive as different creatures from this world and the next."

I never envisioned Nate as a Native mythology nerd. Not that I know him that well. Maybe I could ask him about the spirit box. Or not. I'm not bringing it up tonight, that's for sure.

"The oldest totem pole here is closer to the river. Too bad you can't see it. The Skeena River is really pretty during the day."

I can hear the river as we get closer, the roar of water over rocks. He gives my hand a little squeeze before starting off again. I'm keeping up better than before, although the fog is getting thicker. It hugs the ground up to my knees, swirling with every step. I pull on his hand to stop my feet from sinking. Crap. I'm going to lose a shoe. Does every meeting with this guy have to play out like this?

"Wait a sec. My shoe's coming off." I can't tell in the dark, but judging by his grin, I'm pretty sure he's reliving our little tryst in the ditch last week. I don't blame him—so am I.

"Here, I got ya." I lose one shoe to the mud as he sweeps me up in his arms. "Well, you still have one shoe." My arms instinctively wrap around his shoulders. *Three snaps still undone. One, two, three.* "Here," he says, setting me down to stand on one foot. "Lean up against this totem. I'll go fishing for your shoe."

Totem? It looks like one, but it has tree roots. Teetering on one foot, I take a closer look at the worn, smooth carvings. This totem has gnarled, twisted roots that spread out from the base. They break the surface of the ground, creeping out like grey tendrils, claiming the earth. Nate returns in a second with my shoe, flicking off the last few bits of mud and handing it to me. I take it, still balancing on one foot.

"I didn't think they carved trees while they were still standing. I thought they put them up after carving them."

"You're right. At least that's how people have done it for the past few hundred years or so. This one's not even made out of the same kind of wood they usually use. It looks petrified, doesn't it?"

"So how old is it?"

"I think it's safe to say it's the oldest one here. No one knows its true age, though. No tribe around here has claimed carving it. Try and guess what the bottom carving is. No one's ever guessed it right, but I'll give you a hint: it's not a wolf."

I look at where the roots meet the base while Nate helps me slip on my tiny, useless ballerina flat. He's right. The carved teeth and eyes aren't quite those of a wolf. The hair and limbs aren't quite human either.

A current runs through me when I realize that I know exactly what it is. And all the carvings stacked above it. They've been in my head all week. But here they are, larger than life, exact replicas of the miniatures stashed away in my bedroom.

I recoil, tearing my hand away from the carving but unable to look away. "It's a wendigo."

"Wow. How did you guess that? You must know the story."

"Kind of." My words sound distant in my own head. "I've heard a wendigo story before." A vision of Mason's silver gaze flits in my mind's eye.

"My grandfather told me the story about this one when I was little. It has something to do with the Great Spirits. How they saved their people by cursing them." Nate's hand hovers close to the wendigo totem, just inches from touching it. My eyes feel big as saucers. "But like I said, my grandpa tells a lot of stories. This tree totem could be just some artist's carving from a really long time ago. His story had some sort of box in it, too, that—"

The blood drains from my face as I finish the sentence for him. "Granted wishes." I reach over and take his hand before he can touch the totem. A pretty bold move, but I can't stand the thought of another person playing host to spirits.

"Yeah. You've heard this story?" He tilts his head towards me, surprised. "My grandpa said he's never told anyone but me before." A shy smile creases his lips. "He says a lot of things, though. Sorry. I get so into this stuff. I feel like such a gullible kid. I know they're just stories."

"Yeah. Just stories." My breath huffs out the same colour as the fog. "Can we go back now? This wendigo carving sort of creeps me out." The blackness moves in closer.

"It's just a carving, Rachel. It's not real. But yeah, we can go back."

Right. Not real. If I could convince myself of that, my life would be a whole lot more normal. I loosen my hold on his hand and let it fall. I hear girls' voices close by. I try to make them out, but I can't see anyone through the fog.

"That's Jamey. You all right to stay here a sec? I want to catch her before she's gone with my jacket."

No. Don't leave me in this creepy fog with this creepy totem. "Sure," I say. "I'll be right here. I can't keep up in these shoes, anyway." A nervous giggle escapes my lips.

"Two minutes. I'll be right back. Promise." His hand brushes lightly against mine before he turns and disappears into the darkness.

And here I am. All alone on an island of darkness, my

only company a wendigo totem tree. The fog stirs in front of me, but I can't see what's causing it to move. *It's just the breeze. It's just the breeze.* I'm listening so closely, I hear every internal thump and gurgle my body makes.

Footsteps shuffle in the distance. "Nate?" The steps fall silent and I'm left with only my thoughts. *Not funny.* Heat rises in my face. My heart is beating like a wild animal trying to free itself from a cage. I listen harder, trying to hear over the pounding in my chest.

"I can't believe this. He left you alone!"

The words sound so intimate that I'm honestly not sure if I'm hearing them . . . or thinking them. I scan the fog. Silence. "Hello?"

"Stay there. I'm coming."

It's not coming from out there. The voice is in my head, but it's not my own. *Awesome.* I've finally stepped over the dividing line between sanity and delirium.

"Out for a walk, are you?"

Three guys, standing not ten feet away, emerge from the fog. It's difficult to make out their shadowed faces, but none of them are Nate or his friends. One guy throws an empty can onto the ground, retrieving another from the pocket of his jacket and cracking it open. The acrid smell of stale beer wafts towards me. The other two chuckle to themselves, laughing at some inside joke between the three of them, before the one in the middle composes himself. He looks right at me as he approaches. "What brings a girl like you so far out here on a night like this? All by yourself." He drawls out the last few words.

"I'm not alone. I'm waiting for someone." *Shit. Nate, where the hell are you?*

"You look pretty alone to me." He tilts his head, spreading his arms wide. "What kind of person would leave a defenseless girl like you out here all alone?"

"I'm not defenseless. I'm not alone." No sooner do the words leave my mouth than the other two guys flank me on either side. This can't be happening. A million scenarios run through my head, none of which end well. I'm frozen. I don't know what to do. A silent plea escapes my lips.

My attention is divided among the two on either side of me and the one in front. All of them move closer with each breath I take.

"You could try being little friendlier," the one in front says. "I said I was here to help." The next few seconds are a distorted smear of what my mind can comprehend as reality. I step away when they get too close, but trip. Then I'm on my back on the ground. There's a hand on my stomach and another pressing on my wrist. I don't know what they are saying, but I hear their voices.

Then, as if my unconscious thought has plucked them

from this scene, the two guys that were at my sides disappear. Only swirls of mist remain where they once were. Their departure is almost completely silent. The shock painted across the face of the guy still on top of me tells me that this wasn't the plan.

"Who's there?" He pulls out a jackknife from his pocket and flicks it open. "Who's there?" he screams. He backs away from me in a frantic motion. My hand instinctively goes to the budding bruise on my arm.

"She said she wasn't alone." Mason walks out of the fog between me and the guy with the knife. "Or defenseless. I think you should probably leave now."

"Who the hell are you?" He turns and points the knife at Mason. "I advise you to leave."

Mason blows out a puff of air. "Who am I? The guy you wish you'd never met. I'll give you one last chance to leave. Or you can end up like your friends."

Mason doesn't wait for an answer. He's so fast, a shadow. The end result: Mason, with an arm-bar headlock on the guy, the jackknife now in his hand and pressed against the other guy's throat. "Your call, Rach. How should this one end?" I see the shimmer of silver glaze over Mason's eyes. The guy he's holding at knifepoint looks so scared he might actually piss himself.

How did we get to this? "Mason, whoa, whoa. Don't do this. I'm fine." I look around, peering into the dense fog. "What did you do to the other guys?"

He returns my question with a curt, "They're fine. What do you want done with this one?"

It doesn't take an idiot to figure out what would have happened if Mason hadn't shown up. What does this guy deserve? But I can't start thinking that way.

"Where are they, Mason?"

"God! You care too much sometimes." He doesn't move a muscle, not even a twitch, but the fog does. It runs from him like a scared child, sucking up into the sky and disappearing. The entire field cleared with just a thought, revealing the moon and stars and making the dark night almost bright.

I see two guys lying in a pile about fifteen feet from me, groaning. "See, they're fine."

"Put the knife down, Mason." The adrenaline running though me has made me numb. A frantic Nate is running towards me from across the field. Mason looks at me, blinking, his face relaxing, the metallic shine over his eyes fading.

Without a word and without breaking eye contact, he pushes the guy he's been holding to the ground, keeping the knife. "Sorry."

"You have a *sorry* for her? How about a *sorry* for me, you crazy fuck!" The guy scrambles back like a crab across the wet ground. "You almost slit my throat. And what the hell did you do to my friends?" he screams at Mason.

This guy has no idea. I'm pretty sure Nate's heard everything.

"Rachel, are you okay?" Nate is at my side, out of breath, taking in the scene. "What the hell is going on out here?" I can see his sister and her friends making their way over too. Great, a crowd.

"I'm fine. I—"

"You left her alone, asshole," Mason interrupts, closing the gap between him and Nate, knife still in hand. "These guys your friends?" He spits out the words with disgust.

"What the hell, buddy?" Nate backs up a step, holding his hands up. "I don't know these guys, and I don't know you. I just want to know what's going on here."

"This asshole came out of nowhere and attacked me and my friends." The conscious guy on the ground inches towards Nate, still rubbing the red mark on his throat. "We was just out for a walk and ran into Rachel here. And he jumped us."

"Get the hell away from me, man. I am not your friend." Nate shoves the guy away with his foot.

Mason and Nate are glaring at each other, the other two guys are waking up, and Nate's sister, Jamey, is now here with her friends. I need to get out of here. Evening over.

"Everybody just chill, okay?" I take a deep breath and step in between the two of them, my back to Mason. I'm beyond shaking. I have no idea what I'm going to say but words manage to find their way out. "This is my friend Mason. He"—I clear my throat—"worries about me. He obviously followed me here."

Nate looks over my shoulder and stares back at Mason. "Your friends are not so smart to come out here alone, Rachel."

"Yeah, that's what I told her," Mason spits back at Nate.

"Both of you, just stop." I push my hands up against Nate's chest forcing my back up against Mason's. "I think I should go, Nate."

"Okay, come on. I'll drive you home." Nate takes a step back, offering me his hand, but I don't take it.

"I need to go with Mason." I close my eyes. I can't look at Nate right now. My back is pressed up against Mason's chest. I can feel him breathing, as if he's breathing for me.

"Looks like your date's over," Mason calls over my shoulder.

I do a one-eighty and shoot up on my tiptoes, getting right in Mason's face. "Shut it, Mason!" His eyes soften as he mouths a silent apology.

Turning back to face Nate, an exhausted sigh escapes me. "He's obviously drunk. I can't let him drive home like this." What I really mean is that if I leave him here in this pissed off state, those three guys won't make it out alive. "Trust me, please. I'll be fine. I just think I should go."

Nate searches my eyes, probably trying to figure out how much of what I've said is bullshit and how much is truth. "Call me when you get home and tell me what happened here. I'll be waiting."

I can feel the heat radiating off Mason's chest behind me. "Come on." I turn, grabbing Mason's arm. "Let's get out of here. And get rid of that knife."

The wheels in Mason's head are turning as a smug look appears across his face. "As you wish." Mason strides over to give the knife back to the guy.

"Hey. Here's your knife back." Mason flips the knife around, presenting the handle to the guy. The guy looks at it and flinches back. I don't blame him. "Don't you want it back? It's a nice knife." Mason holds up the knife like he's displaying it. "I would keep it, but I have one just like it. It's beautiful—bone inlay on the handle, stainless steel blade." *What the hell is he doing? Just give the guy the knife,* I plead silently. "Mine's a little tricky though. It snaps shut sometimes, unexpectedly." He closes then opens the knife in his hand. "Yours seems okay, though." He hands it back to the guy again. "No hard feelings, eh?"

"Fuck you," the guy says as he takes it back.

I'm not sure if anyone else heard, but I did: the whisper from Mason's lips as he smiles. "To you too, buddy."

The guy's fingers curl around the handle of the knife. I hear the click of the safety releasing the blade. I hear it snap shut, blade on bone, slicing through his fingers. His cry of pain echoes into the inky sky.

We hurtle down the road, driving way too fast over freshly grated gravel. Mason let me drive, keeping up the charade of being too drunk. His truck feels huge underneath me, like it could crush anything in its path. I can't make it devour the road fast enough.

My clear skies are gathering dark clouds of what-ifs.

What if Mason wasn't there tonight? What if I'd just stayed inside the dance hall? I scream between my clenched teeth, slamming both feet on the brake, feeling a rush go through me. The whole truck fishtails, touching both sides of the gravel road. I don't care. I don't fucking care. I want out of all of this. Now.

What if Mason had no powers? What if wendigos didn't exist? What if I was never given that damn box?

Throwing the truck in park, I unbuckle my seatbelt and reach for the door handle. A blast of cool night air slaps me in the face. It feels good. It feels real. I don't bother to shut the truck door, although I envision slamming it shut, again and again, and then ripping it off like the Incredible Hulk in some fantastic fit of rage.

What if we never made those wishes? What if I never moved

here? What if my parents never got divorced?

I don't run. There's no point. I can't outrun him. I can't outrun this. I slam my knees down onto the gravel road. The pain feels good. The lights from the truck shine on my back. What a strange shadow I cast.

"What are you doing?" Mason calmly walks up to me, gravel crunching under his feet.

What if my brother didn't fight so much with our parents? What if he still lived with us?

"I'm kneeling in the middle of the road."

"I can see that." His hand brushes my shoulder and every cell inside me jumps. My world is in chaos. I am the pebble under the rubble.

"You were going to kill that guy." The words taste dry in my mouth.

"But I didn't. I—"

"You would have, if I hadn't been there. And that thing with the knife? That wasn't an accident. That was you."

I gag on dust. Metallic bile creeps up the back of my throat as I instant-replay the sound of crunching bone and metal slicing clean through flesh. The cold look in Mason's eyes speaks volumes. He doesn't have to say it. He did it. Accidents don't happen in my world anymore.

The dead night air hangs between us. "He was going to

hurt you, Rachel. He was going to do things to you. Things you'd never get over. He deserved it."

Things have already happened that I'll never get over.

A hot tear burns to escape, but I don't let it. "He deserved it? According to—"

"Me. That's who." His words are so cold they slice me.

"You," I say.

"Would you rather I'd done nothing? Just stood by and watched? How about a 'Thanks, Mason'?"

What if I wasn't afraid of the dark? What if my shadow wasn't so scary?

"I told you. I would have been fine. I don't need your help." I can't stop shaking. The rocks are digging into my knees. "What if they found out what you are, Mason?" I stand up, one knee first, then the other. He doesn't help me up. I can do it myself.

"You didn't need my help back there?"

He could easily take one step towards me. He could wrap his arms around me and numb the pain, all of it. And I want him to. I clench my teeth so hard I think they might crack.

What if my brother wasn't dead? What if it hadn't been my fault?

My face is wet, but it's not raining. *Make it stop raining. This was never in the forecast. Make the dark clouds go away.* He stands firm in front of me.

"I'm sorry," I gasp between gross sobs. "I don't know what I need." I step towards him, wrapping my arms around him, burying my face in his chest. I'm on the verge of ugly crying when his arms fold around me, a wave of calm claiming all of me.

My Monsoon subsides to a light drizzle. What if I didn't need him so much?

CHAPTER TWELVE

Hello everyone, and welcome to another Saturday night. I hope you're all enjoying yourselves and are not getting into too much trouble. For those of you heading outside, this evening's a bit cool, but the heat will be here soon. I can feel it. So get out there, have fun, and work on your pre-tan. The May long weekend soon approaches, hopefully bringing with it hot promises of summer.

On that sunny note, I have some great news for our little town of Hazelton. Our very own Jodie and Chloe Fox have most graciously donated the last five hundred thousand dollars needed to complete the new community center building project. Finally, our town will have enough money to build a much-needed place for all you young'uns to hang out. A ribbon-cutting and dirt-turning ceremony will be held at the building site soon to mark the start of construction. I'll have more details on this in the days to come, so stay tuned.

In other news, a public service announcement has been sent out regarding one of Hazelton's longtime outdoor enthusiasts. Professor David Wilkas has been reported missing. Professor Wilkas didn't check in after overnighting north of the Skeena River yesterday evening. The professor is a resident biologist at UBC who often comes to Hazelton to study the rare white animal population that haunts our hills. If you have any information regarding the whereabouts of Professor Wilkas, please contact—

"Julie, can you turn off the radio? My hands are all wet." I plunk another dish in the warm soapy water of the kitchen sink. Water sloshes over the edge, splashing a wet streak down the front of my jeans. Why am I even doing this? It's my birthday and I'm hiding in the kitchen doing dishes instead of sitting outside with everyone else. Still, it's better than facing the reality of *Barbie*, my dad's girlfriend and the woman who is apparently going to be my new stepmom.

My dad's relationship with her is hardly a revelation. I know he's been dating, and my parents have been split for years, but it's just too . . . I don't know. There's a ring on another woman's finger. A gold ring, circling the same finger on the same hand my mother used to wear a ring on, making the same promises. The fact that this woman could pass as my sibling doesn't help things. I drop another dish into the sink, and water sloshes over the edge again.

"How do you turn this thing off? I can't find the button," Julie says, turning the little kitchen radio over.

Rarely is the radio off in Grams' kitchen, and it's always set to the same station, the only one that comes in clear around here. She says it's how she gets her news. Her whole world turns on the little happenings in this town. I'm envious sometimes at the smallness of her world, the simplicity of it.

"Never mind, found it." The radio is silent and Julie goes back to drying dishes. "Too bad you had to hear it on the radio and not from Chloe. It was going to be a surprise. Chloe and her mom have given enough money to completely build the new community center. She's going to tell everybody at Mason's place later." Julie pauses, scratching at a bit of dried food fused to a dish. "So do you think that counts as my wish?"

"Your wish?"

"Yeah. I thought maybe it doesn't count because Chloe donated the money to get the center built. And I haven't seen any —"

"White bears." I say the words without thinking. No matter how much I want my reality to be a memory of a strange dream, it isn't.

"Yeah. The white crow showed up right away for Chloe. Which makes me think maybe the community center is just . . . I don't know. Chloe and her mom are just giving back to the community. Right?" She looks at me as if I'm an expert on the subject.

"I guess. Maybe."

"You guess? Maybe?"

"Yeah, what do you want me to say?"

"Sorry. I don't know. It's just hard to believe this spirit box stuff is real. I mean . . ." She twists the tea towel she's been using into a tight roll.

"I thought you told me that all this wish stuff was just some weird coincidence. Now you're thinking the spirit box might be real?"

"Well . . ." A look of clouded confusion crosses her face. "I'm not sure. I was just thinking. You guys picked spirit animals that are non-aggressive. I mean, what if a bear shows up and decides to come visit me?" She huffs out a nervous giggle. "You know, I bought bear spray after Chloe told me the news. Is that dumb or what?"

In the midst of my self-induced fog, a tiny smile creeps across my face at bear spray and the thought of Julie Ward owning a can of it. I find this very odd. Julie is the girliest girl of all of us. Her hair is always done, nails always painted, and even though most of her jewelry is cheap costume stuff, she never steps out without being perfectly accessorized. A vision of Julie trying to shove a huge can of bear spray into one of her tiny purses makes me laugh.

"What's so funny?" Julie interrupts my private joke.

"Nothing, just thinking." A wendigo makes a bear look like Winnie the Pooh. I dip my hands back in the murky water and pick up a dish from the bottom of the sink.

"So are we going to stay in here for the rest of the night doing dishes, or are you going to tell me what's bothering you already?" She playfully flicks a soapy bubble at me.

Everything's bothering me! All I want to do is tell someone about it, but I don't even know where to start. I want to tell her . . . but, but, but. *My life as a sentence with an abrupt and unknown outcome.* I stare at the dish I've been wiping for what seems like forever, my mouth slightly agape, but I say nothing.

"Your birthday party is sort of happening out there. I mean, I know your parents are out there and your grandma, too, but they're pretty cool. Come on, we can't leave Mason, Chloe, and Ryan alone with the old folks forever. Well, mostly just Ryan. If they knew what he was really like, they'd never let you come out with us again." Julie smiles and reaches into the sink, pulling the drain. "Come on, we're ditching this. I'm not letting you wash any more dishes on your birthday."

I plunge my hand back into the sink, saving the last bit of water before it's sucked down the drain. "I don't want to go back out there." I don't take my hand off the plug. I just let it sit in the murk of the lukewarm water.

"'Kay." There is a pause before Julie starts talking again. I know she's holding back. On a normal day she'd have told me to suck it up and get back out there. Maybe she's cutting me some slack for my birthday. "It's her, isn't it? Barbie or Barb? Whatever her name is."

Yuck. Bile rises in my throat. Barbie. Who names their child that, anyway? Yeah, Barbie is the reason I'm pathetically hiding in the kitchen doing dishes all night. I nod once in agreement.

I let the rest of the water go down the drain and look out the kitchen window above the sink. The bottom half of the window is veiled by faded, blue lace curtains. Through the space between, I see everyone sitting outside around the fire pit. The low flames from the fire barely lick over the top of the metal ring that surrounds it, but it still manages to cast an orange glow across all their faces.

Grams and Mason are both lounging back in low Adirondack chairs. Ryan and Chloe are cuddling together on the wooden garden bench. That forest ranger guy, who apparently my mom is now dating, sits on the stump of wood where Grams usually puts food out for the squirrels. On the long wooden bench are my mom and dad, and between them is her: Baaar-biiie. The life-sized, anatomically perfect embodiment of a reality I'm desperately trying to avoid.

She's the reason my dad isn't staying with us this weekend. It must be too strange to stay under the same roof now that my parents are finding other people. It's strange to see them with other partners. I get it. People move on. It happens with everyone and everything. Not so much with me, though. Maybe that's why I'm still standing here, wondering how, of all possible scenarios, I'm stuck in the same one as Barbie. I'd like to think there's a small part of us that holds on to what was. But for me, that small part is huge.

Julie clinks together the mugs she's putting in the cupboard. "After my parents split up, it seemed like my mom brought home every loser in town. I get it that you don't like Barbie. You don't have to, you know. It's okay." She closes the cupboard door, touching my arm as she turns to face me. "But your dad likes her. So it might make things easier if you'd stop giving her the evil eye."

I break my stare out the window and look at Julie, trying to muster a smile. "Is it that obvious?"

"Just a little." She holds her hand up, pinching her fingers together and squinting. "You know what, though? It's fine. I have just the remedy to wipe that seriousness off your face, 'cuz we only want happy thoughts tonight," she sing-songs as she crosses the kitchen to a bag left on the floor. "Here—I got you a present."

She lifts the tall, slender bag up, presenting it like a game show model. It's obvious the bag contains contents purchased from a liquor store.

"Should I open it now or wait?" I ask, taking the bag.

"Open it! We're having a drink. Maybe it'll help you spill the details about your date last night. I've been dying to know all day. Nate's lucky he's not here tonight, or I'd be giving him the gears."

"He had to work. And you wouldn't." I pull the bottle from the bag. Tequila. "I thought you said *wipe the seriousness off my face*, not *wipe the memories from my brain*."

"Don't be a wuss. And what makes you think I wouldn't grill him about last night? Nate's a big boy. I'm sure he can handle a few questions from an innocent, little high school girl." She bats her eyes and pouts. "I would have grilled every detail out of him an hour ago. Think of it as an initiation. If he's new to our group, there has to be some rite of passage."

She smiles so widely that it creases the corners of her eyes. I find myself smiling too. "But really, are you going to tell me about last night, or do I need to go through your phone to find Nate's number?"

"Okay, okay. What do you want to know?"

Julie hops up on the kitchen counter opposite me, grinning from ear to ear. "From the beginning. What was he wearing?"

I hop up on the counter, too, leaning back against the

cupboard. It feels silly, reliving every detail of my date with Nate. (Well, almost every detail.) But I guess this is what you do with your best friend, right?

I tell her about how unbelievably scrumptious he looked. I mention Nate's friends, and how we danced to my favorite song. I tell her we went for a walk in the fog, out behind the building, in the field with the totem poles. I leave out the last part. She doesn't sniff out any holes in my story.

"Did he kiss you?" She's leaning so far forward, it looks as if she might tip off the counter.

A hitch in my breath catches as the memory floods back. I can almost hear it—my favorite song floating from the speakers. I feel the way everything slowed and disappeared, except for us. I clear my throat to answer. "Um, no. Almost, but no."

"Almost? What happened?"

"This is so embarrassing," I mumble into my hands, covering my face. The memory is bad enough, but admitting that I blew a chance to kiss Nate Grey Hawk is too much. I let my hands open and spit it out. "I choked."

"On what? Your gum?"

It would be easier to wear a blinking *Virgin* sign with the footnote *Never kissed a guy, either.*

"I've never . . ." *Yep, keep going.* "Kissed anyone before."

"Never?" There's a long pause from Julie. "Really?"

Great, now I'm *that* girl.

"It's cool," she says. "It wasn't that long ago for me, either."

Yeah, right. It's nice of her to at least *try* to make me feel like less of a loser.

"Hey, cheer up. There'll be tons of cuties at Mason's house later if you want a birthday kiss. Or not," she adds at the twisted look on my face.

She hops off the counter and takes the tequila bottle from me, cracking the seal. "Does your grandma have any shot glasses? We're doing a shot."

"I don't know. Tequila is not really—"

"Found 'em. You're in luck." Great. The thought of downing a shot of tequila brings to mind images of using a Slip 'n Slide with no water.

As if on cue, the storm door on the far side of the kitchen slams shut. Standing in its wake is Mason.

"She's not really a tequila girl. Her drink of choice is gin. Bombay Sapphire, to be specific. And seeing as it's your birthday, I just happen to have brought you a bottle."

"Gin?" Julie gives Mason a devilish look, taking the blue bottle from him. She runs her finger down the length of the tinted glass. "I'm just trying to loosen her up, not feed her liquid panty remover."

"Actually, it is my favorite," I say. "I used to sneak it out of my parents' liquor cabinet when I was younger. And it's not liquid panty remover."

"Uh, yeah, it is, sweetie," Julie replies. "Pretty much anyone drinking this is looking for a goooood time."

I remember Nate's face when I ordered a gin and seven at the dance. Awesome. My first date with Nate, and he thinks I'm easy.

Mason grabs the shot glasses and another drinking glass from the cabinet, then pours two shots of the tequila and one of gin. "Gin isn't great for shots." He raises the glasses for us to take. "But since you like it so much . . . "

"Whoa. That big glass better be for you. What's that, like two shots' worth?" Julie pipes up.

"It's for Rachel," he says, as he balances the three glasses in his hands. "She'll be fine," he says, giving her drink to her. "She's a lot tougher than she thinks she is."

Mason's up against my knees before I have a chance to hop off the counter. I'm stuck. Even from this vantage point, I feel small. Not because he's towering over me, because he's not. It's a presence that radiates from him. Am I the only one who notices it? Every small, furry forest animal for miles must have run and hid by now. A predator is on the prowl.

I catch his gaze as he hands me my drink. "Let's make a

toast," he murmurs. I'm swimming somewhere in the ocean of his grey-blue eyes. "To the birthday girl." The silence between us catches in my throat. I have to remember to breathe. "May she know what she wants, and find what she's looking for."

What comes next is a blur. The space around me feels strange, but I can't say how. Is Julie still in the room? It feels as though the time surrounding Mason and me has stopped. The dust particles floating through the streams of light from the kitchen window seem to have stilled. They're hanging there now, unnaturally suspended, waiting for permission to move again.

The sound of Julie's throat clearing jolts the dust particles back on their way. "I'll meet you two outside when you're ready to go." She puts her shot glass in the sink and heads out the side door.

Right, Mason's place. Crowds of drunken people from our twelfth-grade class will be there. Well, at least there I can stop hiding out from Barbie. I can just run away.

I lift the glass of gin to my lips, but it's empty. That's when I taste it. The cool warmth of juniper berries on my tongue and in my throat.

"Wow, want more already? You should slow down." Mason has a mischievous look on his face.

I look into the bottom of my glass. Empty. Man, I'm really losing it. How can I not remember drinking it—five seconds ago?

Mason chokes back a laugh. "I'm just messing with you. Do you like my new trick?"

"What trick?" I ask, looking up from my glass.

"Sweet. You don't even remember?"

"Remember what?" I put my glass down, crossing my arms over my chest. "What did you do?"

"Relax." Mason's smiling so widely, he's almost giddy. "I've been up most of the night testing it out on my dog. I just didn't know if you'd remember. I mean my dog can't really tell me if he remembers me taking the Frisbee mid-air. Or why he can't find something that was just there."

"Slow down. What are you talking about?"

"I figured out how to 'pause' things. Only for a few seconds." He looks like his mind is somewhere else. "But you never know when a few seconds could make all the difference."

"Pause things?"

"Cool, eh?" He looks way too proud of himself.

"And you did it in front of Julie. I thought you wanted to keep this wendigo thing a secret. If people find out . . ." A million scenarios run through my head. "What the hell, Mason?"

He rolls his eyes. "Did she look like she thought anything was strange?"

"I don't know. I—"

"She remembers nothing. Trust me." His hand brushes

against my leg and I flinch. "Sorry, sorry." He moves his hand back to where it was on the counter. "I should have told you what I was doing before I did it."

"And what did you do?"

"To Julie? Nothing. To you?" His look softens. "I made you down that whole drink of gin in one shot. I was pretty sure you wouldn't do it on your own, and I figured you might appreciate the sharp corners it'll smooth off your night. I took a guess that you liked gin since I could smell it on your breath last night. At least I was hoping it was your type of drink, and not something Nate fed you on a first date."

"Anything else?" I give him a look, trying to figure out if he's keeping something back.

"Nothing, I swear." His hands go up in defense. "What? Do you think I stole a kiss?"

"You're a mind reader now, too?"

"Nah, I just overheard you telling Julie you'd never kissed anyone before."

"So you're an eavesdropper, then." I'm mad and dying of embarrassment at the same time.

"Listen." He takes my face, gently lifting my chin. "I may do a lot of things, but I'll never steal a kiss from you."

"Oh, so you wouldn't want to kiss me? I'm un-kissable?"

"You girls twist everything." He pauses. He's probably

taking a moment to think about why I'm so un-kissable. "You could wear a dirty paper bag"—his hand moves up from my chin to tuck a stray hair behind my ear—"and I'd still want to kiss you." His gaze trails from my eyes to my lips. "But I will never steal a kiss from you. Unless you want me to."

He could kiss me right now if he wanted to. If I wanted him to. Do I? The electricity that runs between us sparks with every breath.

"Come on. Everybody's waiting." Mason shifts back, taking my hand, guiding me down from the counter. The cool air pools between us, bringing me back from my cloud.

CHAPTER THIRTEEN

I've been here before, both in real life and in my dreams. My skinny, thirteen-year-old legs stick out from under my nightshirt. I'm sitting on my bedroom floor near the door, listening. I shouldn't eavesdrop, but I do. They never tell me anything. Are they protecting me, or hiding things? I don't know.

I know I'm dreaming this time. Seems hard sometimes to separate the thirteen-year-old me from me now. This scene has played over in my head too many times to count, but I swear I feel the chill of the laminate floor beneath my bare legs. It's too real. I'm back in Vancouver, back in my old bedroom, back in my old life.

I know the voices on the other side of the door: Eric, my mom, my dad. I picture them all sitting around the kitchen table. I can't see them, but I assume that's where they are. That's where they sit when they argue.

"*Stealing my credit card right out of my purse? God, Eric. Did you think I wouldn't notice? What the hell did you need so badly that you'd steal from your own mother?*"

A metal chair scrapes across the tiled kitchen floor.

"*Technically, Mom, I didn't steal it. I borrowed your card and got Rachel a birthday gift. Then I put the card back in your purse, fully intending to pay you back. Or at least my share. I figured it could be from all of us.*"

"*That's your version of 'not stealing'?*" There is no love in her voice, just the chill of her accusation. You'd never know it was a mother speaking to her son. "*Okay, I'll bite. So what did 'we' get Rachel for her birthday that cost $345.98?*"

"*It's a leather jacket from that place in the mall she likes.*"

"*And what about this, Eric?*" I hear my dad's voice, monotone yet sharp at the corners. There's a rustling of papers on the table. "*What are these other charges? Looks like some comic book store. I suppose you just had to get a few more stupid comics too?*"

"*They're graphic novels, Dad, and they're not stupid.*" Eric spits out his disdain for the comparison. "*They're like textbooks or industry magazines. I need to know what other graphic artists are doing if I'm going to be any good.*"

"*Oh. Pardon me. You're a graphic artist now. So this is what you're doing for a living? That and stealing your mother's credit cards?*"

"I told you! I didn't . . ."

This is when I should stop listening from behind my bedroom door, when I should quiet the voice inside me that wants to know more. But I don't.

"Save it." My dad cuts him off. *"We all know you're old enough to be tried as an adult now. One more strike on your record and it's jail time. In real jail. That's grown-up, hard-core prison. No more juvie. No more community service. No more slap-on-the-wrist fines. Real prison."*

"So what now?" Mom says. *"Do we turn you in? Let it slide?"*

"It doesn't really matter what you guys decide. Does it? You've already given up on me. You won't let me live here. I'm trying to work and go to school, but it's hard. Things are expensive. I'm probably going to have to quit high school. That'll be just great! I'll become just another statistic, but what do you two care? You gave up on me the first mistake I made. Maybe you had me too young? Maybe your life wasn't in order, so you didn't have time for me? Maybe—"

"Dad and I said you could live here."

"Right—by your rules."

"You brought illegal drugs into the house! And you were selling them! I don't think it's unreasonable to expect you to obey the law if you want to live in this house."

There is a pause. Is it a sound of defiance or defeat?

"Just, please don't tell my case worker about the credit card. Please. I'm trying, okay? I know you don't have to, but please." His voice is flat, the wind sucked out of his sails. *"You guys have your do-over, your second chance, your fucking favorite. Don't give up on her like you did on me."*

There is no answer. Just an acknowledging silence that makes Eric's words true.

I no longer wake up with a start from this dream. I used to, but I think I've convinced myself there's no point in reacting. My parents considered me the favorite. It was unspoken, but obvious. I was too naïve at thirteen to know what that meant, but I know now. I was their do-over. Too bad their second time around didn't turn out perfect either.

By eighteen, Eric had a rap sheet a mile long. When he was fourteen, he was caught shoplifting—twice. At fifteen, he was caught for possession of marijuana. They found it in his locker at school. At sixteen, Eric went away for a while, to what my parents told me was summer camp. Turned out to be some sort of rehab-slash-reform camp. At seventeen, my parents made him move out of our house. I gathered from my eavesdropping that it was because he was selling drugs. Eavesdropping was how I found out most of the details about my brother. I would pretend to be sleeping, and they would all argue at the kitchen table. My parents never once told me about Eric's troubles. Even he never brought it up. And I never once admitted I knew the truth.

Maybe they thought I was too young. Maybe they just wanted to keep me perfect, untainted, a title I did not and do not deserve. Instead, I hoarded my parents' love and attention, keeping my perfect status, falsely displaying a perfect veneer.

Deep breath in. Enough, Rachel. Deep breath out. It's another new day, and I'm still breathing. I let my legs fall lazily over the side of my bed. I usually tramp around in bare feet in the mornings, but today I put on socks. My feet are always cold after the dream.

Walking into my grandma's kitchen, I see it right away: two cups of steaming tea set out on the kitchen table. Crap, she wants to talk. Maybe if I back up real slow, she won't notice I'm out of bed and I can settle back under the covers and forget the day has already started.

I slide my worn cotton socks over the yellowing linoleum, but the creak near the fridge gives me away. Busted.

"Hey, you're awake." Grams' voice floats over the newspaper she's reading. She's sitting in her ratty old La-Z-Boy in the living room. Not sure why she won't get rid of that old thing. It groans in complaint when she shifts her weight. "Were you planning to sleep the whole day?"

"Well—" I blink my eyes wide a few times and fish the last bit of the sleep from them. How many hours was it? My head is still pounding from a well-deserved hangover. I'm not fooling anybody about my level of alertness—not sure why I'm even trying. "I thought maybe I'd spend some time with Mom today. Maybe go for breakfast or something."

"It's twenty after twelve, Rachel." She finally peers over the top of her *Saturday Post*, taking the time to fold it back into its original tight bundle. "Your mom has run out to meet with your dad and Barbie before they leave. Not sure how long she'll be. So I'm thinking breakfast is out."

She's not really staring, just giving me a look only a grandmother can give. Is she mad? Confused? I don't know. My head hurts. She's always one to be out with it, no wondering involved. "Too old to be anybody else but me," she always says. "If they don't like me, that's their trouble."

She's crossing the threshold of living room shag to kitchen linoleum when she says, "I made some tea. Come sit with me at the table."

Whatever she has to say must be pretty heavy if it involves hot beverages. Hot tea, that is. I've never really been a big fan.

The kitchen chair creaks as I sit at the table. I find a comfortable groove and wrap both hands around the welcome warmth of my steaming mug. Everyone has their own mug in this house. Mine's the one with the kitten on it that looks like Grams' cat. My mom has the one with the running horses, and my grandma's is the one with the soaring eagle. Pretty sure they all came from the touristy place in town, along with the dream catcher that hangs in the window above the kitchen sink. Strange place to catch dreams, if you ask me.

Grams takes a long sip from her tea, breathing in the hot vapours. "You're not the only one who's lost someone they love, you know."

We're talking about this now? Everyone knows I don't talk about Eric. He died four years ago. I've dealt with it, or I'm dealing with it. Whatever. I'm fine.

"Your Grandpa Harold died one year and twenty-two days after your brother did." She looks down at her mug of tea like she sees something other than her own reflection swirling back at her. "I know that because I counted the days. I also know it was four days after Harold died that we had him cremated, and two more days after that when we held his funeral. It's been one thousand seventy-four days I've been without your Grandpa Harold. On bad days, I still find myself keeping track."

She gives her tea a stir even though she's put nothing in it. "Keeping track of things was one of the ways I coped with him not being around anymore. Another thing I did was bake. Most times, when someone passes away, your friends bring you things they've made so you don't have to cook for the inevitable crowd of company that's going to show up. For me it was the opposite. I took things to them." She looked up, gazing off at nothing. "I didn't like being alone for any stretch. I needed an excuse to see someone so I wouldn't be alone. I made so many things: pies, cookies, casseroles. Oh, the casseroles: baked-sadness, oven-roasted-pity, bad-luck-pot-luck. I made so much, our tiny grocery store ran out of cream-of-whatever soup, so I couldn't bake anymore. Or so they said."

"Are we still talking about Grandpa?" I have to say something. This conversation is rambling, even for her.

"Yeah, we're still talking about Grandpa." She loosens her grip on her soaring eagle mug. "What I'm trying to say is, we all have our ways of dealing with things when people die. I know how much it hurts to have people go before you, but at some point, it's okay to start living again and enjoying things like you used to, instead of just going through the motions. Life keeps on moving, Rachel. And if you spend forever baking sadness, you won't notice that it's leaving you behind."

Well, what do I say to that? I get it. I do. I'd like to check back in to life . . . I just don't know how.

"Thanks, Grandma, for the tea, but I'm okay. Mom and Dad sent me to this shrink lady a few years back and I'm good now." My sentence trails off as I get up from my chair.

"Are you okay? Maybe I'm just old and worry too much, but . . ."

"But what?" I pause, not looking at her but not looking completely away.

"Nothing, really. It's more a feeling than anything else. Something's just off."

Yeah, something's off. If she only knew the half of it. I take a step over to her chair, give her a bear hug, and kiss the top of her head. "I love you, Grams. Thank you for worrying about me." I've never thanked anyone for that before, but it feels right. I give her one more squeeze before I let go. "I'm going to jump in the shower."

Our gazes meet before I make my way out of the kitchen. Her eyes are slightly glazed. Almost teary, but not quite. "You talk to me if you need to, okay? I'm not so old I don't remember being your age."

I smile in response. Grams can be a nosy person, but perhaps it's because she genuinely cares about other people's problems. Maybe I'll take her up on the talk sometime. Maybe.

I stop off at the fridge and pick up my morning Pepsi before heading back to my room to grab my shower stuff. Strewn on my bedroom floor are the crumpled clothes I wore last night. A blue sort of long shirt-dress thing with leggings. Judging from the smell of booze and bonfire that wafts from the crumpled clothes, I'm amazed I remember anything from last night.

On the back of my computer chair is Mason's varsity jacket. He lent it to me at the party. It smells like peppery citrus. Like Mason. I run my hand over the soft, grey fabric. Last night rushes back into my head, the part where he found me curled up drunk on the swing bench on his back deck. I was trying my best to look invisible to the crowds of people at his party.

"Hey, what are you doing hiding over here?" He has (by my count) his seventh drink in his hand and doesn't even look buzzed.

"I'm tired." It isn't a lie. I've polished off a good quarter of the two-six of gin Mason gave me. I'm feeling pretty awesome—and pretty *tired.*

"Do you mind if I sit with you awhile?"

"'Tis your bench, Mason Allen."

"Oh, using full names, are we? How much have you had to drink?"

I try to pinch my fingers together but my hands are clumsy. My gesture is more like a crumpled fist. "Just a bit." The bench rocks like a huge wave when he sits down. I almost fall right off, except he catches me.

"You're freezing. Here, wear my jacket. I don't need it." He wraps the jacket around my shoulders, and warmth radiates from it. Maybe it's the gin or maybe something else, but I curl into his side and let him wrap his arm around me. He pulls me in tight. It feels wonderful.

"Thank you."

"For the jacket? Anytime."

"No. Thank you for Friday night." He doesn't say anything back, just holds me a little tighter and leans his head against mine.

"So tell me, Rachel Barnes," he says, just loud enough for me to hear. "What is the rest of your story?"

I don't look up at him or move at all, really. I'm in my happy place. "What do you mean, 'the rest of my story?' I've already told you about my brother's . . . accident, and how my mom was messed up but got better. You somehow even got me to tell you about the boxes."

"No, not that part. It's been four years since that happened. Tell me the rest."

I look over at the neatly stacked boxes occupying the corner of my room. A more recent Rachel? That's when it hits me. I have nothing to tell. It's taken me until my eighteenth birthday to realize it, but I'm still that little girl whose brother died. I've been so focused on that, I've become my own sad story.

Who is the Rachel who's existed these past four years? The tape on one of the boxes has loosened and curled at one end. I grab the box and set it on the floor. I still exist. I've just been packed away for a while.

The curled end of the box tape begs to be ripped. Will it hurt less to tear it away quickly? Or should I take my time and be gentle?

I grip the tape and pull. The box gives way in liberation— and so do the last four years of my life.

CHAPTER FOURTEEN

It's eighth-period English and I'm listening to the mousey, small-framed, frizzy-haired Mrs. Fare drone on about summer reading lists. It doesn't make sense to me that she's assigning, or even suggesting, that we read books over the summer. Twelfth grade is over in a matter of weeks. For a lot of us, it'll be the last schooling we ever get.

On the whiteboard at the front of the classroom, Mrs. Fare has scrawled in perfect English-teacher script the date and time of our final exam. It's only two weeks away, and then what? I don't know. Maybe I could stay on at the municipal office. Becoming a lifer? Not the worst thing anyone's planned to do. Or should I say *not* planned to do. I guess my university and college applications fell off the radar when I moved here in the middle of the year.

I may not have some grand plan, but things have been

looking better over the past two weeks. I have a boyfriend. Well, I think he's my boyfriend. Nate and I have been spending pretty much every day together since the dance. My head is still processing the fact that he even called me back after that fiasco of a dance. And he was the one with all the apologies. How he felt so bad for leaving me alone. I accepted his apology and haven't talked much about that night since.

Nine minutes left until the end of the period, and the end of the day. I swear I hear a faint *clang* with every tick the clock makes. My eyes wander around the room. I see Chloe fidgeting with the tag on the hem of her sweater dress. She looks about as zoned out as I am, probably thinking about the next adventure she's about to embark on.

Julie sits two rows over from me. I notice an oversized pink and cream Coach purse under Julie's chair. Definitely from Chloe. Julie got better there for a while—not so paranoid about attacks from white bears. But with the larger purse, I bet her bear spray is in there. I can't blame her, I guess. The news is all over town about the dirt-turning ceremony for the construction of the town's new rec center. It's tomorrow. I guess it's better to have the bear spray and not need it than the other way around. If only a can of air-propelled bear deterrent could solve our problems.

My eyes drift back to the clock. Seven minutes till the end of class. Only two minutes have passed! Clearly, I am stuck in an English class time-vacuum. Time has been sucked out of the room, leaving me here in an endless loop of Shakespeare and *Lord of the Flies* discussions. I rub the kink that's forming at the base of my neck. Just seven more endless minutes. I let my mind drift and my body relax, just enough to pretend I'm not still sitting at my desk.

And I hear something. Softly echoing in my ear, lyrics to a song I've heard many times before, usually blaring out some car radio. But this time it's slow. Like a hazy dream, it sings to me. The words tell me to close my eyes and I do, drifting a little farther from my last class of the day.

The warmth of my own smile washes over me. This song doesn't bring back a specific memory, more like a feeling. It makes me think of the rush of excitement that comes with going into the unknown, or the airy lightness of freedom. Did I hear someone humming it earlier? I let it play on in my head. It sings of new discovery and beckons for me to follow.

The band that sings it is on the tip of my tongue, but I can't quite remember. It feels like this verse sings just to me, but it's not a singer I've heard before. The music makes me want to get up and go. I'm so ready to go! Bust out of this place like Indiana Jones out of the Temple of Doom. Every bone inside me wants to sing along. So I do. The last words of the song pour out of me like a fangirl at a concert.

When I look up, everyone, including Mrs. Fare, is staring right at me. Most are holding back laughs, even Mrs. Fare. Julie looks at me like I've lost my mind. I have no words. My mouth gapes while my face turns beet red. Mason is the only one who *isn't* looking at me. He's got a sly smile smeared across his face, and I realize who was singing in my head.

Mrs. Fare opens her mouth to comment on my outburst of vocals when the bell rings. Everyone but me springs up from their desks and floods out like a herd of wild animals. I'm left alone with a bewildered Mrs. Fare. But instead of getting upset with me for interrupting her class, she pauses. The look on her face indicates that she's entirely forgotten what to say. Closing the book in her hands, she says, "Aren't you going? Have a good weekend, Miss Barnes."

I'm so close to making it outside without anyone stopping me when Ryan blocks my path to freedom.

"Hey, Rachel." It's odd to see him without Chloe in tow. Even odder that he wants to talk to me. "Awesome vocals in English class. That song is a classic."

"Yeah, thanks," I say, trying to move past him to the doors. I don't need his torments right now.

"Wait. I didn't stop you to critique your singing. I wanted to talk to you—about Mason."

I can't help but be suspicious. Ryan never cares about anyone but himself. "What about him?" He looks around before pulling me off to the side.

"Look. I've been the guy's best friend forever, and something isn't right with him lately. All he talks about is you."

"And you think that's bad? Uh—thanks." This time I try harder to make my way past him, but he grabs my arm, not letting go.

"That's not what I meant." His grip loosens but he doesn't release me. "His vibe is totally off. I don't really know how to explain it."

"Get to the point, Ryan."

"You're not like the girls he's usually into. I wouldn't want to see you used up like the others he's dated."

"We're not dating. And why do you even care?"

"Whatever," he lets go of my arm and starts to walk away. "Who's to say I do?"

I watch as he disappears into the crowd. Mason's *change* isn't going to be a secret forever. If Ryan has noticed something, who else has?

The steel door of the school slams shut behind me. Slinging my backpack over my shoulder, I find a seat on the boulder near the front of the school. I can see the whole school parking lot from here. For the past two weeks I've been driving to school in what Julie and Chloe have dubbed the "Barbiemobile," but not today. Nate's picking me up. My mom, Dad, and of course Barbie surprised me with a Volkswagen Jetta for my birthday. It's a few years old, low miles, a nice silver colour. Thankfully Barbie doesn't have a sense of humour like my friends do. Julie and Chloe, on the other hand, think they're pretty funny. They've found it necessary to accessorize my car with what seems to be a permanent *I brake for Ken* bumper sticker. Other than that, it's a pretty sweet ride.

It turns out Barbie works for a dealership in Vancouver and found a great deal on this car. She was the one who convinced my parents that a girl my age needs her own set of wheels. She's won a few brownie points with me for that. The gesture takes her from "most hated" to "slightly uncomfortable with." It's not a "like," but it's a big jump for her. Maybe in time I'll decide that she isn't such a bad person. I just think my heart needs time to adjust to what my head already knows.

"Hey," Mason calls from across the school's front lawn. He's walking towards me alone, which is a surprise. His latest accessory is a girl name Sheri-Lynn. She hangs off him like the absence of his touch causes her physical pain. It bugs me to see him with her. I guess I need to get over that. Not that there's anything to get over. God, she's just so dumb, though.

Last week, I took the time to talk to her. I thought I should get to know her if she's going to be hanging around. So I asked her what she was planning to do after high school. She told me she was going to beauty school. Now all I can think of is her painting other people's nails while chewing gum so loudly you can hardly understand a word she's saying. I'm being harsh, I know. At least she has a plan after high school, which is more than I can say. But she'll never know Mason like I do. She'll never know what he's really like. Or what he really is. He's not the cocky jock people think he is. He's—better than that, and something else entirely.

"I've been looking for you. Thought I might catch you at your locker, but you weren't there." Mason is looking unlawfully good in his tight grey V-neck T-shirt. It's the kind of shirt that looks like it's inside out, but isn't. Its raw, stitched seams strain to keep the bulk of him in.

"I needed some air. Apparently singing in public is my new thing." The smirk he's trying to hold back says it all. "You wouldn't have had anything to do with that, would you?"

"Oh, come on. It was totally funny. Mrs. Fare was going on about plot structure and movies. She'd just finished talking about *Aladdin*. I couldn't resist. When you relax like that, it's so easy to get in your head. I knew you'd figure out that it was me. It wasn't the first time I've been in your head."

"What do you mean, *not the first time*?" My voice is getting too loud. *Chill.* I try to think back but I'm drawing a blank.

I can feel whatever it is that radiates from him as he steps closer.

"That night that I came and found you in that field of totem poles, you didn't hear me?"

I remember the voice in my head. It wasn't my own. I hadn't thought about it much until now. Mason walks around to the other side of the boulder and hops up, sitting beside me.

"Don't be mad. I've gained a few more powers and I've been trying them out. About two weeks ago I figured out that I can let people hear me"—Mason taps a finger to his head—"sort of like a voice in their head. Since then I've gotten a lot better at it. I can put songs in people's heads, and sometimes even convince them to do things. Although it's pretty tough to convince a person to do anything. Animals and bugs are a lot easier."

A moment ago, I felt violated because Mason was in my head. Now I'm ticked off that he hasn't told me about all these new wendigo powers. We had a deal: we'd let things settle for a while and then figure it all out—together. This is exactly how my parents treated me when they talked about Eric's problems: they'd either pussyfoot around it or say nothing at all. It's bullshit.

"Why didn't you tell me about this earlier?"

"Hey, I tried. All you do lately is hang out with Nate. I almost thought you'd forgotten about your whole crusade to rid me of this thing."

"Hey, you haven't exactly been available yourself. Where is Miss Sheri-Lynn, anyway?" Something dark rolls across his face, like the glint of mercury glass when it catches light. "Whoa. What was that? Your skin just changed colour for a second." He closes his eyes as if to compose himself as his colour returns.

"Look, a lot's happened in the past two weeks, and I've wanted to talk to you about it, but this really isn't the place." A small crowd of people walks past, talking about the weekend and filtering out into the parking lot. "Come with me. We can go to my house and talk about all this."

My guilt must show before I even say the words. I know he can tell. "Nate's picking me up. I—"

"You know what? Don't worry about it." He slings his backpack over his shoulder and hops down off the boulder.

"No, I want to talk. How about I come over around eight?"

"Sure. I'll be home all night." He steps out in front of me and puts his hands on my waist. He lifts me effortlessly down from the boulder until I'm wedged between him and the giant rock. My breath hitches. "I'll see you then," he says, sucking in his bottom lip. "By the way, Nate pulled up a minute ago. He's waiting in his truck for you."

I'm suddenly well aware that Mason's hands are still lingering on my waist. Does Nate notice? Mason is always doing shit like this. It's childish and absolutely premediated. Nonchalantly, I brush Mason's hands off, trying to make it look like nothing.

Because it was nothing.

Shoving my backpack down at my feet, I hop into the passenger side of Nate's truck. Sitting next to me, he's calm and collected, as usual. Can't say the same for me. Is it the nervousness I can't seem to get over when I'm around him or the fact that he might have seen me with Mason that's making my heart do flips? Then again, it's been two weeks and Nate and I haven't kissed yet. That has to be causing a teenage hormonal flux.

The scent of him floats over me. I breathe him in. He smells like . . . Nate, which is a mix of the outdoors, manly soap, engine oil, and something else that turns the timid girl in me a little more primal. He doesn't wear cologne. I asked him. That I know his scent is all *him* makes it that much better.

"Hey, how was your day?" I ask, shutting the truck door.

He takes a second to look at me before answering. "It's getting better." A smile creeps up the corner of his mouth. "So, do you want the good news or the bad news first?"

"The bad, I guess." I shift my weight, turning slightly towards him. What possible bad news could Nate have for me?

"Well, I can't get my four-wheeler to start. So quadding is out today. I left it back at my shop until I get the time to fix it." I let out a tiny sigh of relief. This guy has nothing on bad news. "Good news is you get to meet my grandpa."

Not the good news I expected. "Your grandpa?" I try hard not to look underwhelmed.

"Yeah. Remember how he used to tell me stories about the totem poles? Well, I told him about you, and how you knew the story about the wendigo totem. Anyway, I thought you might like to hear some of his stories, 'cuz you seemed interested in that sort of stuff." Nate's voice trails off. Do I detect a bit of rambling?

He goes on about how he has to fix his grandpa's dishwasher. To see Nate nervous like this is cute. He just keeps going on and on. It's nice, I guess, that he wants to introduce me to his family, but it's unsettling at the same time.

It takes about twenty minutes to drive from my high school to his grandpa's place. It feels like we're in the middle of nowhere, although that's my sentiment every time I leave paved roads. I don't have much experience of life on the reserve, but his grandpa's place isn't what I expected.

Turning onto the long, narrow driveway, Nate parks his truck beside a late-model, maroon Oldsmobile.

"Wait here a sec," he tells me, hopping out of the truck and coming around to my side to open the door. He offers me his hand. "It's pretty muddy out here. Watch your step."

The ground is a mess of mud, clumps of long grass, and random stuff. I pick my way through it, finding a path through the scattered debris to the side stairs of the house. The wooden stairs to the front door are so weathered and waterlogged they don't creak at all when we step on them. I'm not sure the doorbell works, but Nate doesn't use it. He just knocks hard twice on the door and goes in. I guess the same rules apply out here as in town.

We step into a cramped kitchen. The first thing I notice is the warmth inside compared to out. It smells of furnace vent dust mixed with the dampness of outdoors. Crammed in the corner of the small kitchen is a worn table circled by four mismatched chairs. Nate pulls one out for me to sit and I do, taking off my hoodie first and slinging it over the back of the chair.

Nate's grandpa shuffles in from the other room, cradling a steaming mug. "Is it cold in here?" he says, taking a sip from the mug.

"No, Grandpa, it's just you," Nate answers, with a smile and a hug.

"Well, turn up the heat anyway. Maybe your girlfriend's cold. Did you ask her?"

Nate stumbles on his words for a moment. "She's fine, Grandpa." I smile on the inside. He didn't correct him.

"Hi, I'm Rachel." I stand up, putting my hand out to shake his.

"I know who you are. Heard a lot about you. You're Ellen's granddaughter." He gives me a look from top to bottom. "You're a lot prettier than I expected." His serious look turns to a wide smile. "You go ahead and sit down. Shaking hands is for business, not friends," he says, leaving my outstretched hand hanging.

He shuffles over to the sink and fills a teakettle with water. "You'll have tea." I'm pretty sure it wasn't a question, so I just nod in agreement. After he puts the kettle on the stove, he sits opposite me with a huff on one of the mismatched kitchen chairs.

"So, Nate, you brought your girlfriend all the way out here to watch you fix a dishwasher? You need to work on your lady skills if that's the case."

I can't help but smile and stifle a laugh when I see a blush cross Nate's face. To know that he gets embarrassed just makes him more—real. Not just the man-god I've put on a pedestal.

"I told you about how Rachel was interested in the totem stories. I thought you could tell her one or two while I fix this for you."

"Yeah, I remember. I'm old, kid, not senile. I just like to see you squirm." His grandpa's smile is as big as Nate's. Maybe that's where he gets it from.

Nate opens the dishwasher door and takes out the bottom rack. "So this thing's been making funny noises? It's probably something stuck in the garburator trap." Nate leaves the dishwasher open and goes over to the kitchen sink. He crawls halfway under it, leaving only his bottom half exposed.

"So, Rachel, how'd you two meet?" Nate's grandpa looks at me with the kind eyes of a very old soul. "Hope he didn't haul you out of a ditch like some of his other girlfriends."

Thud-crash.

Nate's head hits the underside of the sink, sending a few precariously stacked dishes crashing into the steel basin. "What he means is . . ." I hear a wince of pain as Nate rubs the back of his head. "I drive the tow truck sometimes and pull people's cars out of ditches."

"Well, yeah, Nate. What the hell did you think I meant?"

"I don't know, Grandpa. It just sounded kind of . . . bad." At least there's one person Nate knows who didn't hear our mud-wrestling story.

The kettle on the stove whistles and Grandpa is up before I can even offer to help. As if he's done it a thousand times before, the water's poured, the tea bag is dunked, and the steaming mug is set on the table. I can't help but think that the conversation to follow must be important.

I wrap my hands around the warm mug, taking in its heat even though the room is already warm. It's comforting. "We met at his shop. He was fixing something on my mom's truck and I was the one who picked it up."

"Oh," he answers with a smile. "Well, that wasn't too hard to say. Eh, Nate?"

Nate doesn't answer, but I'm pretty sure he's smirking at my version of how we met. Call me old-fashioned. I just don't think the mud-wrestling story should be rolled out the first time I meet Grandpa.

"So, Rachel, you want to hear some of my totem stories? Which one would you like to hear? Or can I pick?"

"Well . . ." Why am I so nervous about this? They have no idea what's been going on. I'm just asking about a carved pole I saw. "How about the story that goes with the wendigo totem?"

"You know the name of it. Not very many people know the name." He looks at me for a moment longer than he should before going on. "But many people ask about that totem. It's very different from the rest." He settles into his chair, taking a deep breath. He looks as though he's filing through a thousand dusty memories to find just the right one.

"That story starts before all my other stories, here in Hazelton, but before there *was* Hazelton. Before there were roads, before countries, and long, long before there was even a hint of the people that live here now. At this time, there were two tribes."

I let myself get lost in his words. Through the veil of steam rising from my cup, I listen as the words flow out of him like history revived. "The two tribes lived in harmony with each other. There was no war or mistrust between them. Each tribe took only what they needed from the earth to survive, and the earth provided. There were animals to hunt, fish to catch, and what grew to forage.

"Every year, when the fall turned to winter, the wide

river that ran between the two tribes would freeze over, erasing the divide between them. This was a time of celebration and friendship; each tribe welcomed the company of the other. Until one very cold winter. That winter, the ice froze so thick over the river that it choked out the fish. The cold was too much even for the animals on land. They began to leave for someplace warmer.

"Both tribes had known hard winters before, but never this bad. Each had saved food for the cold times, but their stores were running low. Soon they would be starving. So the people prayed. They prayed to the Great Spirits to save them. And the spirits heard."

He must have noticed the puzzled look on my face. "The Great Spirits are what make our world what it is. They bind us to all things living and the dead. The Great Spirits do not normally interfere, but they do not like to see suffering, either. So the spirits gave the two tribes each a gift." The table creaks as I lean in closer. "They gave them a way to survive." Nate's grandpa takes a sip of his tea. "Two boxes. Inside each were four carvings. Three white spirits and one black. The tribe's people could ask for anything from the spirit carvings—and they did. The boxes that housed the carvings were beautiful, decorated with the likenesses of the four spirits they contained."

My grams told me before how stories get passed down through generations, but I'm shocked he knows all this. It makes me wonder how my grams got the box in the first place.

Something doesn't add up.

He has a look of reminiscence in his eyes as he speaks. "The gift came with warnings, of course. There are rules, even in the world of spirits."

Here we are, sitting around a kitchen table discussing the wonders of a time that came before us. A time that to them is just a story, just folklore. If they only knew his story held so much truth.

"Hey, didn't you say you saw a white deer around town the other day?" Nate's voice startles me from under the sink.

"I did. Well, I think it might have been white. It was dark." I know Nate is just trying to be nice, but I want him to just fix the dishwasher and stop interrupting.

"It could have been a white deer. I've helped people from the university in Vancouver track white bears around here. Maybe there are white deer, too." Nate's grandpa shrugs his shoulders and takes a sip of his tea. "Where was I? Do you want to hear about the university professor and white bears instead?"

"You were at the part with the boxes," I say with barely controlled calm.

"Right. So the Great Spirits gave each tribe a box containing four spirit carvings. Along with the gifts came many rules and warnings. But, people being what they are, they didn't listen."

"What were the rules to the spirit boxes?" I look at him with all the wonder of a child before they discover Santa isn't real. Before they believe that everything in this world has already been discovered.

"The rules are not so important. It's that they didn't follow them." He rubs the corner of his tired eye. "But you seem to listen. So, I'll tell you.

"The first thing the Great Spirits told the tribes was how to wish on the carvings. 'Take it in your hands,' they said, 'and tell it what you want, but choose carefully.' Once wished, it would be granted. Second, they said, 'Each time you make a wish, that spirit will be released into your world.' And third, 'You can't ask something of the same spirit again until the balance has been restored.'"

"What do you mean, the balance restored?"

"Good question. It means that there is evil for every good. Or how do the Chinese say it? Yin for every yang. The white spirits are pure. They cause no harm when set free to wander in our world. The black spirit does. It is tainted, dark and cursed. The dark wendigo spirit will grant the wish asked of him, just like the others, but upon completion he, too, is released into our world. The wendigo restores the balance of what's good and what's not."

"Released from what?" My breath catches slightly as Nate slams the dishwasher door shut with a jarring thud.

"Look at you, getting all caught up in his stories. Easy there, Grandpa, you're going to give her nightmares." Nate wipes his hands on a dishtowel before sitting beside me at the kitchen table. He sits so close that my leg brushes against his. I swear, every cell inside me gravitates to the point where we touch.

"So you fixed the dishwasher?" his grandpa asks.

"Yep, just some food clogging the lines. All fixed."

"The crappy dishwasher can't even wash away food."

Enough about the damn dishwasher! I reach over and pat Nate's leg, scrunching my nose at him. "I don't scare that easy." Nate slides his hand over mine before I can take it back. My heart pauses, a girlish reaction that sends a smile to my lips. "I think you were at the part where the wendigo is released."

"Yes. Okay. So every time a spirit grants a wish, that spirit is released and allowed into our world. They are then free to do as they want." Nate's grandpa sits up a little straighter and leans forward. "You see, this is where human nature always fails us."

"Because we don't follow warnings?" I answer.

"Maybe. Sometimes." He settles back in his chair, still looking me right in the eyes. "But in this case, it's because we don't know what we want. We are always looking for something more."

If blood can run cold, I'm pretty sure mine just dropped a degree. Was my wish just history repeating itself? The sound of my own voice echoes in my head.

To know what I want, and to find what I'm looking for.

"So when the two tribes received their boxes, they made silly, foolish wishes, soon using up all the gifts given by the white spirits. But the people wanted more, and they knew they could have it. As much as they wanted. All they had to do was wish from the black wendigo." His voice hung in the warm air between us.

"The two tribes gathered together eighteen people, nine from each tribe, to discuss what more was needed to survive the winter. They all agreed, and voted unanimously on what was to be asked of the white spirits and the black. Three times from each box, the black wendigo was wished on. And when their wishes were granted, six wendigos were released into the world." Nate's grandpa pauses, rubbing his tired eyes again.

"The people, they learned quickly of the curse the wendigos possessed. Unfortunately, it was their undoing. You see, a wendigo is cursed to collect its toll for the rest of its days. Which is a very long time, because as long as it collects, it'll never die."

"What's its toll?" I ask.

"Its toll is the price it pays to stay in our world. It collects"—he pauses to find the right words—"souls. The thing that gives life to the living. Each time it collects, it receives that person's memories and more."

"Okay, Grandpa, now you're just telling campfire stories." Nate rolls his eyes. "How about we finish this up another time?"

"No, wait," I say before I can even think. "I want to hear the rest." I give Nate's hand a little squeeze and he settles back into his chair. He probably thinks I'm weird, but I'm beyond caring right now. I don't know how his grandpa knows these stories, but it's the closest thing to actual research I've done in weeks. "What did the people do to get rid of the wendigos?"

Nate's grandpa starts out again. "The people prayed to the Great Spirits again for help. And they took pity on them, again. That is when the spirits created the totem, carved with the likenesses of all four gifted carvings. The story goes that the spirits gave them a choice. They could return the boxes back to the earth from which they came. Or they could try to solve the problem in their own way. Sounds simple, right? But there is a catch. There always is. If the boxes are returned, so are the wishes. It's all or nothing. Go back to starving in the cold winter or deal with the evil you've created. Not a very happy ending, eh?"

"So what did they do?"

"That's where the story ends, Rachel." He takes a long sip from his tea. "But you know what I think? I think most history is told by the victors. Maybe they didn't want the rest of the story told."

"History, eh? Oh, you've really caught him telling stories

tonight, Rach." Nate pushes back his kitchen chair, scraping it loudly against the floor. "Sorry to cut this short, you guys, but I have to get back to the shop to finish up a few things."

And that's it. That's all the information I get. It's probably all there is. The two of us are almost out the door when his grandpa stops me with a hand on my shoulder. "You come back to visit sometime. I have lots more stories."

Stories or histories, Grandpa?

We pull out of his grandpa's driveway, turning back onto the main road. But we don't get far before the truck slows. Without saying anything, Nate pulls over to the shoulder and stops.

"Is something wrong?" The sun's going down. There aren't any lights for miles, just the fading silhouettes of trees.

"I'm just thinking—and it's distracting." He's not looking at me. His face is half in shadow, but his smile is still bright.

"So distracting you had to pull over?"

Shifting the truck into park, he turns to face me. "Yeah." He speaks so quietly, like he's almost afraid to be heard. His eyes catch mine and I forget about how dark it's getting, about being alone with him. "Let me see your hand."

The giddy schoolgirl in me craves any excuse to touch

him, so I don't ask why. I hold my hand out for him to take. He takes it in his, kissing the top of it. I can't explain the shiver that runs through me. "What was that for?"

"Because you surprise me. Because I've never met anyone like you. I watched you listen to those stories in there and—I saw something." He presses his lips together tight. "I don't know, I'm just . . . We can go now. I just needed to stop and kiss you before I went crazy."

I am the white deer caught in headlights, silhouetted against a black forest.

"Oh," is all that comes out. The flicker fades from his eyes as he sets my hand down. *Crap.*

Before he can turn away, I unbuckle my seatbelt. I'm on autopilot, letting the oldest part of me take over. Older than the part that breathes and makes my heart beat. This part is more primal, the part that craves. My lips find his as if they'd been there before. Can't say how long we stay like that. But it's much darker when we finally come up for air.

CHAPTER FIFTEEN

Mason's mom answers the door when I get to his place. I've never met her before, but the resemblance between them is unmistakeable. They both have the same pale, soulful eyes, high cheekbones accenting a slender face, and rich, dark hair with a slight wave to it. She shows me through to the back deck, where Mason is sitting on a timber-framed swing bench. His head's back, looking up at the night sky, rocking gently back and forth.

The back door creaks and announces my arrival, although I'm sure he knew I was here long before that. Judging by the absent look on his face, whatever he wants to talk to me about can't be good. He just keeps swinging, keeping a slow rhythm, looking up at the night sky.

"Sorry I'm late." I sit beside him on the swinging bench. "I got caught up."

"Making out with your boyfriend."

My mouth falls open. I should be used to his unfiltered comments by now, but somehow this has more sting to it. "I didn't say that. You're putting—"

"You're not denying it?" He still won't look at me. I can't decide which is more annoying—the words coming from his mouth or the fact he won't make eye contact. He's started picking at something under his fingernails, too.

"Fine. Yes, I kissed him. Happy?" Why are we even talking about this? I get that he doesn't like Nate, but he never says it out loud. It feels wrong, talking about Nate with Mason. Like I'm admitting to something I hoped he wouldn't notice.

"Sure, I'm happy for you." His words drip sticky with sarcasm. "You got your first kiss. Way to go, Rach." *Is he pouting?* He seems to have gotten whatever is bothering him out from under his fingernails. I hear him inhale deeply. "God." He makes a scrunched-up face, like he's gagging. "You smell like the inside of his mouth."

I stutter to find words. "What the hell?" I straighten up a little taller on the bench. "I came here to talk to you, not to have you bad-mouth who I'm kissing. I don't talk about your girlfriend that way." *At least not to your face.*

"Well, maybe you should," he mumbles, almost inaudibly. At least I think that's what he says. "Listen." He adjusts in his seat, finally looking at me. His eyes are glazed over. Not like he's been crying—something else. "Sorry. For being rude.

I'm just . . ." He cuts himself short. "Thanks for coming over here. You're my best friend. You know that? You know almost everything about me, and you still want to hang out with me, which makes me wonder about your ability to judge character." His lips hint at a smile.

He's trying to lighten the mood before he delivers the bad news. I know that game. Wrapping my arm around his shoulder, I give him a squeeze. "Almost everything? Like what? I don't know your favorite colour. Blue?"

"This is serious, Rachel." He shrugs out from under my arm. "Things have gotten—complicated. And I just want you to know that you're my best friend."

"Okay. What am I missing here? You sound like you're dying or going away or something. What's happened?" The look on his face is somewhere between *my dog died* and *I think I'm going to be sick*. His eyes focus deeply on mine.

"I meant what I said that first night the spirit box was opened." His face turns solemn. "I will always protect you from the wendigo."

I think back to that night, all of us sitting around my living room coffee table. We had no clue what we were unleashing. That night will be forever burned into my memory. It seems so long ago, but really it's only been a few weeks. Crazy how a few weeks can change everything. And everyone.

"Hey, I know you're not going to hurt me, Mason. You're

not like other wendigos." I almost need to reassure myself more than him.

"How do you know about the others?" His sudden worry surprises me.

"Calm down." I gesture with my hands for him to relax. "I just meant that I talked to Nate's grandpa tonight. He told me this folklore story about the wendigo totem. You know, that weird totem-like tree by the community center out on the reserve? Nate's grandpa knows all kinds of—"

His face turns a shade of red I've never seen him sport. "You told Nate and his grandpa about the spirit box—and me?"

"Hey. No! Chill. You know I'd never do that." I enunciate every word, not backing down from the steaming face in front of me. "Now you listen. I don't know what's put you in this hideous mood, but I'm talking now. And when I'm done, it'll be your turn. Okay?" Not a sound comes from his tightly creased lips. The look on his face tells me his temper still bubbles near the surface.

"Okay," I go on. "No, I did not tell Nate or his grandpa about you or the spirit box. The only people who know about the spirit box are Chloe, Julie, Ryan, and the two of us. Although Chloe, Julie, and Ryan don't seem to remember the details of that night very clearly." His lips part slightly to speak. I shoot a look at him that silences any words. "I get why you wouldn't want them blabbing on about it. Don't act like it wasn't you that changed their memories. I'm not stupid. I noticed.

"I've told no one about you or your powers or this wendigo thing. What the hell would I say, anyway?" I'm almost yelling. I just need to say it. "You are *my* problem to fix. And I've been working on it. It's what I've been trying to tell you.

"So, like I was saying when I started, Nate and I were out at his grandpa's place. His grandpa was telling me a story about the wendigo totem tree. His story told me how to get rid of the wendigo spirit. So, long story short, all we have to do is return the spirit box to the earth from which it came." His silence falls heavy on me, like a damp weight. I don't get it. He should be happy I figured it out. I know how to fix this. "So . . . ?" I let the word drag out, trying to gauge his reaction. "I've figured it out. Aren't you happy?"

He slowly lets out the air from his chest. Was he holding his breath this whole time? "So, you know exactly how to rid me of the wendigo?" His words are slow and deliberate. "And you're willing to do that—for me?" His words are far too calm for how worked up he was just minutes before. Something about the way he says it isn't right.

"Well, I know basically how. The story goes that all that was needed was to return the spirit box back to the earth from which it came. I figure that means bury it. Probably at the base of the wendigo totem. Sounds easy enough."

"And what about the rest?"

My eyes focus in on his. They've gone hollow and cold,

but deep below their surface I see something. Maybe he allows me to see it, if only for a fleeting moment, and then it's gone. "What do you mean, the rest? You mean the part where all the wishes get taken back? We weren't meant to have them anyway. Julie and Chloe will get over it. They'll have to. You can't go on like this." There must be more to the story, but how could he know? "What aren't you telling me?"

A sigh escapes his mouth before he speaks. "Have you ever considered that some things in life are less an affliction than they are a choice?"

I know what he's saying. I know exactly what he's saying, but I don't want to believe it.

The reality of the two of us sitting here on the deck drains away, and the foggy haze of an almost-forgotten memory floods into my head.

"Eric, that's enough. You're going. We already talked about this." Eric's bedroom window is open a crack. My mother is talking loudly inside. I'm supposed to be over at a friend's house, but I came back for my jacket. I crouch low in the flower bed where no one will see me. It's cold outside. "I've already told Rachel you're going away to camp, so just play along."

"Why do you lie to her, Mom? Am I that much of an

embarrassment to you?"

"It's not like that, Eric. She's too young to understand what rehab is. I don't really want to explain drug addiction to a child."

"So sending me away to this place is just about fixing my addiction, eh? I got news for you, Mom. I chose to do drugs. I chose to stick things in me to mask my problems. Do you understand? I chose this."

I hide in silence, my back pressed up against the cold brick wall of the house. No one will notice me here. I understand what they say. I understand everything. My mind just refuses to believe it.

Eric goes on. "Life is choice and consequence. That's all it is, Mom. I don't need rehab to tell me that. I need you to stop believing that I'm the result of a chance mistake you made along the way—that this is your fault. Because it's not. I did this. I chose this."

Eric's words echo in my head. *I chose this.*

My words croak out from a mouth that's gone bone dry. "So all this time it's been your choice to be a wendigo? You've known all along how to fix this, and you just let me think I could cure you. You've had the answer all along."

I'm that little kid again. I feel like I'm going to puke. No, faint. No, puke. Ah, fuck it. I wind up my fist, punching him as hard as I can in the chest. "You bastard!" I scream through clenched teeth. "Fuck!" I might as well have punched a brick wall, his chest is so solid. My hand wails from the punch. I'm pretty sure it's broken. "What are you?" No matter how hard I will it not to happen, a tear rolls its way down my cheek.

"I'm sorry. I shouldn't have let you do that. Here, let me see your hand."

I stare at him as he reaches for my broken hand. I guess he's right. He could have stopped me. The anger rises off me like steam. He's been lying to me. I want to burn a hole in his head with my dirty looks.

"Just give me your hand. It's probably broken."

I let him take it. God! He's lied to me this whole time. He's known all along how to fix this problem and . . . he didn't. Mason gently smooths his hand over mine. A strange sensation of heat and then sharp cold pass through my hand where he touches it. Within seconds the cold subsides, and I'm left with only the soft touch of his hand caressing mine. The throbbing pain is completely gone. It's like I never hurt it, but the not-so-distant memory of slamming it into his chest still remains. I take my hand from his. It's completely fine. I sniff back a tear. There'll be no more of that.

"You say in one breath that I'm your best friend, and in the next you lie to me. You'd better start talking, or I'm leaving."

"Where do you want me to start?" His eyes are deceptively kind. It makes me wonder what lingers behind them.

My mind reels. "Start with what you know about getting rid of a wendigo."

Mason's lips crunch together. "First, can I just say that I never thought you'd figure it out?"

I can almost hear the cartoon clank of my jaw hitting the floor. "So you think I'm stupid?" My voice cuts sharp.

He puts his finger up to shush me. I want to bite it off, but I know that will never happen, so I just shut up. "I don't think you're stupid. I think you're the smartest person I've ever met."

"And how's that?" I ask in a caustic voice.

He pauses again before he speaks. "When I became a wendigo, there was knowledge that came with it. I know the story of how the spirit box was created. I know how and where to return it. And I know the consequences of returning the box to the earth. There's a reason why the box still exists, Rachel, and why the stories surrounding it haven't entirely disappeared. It's amazing you were able to find even part of the story."

"What do you mean, *part*? I know that when the box is returned all the wishes are returned with it." I'm deflated he isn't even considering putting the box back where it came from. "I'm not that attached to my wish. Yeah, Chloe will be pissed, and so will Julie. But they don't need to know it was because the box was returned. I mean, thanks to you, they're not even sure the spirit box grants wishes. They would think it was just bad luck. Come on, Mason. It's cool and all that you have these powers, but it's time to go back to what you used to be."

"There's no going back. Don't you get it?" A sort of hope fades from his eyes. "You're not getting the entire story. Think about it. If it was that easy to just return the spirit box, why does it still exist today?"

"I don't know. Maybe they were all too greedy and couldn't part with their gifts. Just tell me. What am I missing here?"

He fidgets in his seat. "The box still exists because the price of returning it is too high. The price was too high for the people then, and it's too high now. To return everything to the way it was, the box and all its contents must be returned to the earth from which it came. And the toll must be paid."

The toll. I remember what Nate's grandpa said about the toll. It's what the wendigo collects. It's what makes us alive. Our souls. That which powers us and connects us to everything. The realization hits me. "No one was willing to give their soul to send the wendigos back." My words sink in deeper. "No one was willing to die."

"There might have been someone willing to die, but it obviously didn't play out that way. And there's no way I'm letting you do that."

"No. I mean, of course I don't want you to die, but you can't stay like this forever. There has to be another way. We have to figure out what the original people did." God, his head is like a brick wall too. He's just being thick. This is *not* the way this ends. Why can't he see that?

"The original people just let their wishes run their course. Which eventually released the wendigos into our world."

There's that word again. *Released.* "What do you mean?"

"After my wish is complete, I can leave."

"So the wendigo can leave? The spirit will leave you?"

"No, Rach. I am a wendigo. It's not leaving me."

Closing my eyes, I let the air rush from my lungs. What's the point? I can't fight against a power that's won before I've even started. The world will keep on moving, no matter how much I want it to stop. Lifting my feet, I let the bench swing. It cradles me as it glides.

"So you're a wendigo, and that's it. And when you're done here, you're leaving Hazelton." The distinct taste of defeat lingers in my mouth. "What about the curse? The story says that a wendigo is cursed to collect souls for all eternity. What about that?" I let a sigh escape from the depths of me. "Are you going to start collecting souls too?"

I open my eyes to find myself alone and cold. Mason got up, and I didn't even feel the shift of his weight. He's standing at the far end of the deck, leaning over the railing and looking off into the tree line. I try in vain to see what he sees, but something inside me tells me I never will. I get up from the bench and walk over to him, crossing my arms, warding off the evening's chill.

His voice is soft as he speaks, a tone of apology even before the wrong is done. "That's exactly why I have to leave here. It's not about *when* I start collecting. I do collect."

If the cost of knowing was the burden of the truth, would you still ask the question? He does collect . . .

My whole body is numb except for my hands. Without thinking, I touch the small of his back, where his muscle dips towards his spine. He still feels like Mason. Only a thin layer of cotton T-shirt comes between his skin and mine. I let my hand linger there. I feel what radiates from him, and part of me wants to lose myself in it. I want it to wrap around me and protect me from all the ugliness in this world. But I find that part inside me that's still brave and not so damaged.

"I can't change you back." Saying it out loud hurts, like years spent with the Weather Lady just came crashing down on my head. "But I can be here to listen." I swallow down the butterflies that try to escape. "What kind of friend would I be if I didn't do that?"

He turns to me, his eyes looking a thousand years older than they did just a moment ago. "I'm exactly like every other wendigo that has come before me. The stories are true. What keeps you alive sustains the life in me. I take—and have taken—what serves my purpose." The spot where my hand touches the small of his back goes cold as I slip away from him.

Did I expect him to say something different? I slide against the railing of the deck, wrapping my arms around my legs as I sit. I am hollowed out of everything I once knew. He slides down and sits beside me. He takes my hand in his, and the numbness inside me subsides just a little. I don't want to hear this. I must hold on to the bravest part of me . . . but I don't know where it is.

"At first, it was like a dream," he says. "Except I wasn't waking up. And then the hunger grew stronger."

I listen to him tell me about the lives he's taken. He talks about taking the lives of deer, bears, cougars, and whatever else he found in the woods. He told me about how they died. How he killed them. He describes his methods as unrefined, amateur. Like it's a skill. Bile rises in my throat and I cover my mouth to keep from throwing up. To keep from screaming.

Steve, the ranger, passed out flyers to figure out what was killing all those animals. I want Mason to stop talking. I don't want to know anymore. This is nothing like one of those vampire books. There is no romanticizing the taking of life. It's disgusting, it's brutal, it's savage. The nauseating effect of listening to him speak saves me from hearing every detail, but I catch this: "So I had to get rid of the university professor."

"Wait, what?" I didn't think I had words left in me, but there they are. I blink hard. "You did what?"

"If that professor turned in a report that said the

population of rare white bears in this area was on the rise, my father's oil projects would never get approved."

"Oil projects." My own voice sounds strange to me. I remember that first night with the spirit box. Mason wished his dad's company would finally get some projects going in this town.

His hand is still tangled in mine. I am still here, listening to all this. This is real. I look across at his chest, rising and falling. His breathing is not quick. He looks at me only with kindness, yet he talks about killing. Animals and people. I try my best to imagine him as a fictional creature—a monster. I can't. This is Mason. He is a wendigo . . . and he kills people.

"You killed him?"

He lets out a breath as he rests his head against the slats of the deck railing. "Look, it's like—" He seems to be at a loss for words. "The difference between taking the life of an animal and taking the life of a person is like the difference between cold cuts and prime rib."

My stomach threatens to revolt. "Just wait—stop. I thought I could sit here and listen, but I can't. The thought of animals and people dying is scary enough, without hearing you compare them to pieces of meat." I pull my hand free of his to cover my mouth, keeping everything in. "I can barely stomach the thought of people I don't know dying, but eating them . . ." I want to get up. I want to leave, but there's no place far enough away to pretend this conversation never happened.

"I don't eat them. I—"

"No. no," is all I manage to get out, shaking my head. The hand that covered my mouth clenches into a fist. Leaving one finger to my lips, I hiss, "Shh."

Both Mason and I just sit on the deck, pressed up beside each other for what could be a moment, or hours. We sit here, while I crumble in upon myself. I think about how permanent some things are once they're done. I think about how the two of us were before all this happened, and who we are now.

If the cost of knowing is the burden of the truth, would you still ask the question?

No.

Maybe next time I would say no.

CHAPTER SIXTEEN

My body aches like it's been on a two-day bender, but I haven't swallowed a drop. I got home late last night from Mason's place. Not sure what time. Not sure who drove. My mom and Grams had already gone to bed when I came in. Good thing. Rehashing my evening was not high on my to-do list.

The belt I wore with my jeans is cutting into me. I didn't bother to change out of my clothes before flopping into the oblivion of the tangled blankets on my bed. It feels like I stared at the ceiling the entire night, waiting for morning. My eyes burn, begging to close.

Voices waft from the kitchen: Mom, Grandma, and someone else. A man's voice. My body aches in protest as I roll onto my side. I can't hide in here forever. Eventually someone will come knocking and find me. Time to put on a smiley face and confront the day. No more boxing things up. I can do this.

It's mid-morning with dark skies. More ominous clouds could be on the horizon, but perhaps the day will warm up later on.

Today I'll forget what the weather's like, put on my sunglasses, and act like it isn't dark outside.

My tiny bedroom looks the same as it did yesterday. Yet somehow, everything feels out of place now that I've unpacked, dusted things off, and set them on shelves. Everything's out in the open, on display for the world to see. I thought I was ready to unpack, but everything feels too raw, and I wish I kept my cardboard boxes.

Breathing out the remnants of last night, I sit up. I let my feet drape over the edge of my bed and touch the cold floor. Raking my hair back into a messy ponytail, I smooth away some of the disarray. Yesterday's shirt looks no better than my hair, but I don't bother to change it.

Rounding the corner into the kitchen, I see the man belonging to the voice I didn't recognize. It's Steve, the Fish and Wildlife guy my mom's been seeing. He's been over here more and more often lately. A part of me thinks that if I ignore the fact that my parents are dating other people, the other people might go away. Apparently, this method isn't working. I'll rethink my coping mechanisms another day.

Steve is nice, though. Nicer than Barbie at least. Or maybe it's the fact that he doesn't look like he jumped from the pages of a *J. Crew* catalogue that makes him a little more approachable.

Not that he's bad looking. He's decent, for a guy my mom's age. His kind eyes match his dark brown hair, which is always a little on the shaggy side. He also sports a five o'clock shadow that never changes no matter what time of day it is. He's wearing his sage green and black work uniform this morning. I hardly ever see him wear anything else. He must have just come from work.

"Good morning. I was wondering when you'd get up," Mom chirps between sips of her mug. "There's coffee made if you want some."

My hand pauses for a moment on the fridge door. I think about grabbing a Pepsi, but I decide to go with the offered coffee. I'm not in the mood to be criticized about my choice in morning beverages. "Thanks," I say.

Rummaging through the cupboard, I look for my cat mug. I can't find it, so I grab whatever touches my fingertips first. Not being a coffee drinker, it takes me a minute to decide if I want milk and sugar. Both is probably best, since I'm so used to the caffeinated sweetness of a morning cola. The conversation between Grams, Mom, and Steve continues at the kitchen table without me, which is good. Quasi-social interactions are about my limit right now.

"So like I said." Steve's voice is calm, with a slight edge. "I'm still a bit shaken up about it. I don't usually get called out to accidents like that."

Accident? I perk up. It's strange how everyone says they

don't want to hear about accidents, but in reality we're all a bunch of gawking voyeurs. *Ignore it. How much milk do you put in coffee?* If there's one thing I don't need today, it's more details about gruesome things.

"Well, we're glad to have you around to deal with those sorts of things," says Grams. "The police were called out too, though, weren't they? I mean, animal deaths are one thing, but the police have to deal with people, right?"

People? Some poor guy probably hit a deer on the highway and Steve got called out to deal with it. I concentrate on my coffee. *Where's the sugar?*

"Yeah, there were a couple of cops there." Steve lingers over the steaming cup in front of him. "It wasn't so much that the guy died. I mean, I've seen accidents before where people have hit animals and died. It's just, I kind of knew the guy. Well, not like we were friends or anything, but he interviewed me two days ago. We sat and talked for over two hours.

"Him and his news crew were here doing a story about the big lottery win, but they caught wind of another story about white animal sightings. He told me about a few local sightings he'd heard about. There's been a white crow, a white bear, and someone saw a white deer too."

Clink, clink, tink, tink . . . tiiiiink. The sugar spoon bounces off my coffee mug, off the counter, through my fumbling fingers, and ricochets off the lower cabinets before landing on the yellowed linoleum of the kitchen floor. If I wanted all eyes off me . . . I have successfully *not* achieved that.

"Everything all right over there?" Grams says with a look of concern.

"Fine. Just fine. I'm fine." I'm pretty sure repeating the word *fine* isn't selling my state of well-being. Perhaps I'd be more convincing if I'd showered or at least changed my clothes.

"Okay, Miss *Fine*. Are you going to come sit at the table with us, or are you trying to see how many spoonfuls of sugar it takes to make your coffee a solid?" Grams is going easy on me because Steve is here.

I retrieve the fallen spoon from the floor and put it in the sink. I sit on the last kitchen chair between Mom and Grams and take a sip of my coffee, trying to keep my face straight. Grams may be right, judging from the sweetness of it. Sugary solidity is not far off.

A choked laugh comes from Grams as she pats me on the knee. "Maybe coffee's just not for you, eh? Do you want me to get you a Pepsi from the fridge?"

"I'm fi— No thanks. This is good." I wrap my hands around the warmth of my mug.

Mom starts up the conversation with Steve again. "It's sad to hear that he died. I would have liked to read what he wrote."

"Yeah, too bad." Steve blinks like he's coming back from somewhere else. "There's another thing that's not sitting quite right with me. The moose he hit. I mean, I've been to a lot of animal crash sites in the past, but this one was strange. Usually if someone hits a moose or deer on the road, they hit it while it's trying to cross. So the vehicle hits its legs first, which causes the animal to roll onto the hood or the windshield." Steve talks with his hands a lot. It's like watching a disturbing mini-puppet show all about animals rolling over vehicles.

"But it doesn't look like the moose rolled up over any hood. It looked like it was lying down on the road when it was hit. A moose lying down on the road?" Steve looks like he's trying to convince himself. "That just doesn't happen."

My mind turns down the volume that surrounds me as I watch the charade Steve puts on. I can't bear to hear the words anymore. His moose hand slamming into his car hand makes me shudder. *Why would a moose lie down on the road?* The question rolls around in the silence of my mind. Then it comes to me.

"I've gotten a few more powers this week. I can put songs in people's heads, and sometimes even convince them to do things. Although it's pretty hard to convince a person to do anything. Animals and bugs are a lot easier."

I tell myself not to think about it. I can pretend for today. But the memory of Mason's voice slides back into my head.

"If that professor ever turned out a report saying that the

population of white bears in this area was on the rise, my father's oil projects would never get approved."

My warm grip on the coffee mug goes cold. Any excuse or explanation for the conclusions rushing through my head might be a comfort, but they don't come. I push back my chair from the kitchen table and stand up abruptly. All eyes are on me for the second time this morning. My mouth opens to say something, but what can I say?

Knock knock knock..

The sound at the kitchen door startles me.

"That must be Julie. I'll get it." Stumbling backwards, I squeeze between my chair and Grams'. By the time I make it to the side kitchen door, Julie has let herself in. Knocking is just a courtesy, an afterthought, before she walks right in, without a clue what's on the other side.

Julie and I head to my room, away from the prying eyes in the kitchen, but it's not the refuge I seek. What I want is a better place to hide. She lets her weight fall heavy as she sits down on the edge of my bed. Tiny dust particles flit into the rays of light streaming through my window. I wish I could fly away like a tiny speck, barely noticed.

"Wow, you unpacked!"

It only occurred to me recently that toting around my whole life in boxes affected people besides me. When I look at Julie, I see the effect it had on her—she's relieved. Grams always says, "You'll know a true smile when you see one. A person who really means it smiles with their eyes, too."

"I knew you'd settle in sooner or later," Julie says. "Pretty soon they'll be calling you a lifer."

A lifer. I liked living in the same house in Vancouver for as long as I did, but I wasn't so much attached to the house as I was to the *sense of family* I had in it. Now, after moving so many times, no place feels like home. Another one of Grams' quips of wisdom pops into my head. "The dirt has never clung tightly to your roots." She told me that when I was a kid. I never got it then, but I do now.

"Yeah, this place is growing on me. I'll stick around for a while." I huff as I fall down beside her on my bed. The heaviness of last night still clings to me.

"Good. I don't think I could handle both my besties leaving town without me."

"Chloe's leaving?"

"Yeah, of course she is." Her words come out dryly. "I guess I don't blame her. If I had all that money, I'd want to see the world too. Part of me just thought she might stick around. But she's leaving right after finals."

"Hey, you still got me." I sling my arm around her shoulders, giving her a squeeze. "Come on. I'll let you do my hair and makeup before we go over to the community center ribbon cutting."

Julie gives me the ol' once-over. "Well, I should hope so. Don't take this the wrong way, but you look like hell. Are you still wearing yesterday's clothes?"

Only Julie would notice. To her, that's a fashion felony. "Busted. I put on the same T-shirt and jeans when I got up." It's not a complete lie. If she knew I crawled into bed like this, she'd wonder why. "I was pretty sure when you got here you'd want to pick out an outfit for me anyway."

"You know me all too well." The genuine smile returns to her eyes. Hopefully my fashion crisis will take her mind off things, at least for a little while. Julie is up from my bed, unfazed. She's a girl on a mission. While she pillages through my closet for a top she deems wearable, she orders me to find bottoms that will match what she's picked. "Get your skinny jeans. The ones with the white stitching. Those are nice." She lines up her three choices on my bed as I get the jeans from my dresser. "So what do you think?"

Truthfully, I think I'm going to wear whatever she thinks I should wear. I'm just relieved that she's picking an outfit from my clothes and not hers. Julie's shorter than me, so whenever I wear her clothes, especially her dresses, they can almost pass as shirts. If I protest the length of anything, she says she wishes she had "model legs" like mine.

"How about the light blue one?" I pick the one I think she prefers so I don't have to debate the merits of each outfit. I don't usually mind talking fashion, but today, the fewer words the better.

"Yeah, it goes with your eyes. But what about the black?" I shrug. I don't know—I don't care. "You're right. It's too nice out for black. Now to accessorize." Julie takes a Ziploc bag out of her purse. It's filled with costume earrings, necklaces, and rings. She smooths the covers on my bed and empties the bag. "Get dressed and I'll pick out a necklace to go with it."

The shirt's too tight across the chest, which makes the three buttons at the neck pull. I button them all up anyway. Maybe no one will notice. Julie turns to me, holding up a short, chained necklace with a mini rhinestone golf ball hanging from it.

"Um—your girls are trying to bust free of their cage. You might want to give them a little air before someone loses an eye."

On a different day, I would argue the virtues of leaving something to the imagination. Today I pass, so I don't have to try on every top in my closet. I undo the top two buttons as she clasps the necklace on me. I look at the outfit in the long mirror attached to the wall beside my bed. I could almost pass for human, if it wasn't for my bird's-nest hairdo.

"You look nice. Let me do something with your hair and

we can go. Sit." She pulls out my rolling desk chair for me. "Do you still have that gold hair clip you wear sometimes? I'll just clip your hair back."

"Check my jewelry box. It's in there somewhere." I sit on my computer chair and wait for her to find it.

She sets it in front of me on the desk. Standing behind me, she brushes long strands of my hair with her fingers while I flip open the lid. Staring at us both, resting on top of a jumble of cheap jewelry, is the charred black wendigo carving. My hand pauses with a twitch. I forgot I put it there.

"The wendigo piece," Julie says, pulling back on a tangle. "Last time I saw you with that, you were holding it with a pair of pink oven mitts." The air escapes her mouth in a huffed laugh. She stops combing her fingers through my hair and lets it fall around my shoulders. "Did you ever fix it?"

If she only knew what she was really asking.

"Actually, it was never broken." I taste the words as they come out of my mouth. Their metallic tang lingers on my tongue. "I was wrong." Picking up the wendigo piece, I hold it between my thumb and my forefinger. "This is exactly what a wendigo is supposed to be like. I just thought it was different."

Julie brushes her hand past my shoulder, stretching out her palm in front of me. "Here, give it to me. These spirit animal carvings give me the willies. I'll put it back in the box where it belongs."

I don't protest at all. Her small, slender fingers wrap around it as she takes it away. I'd left the spirit box on the shelf right beside my jewelry box. There's a soft click as Julie opens the box to put the wendigo piece back.

"You know, part of me wishes that we'd all listened to you that night. About not messing around with this box." Julie clicks the lid shut and starts again with my hair, putting in the clip I give her. "I mean, it created all this stuff that's happening, right? Stuff that shouldn't be happening. Right? Or am I just going crazy?" With the way Julie tugs on my hair, I'm going to have a bald spot if I don't say something soon.

"Ouch. Easy."

"Sorry." She finishes off my hair and plunks back down on the edge of my bed. "I'm just frustrated." She covers her face with her hands and takes a deep breath before going on. "Chloe wished to be rich and famous. She got it. And now she's leaving. She's leaving the place where her life runs so deep it's laced between the bedrock. You don't know her like I do." Julie slowly shakes her head. "This isn't her. She's different now, and it's not just all that money. She's still Chloe, but she's different. What if we all change?" She seems to deflate as she breathes out the question.

I look at my hair in the mirror. She's done in minutes what I couldn't have achieved in hours. I want to tell her that she's not crazy, that it's not all coincidence, but I don't. I look her straight in the eye and say what I wish was true. Because I don't want one more person suspecting the horror of this reality. Or that's what I tell myself.

"Chloe's still Chloe, you're still you, I'm me, Mason's . . ." My tongue ties for a moment like I'm trying to convince myself. "Still Mason. And Ryan? He's never going to change even if we wished him to. High school's almost over, and as much as we might want to freeze time and be like this forever, it's not going to happen. People are going to change, and they might move away, too. You just have to keep faith that things happen for a reason. Reasons that we might not understand."

Julie offers a faint smile. "Wow, deep thoughts by Rachel Barnes." She lets out another long sigh. "I get it that things change and people too. I know that, but it doesn't mean I have to like it."

Pushing herself up off my bed, she heads back over to my closet. "What do you say we get out of here? Gloomy conversations on how we're all going to change and move away are not on my to-do list today." She flicks quickly through the hangers to the end of the closet where I keep my dresses and coats. "It's supposed to get chilly later. You might want to bring a jacket."

Her fingers stop on the one article of clothing I hoped she wouldn't pick—the leather jacket my brother gave me for my birthday. That jacket was one of the first things to go into a cardboard box and one of the last to come out. It hasn't seen the light of day in years. In fact, I think the only time I ever wore it was the day Eric gave it to me, just to try it on. Shortly after that it got sealed up in a box, like everything else I pretended didn't exist.

"This is cute. How come I never see you wear it?" Julie has the leather jacket off the hanger, inspecting its details. I'd almost forgotten what it looks like. Soft charcoal grey with vintage-style snaps at the collar and sides. Its heavy, brushed-chrome zipper is exposed, and it's finished with a cropped collar.

"It's old. It probably doesn't even fit me anymore."

She tosses the jacket at me and I catch it. "Try it on. Let's see."

Her words are so casual. She doesn't know the story about my brother. Not many do. I feel bad that I've never told her, but conversations like that rarely come up. I feel the soft leather between my fingers and think of the words I just said to Julie. *"As much as we might want to freeze time and be like this forever . . . it's not going to happen. People are going to change."*

I slip one arm down the sleeve of the jacket and then the other. I remember now, that when Eric bought it for me, he said it was a little big so I'd grow into it. It seems to fit perfectly now, hugging every curve like it was part of me.

"Fits like it was made for you," Julie says, as she gathers the last of her jewelry off the bed. "Come on. Let's get out of here. I'll drive."

CHAPTER SEVENTEEN

Judging by the number of vehicles parked everywhere, the whole town must be out for the ribbon cutting. It's just as fast to walk to "downtown" Hazelton, but Julie insisted on driving. I know why when she steps out of the car. Her four-inch cork-wedge shoes teeter on the uneven pavement as she stands up.

"Nice shoes," I say. "But can you walk in them?"

"Oh, ye of little faith. Jogging or running is probably out of the question, but I don't think it's a requirement at today's particular event." Her shoe catches on a raised crack in the pavement, almost toppling her.

"All in the name of fashion, eh? Do you want me to walk in front of you or behind you?" I ask.

"Why?" She scrunches her nose when she asks.

"Just wondering which way you're most likely to fall when you trip in those shoes." That was awesome. Maybe Julie's "lifer" comment wasn't too far off. I seem to have the teasing down to a science now.

Julie's smile says she's in a good mood despite all the changes. She lives so much in the moment, which is one of the things I love about her. Right now—in the moment—it's a beautiful day. People are getting together; you can feel a buzz of excitement and hope for the future.

The sun peeks its rays through the lingering clouds. They warm my face.

"Come on, smartass. I'm never going to get any better at walking in these totally awesome shoes if I don't try." Julie adjusts her purse over one arm and loops her free arm through mine. "Just walk beside me. There's a better chance of catching me no matter which way I fall."

There's a small stage set up in front of the old community center. A crowd lines its edges, at least twenty people deep. The old community center looks like one of those pre-fab buildings that's been slapped together and added on to a few too many times over the years. What a mishmash of dated construction. Giant evergreen trees dot the large grassed area surrounding the building, shading most of us. All the lower branches on the trees have been trimmed away, allowing everyone to mingle under their immense canopy.

We slow to a stop at the edge of the milling crowd, scanning for familiar faces. Chloe is here with her mom, up on the stage. They're standing beside a few official-looking people in dark suits. One of them is probably the town mayor. I don't see my mom, my grams, or Steve, but they should be here somewhere.

I don't see Mason either. I'm not sure if I'm relieved about that or disappointed. The memory of last night still swirls in the recesses of my head. Even after everything I heard, there's got to be a way to fix this. Change this. I haven't given up, even if I'm currently at a standstill. What I need is a little distraction from my current reality. And today's a good day for distraction—if I can find it.

A warm hand runs over the small of my back. I know exactly who it is before he says a word. It's the familiar tingle of his hand touching my skin and his woodsy scent that drifts over me. My whole body relaxes and excites in the same moment. He's become my safe haven, my place to forget. I swivel around, turning myself into the warmth of Nate.

"Hey, I've been looking for you. Did you guys just get here?"

He asks us both the question, but doesn't look away from me. Oh, that look . . . He looks at me like our clothes are lying tangled on the floor of some secluded room. I return the look, and for a second, I contemplate Julie's reaction if I were to ditch her and run off with my boyfriend. The memory of kissing him last night still lingers on my lips. Can he tell what I'm thinking?

Probably. Sometimes I feel like I'm an open book, and I'm the only one who doesn't know what's on the page.

"Yeah." Julie clears her throat. "We got here just a minute ago."

"My friends are over by the picnic tables." Nate motions towards a grouping of trees that shades a line of picnic tables and barbeques. "Do you guys want to join us?" I notice a blush rising on his face as he looks away.

I know Julie has been curious about meeting Nate's friends for a while. She's joked before about his friends and if they look just as Spartan-warrior as he does.

"Yep. Lead the way." Stepping back from Nate, I loop my arm through Julie's. "Come on. I'll walk beside you."

I recognize Nate's friends—Finn, Mark, and his sister, Jamey—from the dance. Even though I've only met them once, it feels like we're friends now. I guess being upgraded to girlfriend status does that. Nate quickly glazes over the introductions of Mark and Jamey, but takes a little more care introducing Finn. I'm pretty sure I'm not the only one who notices this. Nate even shifts position to make room for Finn to stand next to Julie.

I remember when I first met Finn. He looked so similar to Nate that I thought they might be related. A tiny smile touches my lips. Finn looks much the same as he did that night. His hair is long, straight, and black, just a little shorter than Nate's. Any girl would be jealous.

I'm curious about Julie's reaction to this obvious introduction. I haven't lived here long enough to know, but she's been single for a while, I think. Maybe a little distraction on this beautiful day will be good for her too.

A tall, blonde librarian type woman is up on the stage trying to get everyone's attention. Her squealing microphone does the job. "Welcome, everyone. Thanks for coming out today. We'll try and keep the speeches to a minimum so that we can get to enjoying the music and food before it starts to rain again." The smell of grilling hamburgers and hot dogs wafts from barbecues just a few feet away. The grumbling of my stomach reminds me that it's been a while since I've eaten. "Without further delay, I give you Mayor Falen."

Applause chatters through the crowd. A large man in a navy blue suit makes his way to the podium set up on the stage. "Thank you, Catherine," he says, adjusting the mic to the proper height. "News travels fast in this town," Mayor Falen's voice booms. "I'm sure you've all heard about the large lottery wins of our own Hazelton residents, Jodie and Chloe Fox."

A few congratulatory hoots and hollers come from the back of the crowd. "The Foxes' lottery win will benefit our entire community, as Jodie and Chloe have decided to generously donate the remainder of the funds needed to build our community center." I drift in and out of the mayor's speech. I've already heard this story about a million times.

Mayor Falen's booming voice carries over the crowd. "The community board members have voted and come up with a new design for the center's logo. We hope everyone will like it as much as we do."

The mayor yanks a rope attached to a sheet, revealing the new sign. It says *Hazelton Community Center* in raised brass letters against a black background. Decorating the right-hand corner, starkly set against the black background, is an artist's rendition of a white bear. My eyes focus on its white and brass details. "We decided on the spirit bear," he boasts. "It's a symbol of strength and hope, which we hope will come back to our great community with the construction of this new facility."

Chloe and her mom have come to stand beside the mayor and the big sign. All three of them pose with a pair of giant, gold scissors. After a few cameras flash, they use the scissors to cut a red ribbon that has been strung from each end of the stage. I shouldn't be able to hear the sound of the ribbon being cut over the crowd, but I do, if only in my head. With a *snick,* the metal blades slice through the ceremonial velvet ribbon that, under normal, non-spirit-box circumstances, would never have been cut. I'm almost pained by the unnatural wrongness of it all, but this is just another day for everyone else. *Just another half-sunny, half-overcast day.*

Julie's gaze catches mine as she shifts her weight uncomfortably. For a moment I think she gets it. All this change is our doing. None of this would be happening if it weren't for the four of us messing around with the spirit box that night. But it's a good thing, right? Everyone looks so happy. Yet my stomach sinks. This much good does not come without a price. Julie's eyes dart around the milling crowd of people. I know what she's looking for. The white bear. Even if Mason clouded her thoughts about certain details, she can't deny what happened at Chloe's. The white crow showed up as a live animal, and so did the deer— and the wendigo, so to speak. The crow had brought all his friends. I hope this bear doesn't bring his buddies too.

The crowd of people next to the stage suddenly shifts towards us with unexpected force. We're backed up against a line of picnic tables, which have been pushed together to form a long chain. Screams erupt. People are yelling out in front of us, but I can't see anything through the crowd. Looking up to the stage, I see Chloe staring down at Julie and me. Even from this distance I can tell her face has paled.

"Here, take my hand." Nate helps me step up onto the picnic table where he's perched. I see Finn doing the same for Julie. Except Julie, between her nerves, the pushing crowd, and those damn shoes, can't seem to get up on the table.

I leave Nate's hand hanging and push against the crowd that circles Julie. "Hey, back up!" I yell over the crowd. "Julie, this might be easier if you just take off those shoes."

Julie's smile breaks into a nervous laugh. "I guess, eh?

These aren't made for climbing either."

She quickly sits on the picnic table bench to take off her shoes. I hold off the pushing crowd as well as I can while she jumps onto the table in her bare feet. With shoes and purse in hand, she reaches back to help me up, and her purse falls open. Out comes the unmistakable can of bear spray, rolling on the ground like a dirty secret. Without a second thought, I kneel on the damp grass to retrieve it from under the table. I should have just left it. Why did I go back? People are pushing past me, making the picnic table teeter and rock over my head. The can of bear spray slips in my fingers a few times, but I finally get hold of it. I can hear Nate calling me.

Backing up blindly on all fours, I make my retreat from under the table, when *bam*. I'm pushed from behind. My head bounces off the wooden planking of the bench. I yell and curse under my breath. I can already feel a bump starting to swell.

Standing up, I spin around to confront whatever jerk just punted me into the table. "What? Not even an 'I'm sor—" My words don't make it out when I realize whom I'm speaking to. Or *what*.

Standing in front of me, five feet away, is Julie's white spirit bear.

I can't move. If I turn to climb over the table I'd be turning my back on it. It rises onto its hind legs and stands tall. It towers over me, its five-foot-something stature quite intimidating. And it definitely has a few pounds on me. It's so close that I can smell its fur, damp and matted from the recent rain. I'm alone on this side of the long line of picnic tables.

The crowd lets out a gasp. The bear sniffs the air, searching the crowd. I'm no expert on bear language, but I feel like the right thing to is to make myself look small. Right? Crap, I don't know. I feel like such a city girl. Bear attacks are not even on the spectrum of bad things that could happen to me. Everyone but me has made it to quasi-safety on the other side of the tables. My palms are sweaty, my heart pounding. The can of bear spray starts to slip from my hands.

I have a can of bear spray.

I put both hands on the can.

"Rachel Barnes, don't you dare spray that bear. It's not going to hurt you." The voice inside my head stops me short. It's Mason, as clear as if he were standing beside me. Maybe I've finally gone crazy. *"You're not crazy. It's me."*

I glance around, not straying my focus too far from the bear. I don't see Mason anywhere, just a sea of stone-faced people wondering how this bear drama is going to play out. *"Just take a step back and have a seat. I promise the bear won't hurt you. Trust me. It just came here to see the wish. But you're making it nervous, standing there with a can of bear spray in your hand."*

"I'm making it nervous?" I'm having a screaming match in my mind. *"It's the one standing on its hind legs!"*

"It could say the same about you." I can hear every sarcastic inflection. *"Sit."*

I take a step back, feeling for the wooden bench behind me. Slowly lowering myself onto it, I set the can of spray down beside me. The bear lets out a snort and falls back onto all four paws. He takes me in with his deep brown eyes, tilting his head.

"I convinced him that you're a spirit bear just like him. He believes me, but he thinks you look—and smell—funny." The bear flops down hard into a sitting position in front of me. Its expression looks almost bored.

"Okay, well. Tell it to go away or something."

"Wait. I need to talk to you first."

"Here?" The people on the other side of the table are trying to formulate a plan to get me away from the bear.

"Last night at my place, you totally shut down when I started to tell you about everything. You didn't let me finish explaining." I don't just hear the emotion in his voice, I feel it. I feel the hesitation—the insecurity. *"I'm not some monster. I'd never do anything to hurt you. I just want you to hear me out. Please, give me another chance to explain. You need to understand."*

I mean to answer, but my train of thought is interrupted by laughter. Some of the people behind me are pointing at the bear, which to my surprise has started doing tricks for the crowd. It's moved a few feet away from me, giving itself some room to do roll overs and hop around in a circle.

"What did you do to the bear, Mason?"

"Relax. I just need a few more seconds to talk to you. I may have convinced it that it's a circus bear that loves to do tricks."

"God. Is nothing serious to you?"

"Yes. Just listen. When you left my place last night, I thought that was it. I could see in your eyes what you thought of me."

I don't know how to respond. I try and keep my thoughts silent.

"I'll be out at Ross Lake with everyone tonight. Can I talk to you then?"

The bear is still entertaining the crowd. It's moved on to playing dead. Its paws flail wildly until its movements cease. Even the slight rise and fall of its chest becomes still. The bear looks dead. Much like that moose on the highway must have looked before that reporter's van ran into it. I'm taken back to the scene around my grandma's kitchen table this morning, Ranger Steve's hand-puppet show acting out the crash. For a moment, I swallow down the bitter thoughts and close my eyes.

My eyes open to see people whistling and thumping their hands on the picnic tables about twenty feet away. They're trying to draw the bear's attention so I can climb over to the other side.

But its reaction is not what they expect. Its whole body tenses. Whipping its head towards the thumping hands, it lets out a low growl.

Enough! I'm not afraid of you. I stand up from the table and march towards the bear. I am a runaway train on a downhill track. Nothing is stopping me.

"Get out of here!" I'm yelling at the top up my lungs at an animal that can probably kill me in one swipe. "Go! Just go!" My hands are shaking. "Get out of here before someone figures out you're not as harmless as you pretend to be." My feet are planted. I'm not backing down. I am strong.

I'm blocking the path between the bear and the people banging on the tables. The bear stops with a huff, shaking its head in frustration. But I stand. I feel its warm breath on me. I see into its eyes. I know Mason is still in its head.

I whisper to it, low enough so only he and I can hear. "You may tell that bear what to do," I say, "but you don't tell me." Mason's voice is gone from my mind. My walls are back up. Just the way I like it. I say one last thing before straightening and pointing towards the woods. "I will find you at the lake. I haven't given up on you."

The white spirit bear turns and trots off towards the tree line. In only a few seconds, it's swallowed up into the shadowy lurch of the tightly knit trees. I'm left all alone.

And I can't help but ask myself, would I rather count myself among the blissfully unaware crowd or be in the good graces of a monster?

"Rachel." I hear Nate's calming, even tone. "Are you okay?" His hand brushes the arm of my leather jacket. The one my brother gave me.

I know which side I'd rather be on. It was never really a choice.

I turn towards Nate and the advancing crowd. Pretty much everyone's knee-jerk reaction to the question 'are you okay?' is 'yes,' but today when I say it, I really mean it. "Yeah, I'm okay. I'm better than okay."

Julie is coming towards us, and close behind her is Finn. The rest of the crowd, with their prying eyes and questions, aren't much farther. They'll all ask me about the white bear. They'll want to know why I acted the way I did. I mean, what kind of crazy person chases after a bear?

I reach for Nate's hand and give it a squeeze. He's already crossed to my side of the tables. "Let's get out of here." Standing on my tiptoes, I try and peer over the sea of heads. My pathway to freedom is narrowing quickly. I pull him to follow me. Julie reaches us before we can leave. "I'm okay, but I need to get out of here. I—"

"It's okay. I'll see you tonight at the lake. Just go." How good it is to have a friend who understands you in so few words? I flash a tight smile and turn towards the parking lot, dragging Nate behind me. I don't slow down much, weaving through the crowd.

"Where are we going?" Nate asks.

"I don't really know. I just want to get away from here."

We've made it past the majority of the people. No one is following us, but I'm not slowing down. I can't believe I just did that. Who stands up to bear? Me, that's who. I want to climb to the top of some mountain peak and roar till the breath is gone from my body and there's nothing left but me—the girl I used to be, before all the bad things came to stay. I feel, if only for a moment, like I saw the person I wanted to be.

"Hey." Nate pulls on my arm. "Slow down." He draws me towards him. My heart is pounding from the freight-train load of adrenaline coursing through it. "Whoa. Just stop for a sec." His eyes dive into mine. "Hey." His warm arms hold me to him. My breathing tries to match the rise and fall of his chest. "You look like a wild animal just let out of its cage. Are you really okay?"

How do I explain to someone that picking a fight with a bear was one of the most eye-opening experiences I've had in my life? I don't know, but I know where I'd like to start.

I push up onto my tiptoes, letting my lips find his. His mouth is warm and soft, but I don't want warm and soft. This current, this need that runs through me when we touch, has every inch of me buzzing. My heart is pounding, I need to come up for air. I push back just far enough to speak.

"I'm really okay." I look into his beautiful, dark eyes.

"Let's get out of here."

Luckily, we've been walking towards Nate's truck. He opens the passenger door for me, like he always does. Shutting it, he goes around to the other side. Out of the corner of my eye, I catch a glimpse of something in the truck's side mirror.

My white deer.

Its antlers look larger than before. They have more points, and their fuzzy velvet is shedding in spots. Turning its head slowly towards the truck, it catches my gaze in the mirror. My eyes are fixed on its reflection. It's no more than a second or two before it turns and continues on its path, disappearing into the shadows of the tree line.

Where's it going? Why doesn't it stay? Has my wish been granted?

Not yet. I still don't know what I want, what I'm looking for. Maybe that's why the visions of my white deer are so fleeting. They're only glimpses of the thing I want most.

CHAPTER EIGHTEEN

If you asked me a year ago if I'd go to a party like this, I'd have probably said no. I never even got invited to parties like this a year ago. Events like this were reserved for the popular crowd. I wasn't part of any crowd really. I wasn't sporty or geeky. I didn't play in the band or perform in the drama club. I didn't stand out as any one thing. I had my camera, though, and the photography class I took for extra credit, which let me view life behind the safety of a telephoto lens. That was me. The girl who hid from real life, who blended into the scenery. That was my quiet reality.

But not anymore. Out here in Hazelton, it seems this is my new normal: parties every weekend, ample booze, music so loud you feel it more than hear it, acres of wilderness and fresh air to get lost in, and minimal adult supervision. Technically there are adults at Ross Lake, if you consider those old enough to buy under-agers alcohol adults. It's a virtual carefree paradise.

A squealing girl wearing a bright pink hoodie darts past me into the crowd and glances off my shoulder hard as she passes. A few steps behind her is a guy I recognize from my English class. Andrew. He sits two desks in front of me. His frame is hulking, and he's always sporting a military haircut you could set a watch to. He catches her effortlessly, overtaking her in a few large strides, scooping her up and over his shoulder like she weighs nothing, and carrying her off. She laughs and screams at the same time, expressing both ends of an emotional spectrum. I get it. I think I've run through the whole rainbow today.

The crisp air from the lake fills my lungs. It's a beautiful night. The rain clouds from earlier have moved away; maybe it won't rain after all. I scan the mingling faces of the crowd near the edge of the water. I don't see anyone familiar, and I'm kind of glad. It would be nice to get tonight's conversations over and done with, but I'm good just standing here on my island of one, taking everything in. Right now, I am Rachel Barnes. I'm wearing my faded, comfy jeans with the rips in the thighs and the leather jacket my brother gave me over a thin, navy blue hoodie. Julie would have a million labels for this outfit—including dull and tomboy—but I don't care. This is me in my own skin.

As I get closer to the water's edge, the hard-packed grass turns to small pebbles and coarse sand. The days are getting warmer, but a cool breeze comes off the water. I'm told no one goes swimming in the lake until very late summer. Now it would be like taking a polar bear dip, since the lake is fed by snow runoff from the mountains.

"Rachel!" I hear my name over the din of music. I see Julie waving from one of the docks. As she starts walking towards me, I notice she's with Chloe, Sheri-Lynn, and a few others I don't recognize.

As soon as she sees me, she wraps me into a hug, which is surprisingly crushing for a person her size. "How are you? Are you okay? I was so worried about you after you left the ribbon cutting. I mean, I totally get it. Everyone was talking about you going postal on that bear. It's probably gone viral on YouTube by now." Julie can ramble like an endless, looping newsreel, especially when she's been drinking.

She breaks to take a breath so I jump in. "I'm okay, Julie. Today's been interesting, but I'm all right." I look down at her hand and see she's holding a drink. "Did your cousin boot for you again? I could really use a beverage." Another thing I never would have said a year ago.

I follow Julie to a blue and white cooler near a cropping of tall, spindly pine trees. I immediately crack open and chug at least half of the drink she hands me. It goes down too easy. I can tell she's surprised. Maybe the Rachel she knows doesn't chug drinks. We find a seat on a large rock jutting out of the ground beside the cooler.

"So—that bear?" Julie starts slowly. She seems to have

slowed her train of thought.

"Yep." I take another, more dignified, sip of my drink. "That bear."

"Can I just ask you something?" She doesn't wait for my approval. "Why did you get in front of that charging bear? It was going to rip those people apart. The Rachel I know doesn't have a death wish."

I'm not even sure if I know that Rachel. A million versions of the truth run through my head. Telling her the entire truth would reveal too much. I can't decide which bothers me more: the fact that I'm lying to a friend or the fact that I'm getting good at it. I used to suck at lying.

"I guess I just reacted," I say. "I could see it was going for those guys banging on the tables." An image of the white bear flickers in my mind, its eyes not quite its own. Mason's eyes. A silver glaze crosses its vision as it focuses on the sound of drumming hands. I see, I feel, its frustration. Its anger. I feel the disconnect between Mason's control and the rush of something more primal. "I had to do something. I couldn't just stand and watch it attack those people. I thought I had a better chance of stopping it than they did."

"A better chance at stopping it?" Julie repeats, unconvinced. It wasn't a lie, just not the whole truth. "Well, you were right, I guess. You stopped it, and gave everyone watching a freaking heart attack. Did you call your mom and tell her you're okay? She called my cell, like, three times. I didn't answer. I didn't know what to say to her. I mean, it can't just be coincidence that all these animals are showing up around town. This is from messing around with that spirit box. I've even heard people talking about a white deer. If that's true, what about Mason's animal? The windy—"

"Wendigo."

"Yeah, the wendigo. We don't even know what that is. What if the wendigo has come here? I saw Mason around earlier, but I didn't want to ask him about it and look totally stupid."

I guess the question had to come around eventually. I let another swallow of my drink slide down my dry throat. I don't want to lie, but the truth isn't much better. "First: slow down. Yes, I texted my mom. I chickened out about talking to her, too. I don't really know what to tell people about that bear. Yes, the crow and the bear probably have something to do with the spirit box, but it's nothing we can't handle. It was just a crow and just a bear. And the deer will just be a deer." I feel like I'm trying to convince myself.

"And what about the wendigo? Has Mason said anything to you about it?" Julie continues. She breathes in deep and scrunches up her nose. Even though we've only been friends for a few months, I know her tells. She does that when she's trying to choose her words carefully. "Maybe I'm being overly sensitive here," she drawls out, "but is there something going on between you and Mason? I know you and Nate are together now, but ever since your birthday you and Mason are different around each other. It's hard not to notice. I can't decide if you love or hate each other."

"I—" My thoughts are frozen, my whole world spinning inside my head. Love, hate? In my world they exist right beside each other, with a thin line drawn between. A cold drip of condensation from my drink rolls over my hand, and then another.

"I'd say it's an equal split." Julie and I both jump at the deep, even tone of Mason's voice. "Hopefully a bit more of one than the other."

My eyes lock onto his. How long has he been listening? I'm beginning to realize that if he wants to hear something, chances are he will.

"Oh my God, how long have you been standing there? You scared the shit out of us," Julie says with a nervous giggle.

"Oh, long enough," he answers, flashing a smile at her.

I know what he's doing. He's trying to distract her with that whole hey-girl-I'm-totally-good-looking-and-hanging-on-every-word-you-say act. Well, it won't work. But Julie's cheeks are flushed pink and a goofy smile is plastered across her face. *Seriously, Julie?*

"Mason." The volume of my voice is too loud, and the

tone scolding. I don't say anything more—the glare I shoot speaks volumes. He clears his throat and stands taller. The dazed Bambi look flickers and fades from Julie's face.

"Sorry to interrupt." His eyes don't leave hers. He goes on talking as if I'm not even here. "I've been looking for Rachel all day. Would you mind if I steal her away from you for a little while?"

"No problem," Julie responds instantly, looking at me like our earlier conversation just vanished into thin air. "I'll catch up with you later, Rach. I'll be out on the docks with the rest of the girls." She scoots past Mason like his hotness might actually burn her, trotting back off to the docks without a care in the world.

He sits beside me on the uneven rock, his shoulder pressing into mine.

"What did you do to her, Mason?" My words are slow.

"I just distracted her a bit. It was nothing. It's not like I did some zombie brain scan and erased her thoughts. She remembers everything. I just made her think it wasn't very important to know the answer to her question." He nudges into my shoulder. "And it sounded like you needed rescuing from the conversation. I was just trying to help."

"You can erase thoughts? Wait. I don't want to know. I don't want to know anything more about strange supernatural things that shouldn't exist."

I pound back what's left in my giant can of whatever. The lightheaded buzz is a welcome retreat. I set the empty beside the blue cooler and take another one out. Bubbly foam runs down the side of my hand when I open it. I slurp it up quickly so it doesn't get my sleeve wet.

"How many of those have you had? Didn't you just get here?"

"What?" I say between gulps. "You don't know? Haven't you been spying on me the whole time?"

He takes a second before he answers. "I wasn't spying on you. I was looking for you. You said you'd meet me out at the lake tonight."

"I said I'd find you out here. Maybe I just needed a minute to . . ." The electricity between us makes my head spin. Why do I want so badly to wrap my arms around the biggest problem in my life? Why does it feel like that would be an answer to everything?

"To what?" he asks. "To get drunk?"

"Do you ever think that you're a lot to handle right now? My day has been a bit of a roller coaster. Maybe this"—I hold up my can—"is my way of dealing with that. I got in a fight with a bear, you know." I almost spit the words in his face.

"It was me you were 'fighting' with, not the bear. Don't be so dramatic. The bear was never going to hurt you."

"Don't be so *dramatic*?" The words come out of me with a seething hiss. "Pardon me. I'll remember that next time my friend possesses a bear and tries to attack people." I touch the cool can to my lips again for another sip.

I see his jaw tightening. "Stop drinking so fast, Rachel. You're going to make yourself sick."

"So you don't deny it?" I look directly into his eyes. "Were you going to let that bear rip those people apart? All because you were frustrated? You were having a bad day?" I whisper the last words. "And no one would ever suspect it was you. God. You're better than this."

His lips brush against my cheek as he leans in towards me. I wonder for a moment if he's going to kiss me. Dam it. He's probably in my head right now listening to my girly thoughts. His sweet breath lingers near my cheek as he whispers, "No. I'm better *like* this. Come with me. Please. Let's take a walk."

"Hey." I push against his solid shoulders. Too much alcohol so quickly is swirling my brain. I stumble to my feet and step back from him. "Don't you use your mind voodoo on me." God, that sounded stupid. I should just shut up.

"Hey." His voice softens. His strong hands reach out to steady me. "You're my friend. My real friend. No matter how screwed up things are, that's real. I would never use my powers on you to change that. No matter how much I wish things were different."

I want to be mad at him. I want to treat him like some beast that should be shunned and feared. I feel the weight of my drink in my hand, its contents half-gone. I want to crush it, put all my frustrations into my vice-like grip. But I set it down gently onto the rock. "Where to?"

His fingers trace lightly over my hand as he stands in front of me. "Thank you," he says in a soft whisper.

It doesn't take long before we are away from the crowds.

"I remember this place," I say without thinking, "from the last time we walked here."

Mason slows to a stop in front of a looming tower—a pine tree so large its branches must span twenty feet. His body relaxes as he looks up towards the spanning branches.

"This used to be my place, where I'd come to get away from the real world. My sister and I spent a lot of time here when we were younger. She and I created these fantastic realities here, where people had magic and could live forever. Where people would never die. This was our fortress."

I step towards to him, not to touch him, just to be closer. "We don't have to talk about her if you don't want to." I'm doing my best to keep my voice low. I don't want to argue anymore.

"No, I wanted to bring you here to talk about her. I think

maybe if I explain things this way you might understand." He swallows hard. "You might understand why I won't change back. Why I'm better like this."

I fold my arms, shaking my head. "I agreed to come and listen to what you had to say. So tell me, but I don't promise anything."

"Okay." He sits on a fallen log in the middle of his forest castle. With the surrounding rocks and shrubs, it mimics a throne. "Do you want to sit?" he asks. I don't answer. I just sit beside him, our legs and shoulders touching slightly.

"After Angie died, I decided I was the one who had to be strong. My mom was a wreck. So was my dad." Mason's gaze was distant. "But what did I know about being strong? I thought being strong was to carry on, to be happy again, to continue living. But that all hurt too much. So I did what I needed to do. I created a me that didn't hurt. I was tough, smart, athletic. I was the life of the party. Girls liked me, and I liked girls. But I never got to know them, and they never got to know me, because there wasn't anything to know. I was about as deep as a puddle. I had to be. Because I was only strong enough to create a thin layer over the hurt. Just thick enough to keep it from getting out."

My body snuggles closer to his warmth as he talks. I listen. I don't say anything. I understand about trying to be strong, but it still doesn't make this wendigo thing right.

"But now I'm this. This is more the real me than I've been

in a long time." He pauses, running his fingers over a leafy branch like an armrest. "Do you remember how I told you everything is connected?"

I nod my head in silence, trying to absorb his words. Trying to understand.

"Everything and everybody who came before us still exists. Just because we die and our bodies go away doesn't mean we just disappear. My sister still exists. The energy that made her alive still exists."

"Like in that bush?" The instant the words leave my lips, I feel stupid.

"Sort of, but no. I'm not saying my dead sister is now a bush in the forest. Think of it like this." He looks at me with sparkling, blue eyes. "When a raindrop falls into an ocean, it doesn't disappear. It just becomes part of something bigger. When I come back here to this spot in the forest, it feels like she's still around. I can find the part of her that still exists. Being a wendigo connects me to all that."

I take a moment to look at him. Him. This—wendigo. "I understand, I guess."

"Being a wendigo makes the hurting parts of me bearable. It makes me more like who I was before."

"Yeah, except the part where you have magical powers and kill people." My words taste sour.

"Right." He clears his throat. "This isn't perfect." His shoulders slump, he looks defeated. "So how do I convince you that the good in me outshines the bad? How do I convince you I'm still me, not a monster?"

"Give it up. Get rid of the wendigo. You know how to do it. I know you do. Why won't you?" We've fought this fight before, back and forth, rallying, with neither side willing to give up. It's like despite whatever progress we've just made, I'm putting us back to square one.

His gaze focuses on me again. "Listen to you. Such fight." A faded smile crosses his lips. We stare at each other. Any other person would have looked away by now—but I don't. I take him for what he is. No preconceptions. No bullshit. "For me, giving up the wendigo would be like you having to relive the night your brother died, every day, forever. Eternally stuck on repeat. I'm not strong enough for that. I'm not like you."

"I've been stuck on repeat for years. Every nightmare, every dark corner, every sunrise and sunset is my perfect storm. There are whole almanacs on my unchanging weather." Swallowing down the searing rush of adrenaline, I try to calm the tremors that want to take me over.

I understand his pain. I understand the broken parts that clang around, never getting fixed. I understand why he needs it. There might even be a part of me that envies him. What I wouldn't give not to hurt anymore. "So, what now? There's no way we're going to be able to keep you a secret forever here in Hazelton."

"I know, and I've been thinking about that. It's what I wanted to talk to you about next. I just had to make sure you didn't hate me first."

"I don't hate you!" My words come out with burning ferocity. I can feel the heat coming to my face. "I'm not afraid of you. I've never not hated someone so much in my life." I want to cry. "I get it. I get you. I understand why you do it. That's what scares me." My last words escape in a whisper. "I should hate you, but I don't. It makes me think there's a part of me that would do it too. Horrible things—just to hurt less. Because killing is horrible, and that's what you do. You kill. That is the price you pay for all this." My whole body vibrates with the emotion inside me. He presses his forehead against mine. I feel safe here. I want to feel safe here. Not because of some magic he's projecting, but because, for once, someone understands my broken pieces.

"I won't ever lie to you about what I am. But you're right, I do need to leave Hazelton. Which is why I'm moving away after graduation."

"You're leaving?" Of course he is. He can't stay. A person who needs to feed on the souls of others can't exactly stay in a small town without being found out.

"Yeah, I thought I'd try out Vancouver for a while. Maybe go to school in the fall. I applied to a bunch of schools and got accepted on almost all my applications. I can take my pick. I thought you might want to come with me."

Wait. What?

"I can't go with you," I stutter. I can't make plans like that. I don't make plans like that.

"Why not?" He makes it sound like *my* answer is the ridiculous one.

"Because. I have friends here. I finally have a normal life. At least, I'd like to have a normal life here."

"You don't have to decide right away, but you'll be the only one left if you stay."

"No. Chloe is the only one leaving, and I don't think she really likes me anyway. Julie and Nate will still be here. They're lifers."

"So they haven't told you yet?" His voice trails off.

"What are you talking about?"

"I was here about a half hour before you. I overheard Julie and Chloe talking." He pauses for a moment, just looking at me. "Chloe is taking Julie with her when she leaves." He says it quickly, like ripping off a Band-Aid.

"No. Julie told me just this morning she didn't want to leave."

"She also doesn't want to be without her best friend. Chloe is going to pay her way. She couldn't pass it up."

And what about me? I'm not a best friend too? "She would have told me if she was going with Chloe. You must have misheard."

"I'm sure she was going to tell you. It sounded like they just decided tonight. She probably would have told you if I hadn't interrupted."

I lean forward and let my face rest in my hands. "Great." My words muffle into my palms. "So what about Nate? How do you know he's leaving? Don't tell me you two have gotten all chummy on me?"

"Nate and I are not friends. I know he's leaving because my wish has been granted."

I let my hands slide from my face. "What do you mean? You didn't wish him gone. You wished that your dad's company would get some projects going in this town. How could that make Nate go away?"

"My dad's been working to get site plans approved by the municipality, but for years, he never had any luck. Not until Nate offered his guiding services. He was the one to find new places to drill. With his help, the plans got approved by the municipality, and projects finally have the go-ahead. My dad was so impressed with Nate that he offered him a job. Nate accepted. He's going to be a Native relations leader for Western Canada. He might still call Hazelton home, but I doubt he'll live here much longer. Not with all the traveling he'll be doing. My dad said they want to put him in one of their southern offices, probably Vancouver."

All the adrenaline from earlier drains from me. Mason wouldn't make this up. It would be too easy to find out the truth. "But he would have told me. I was at his place all afternoon."

"Yeah, listen. I try really hard to stay out of whatever goes on between you two. I don't need the details. I'm just telling you what my dad told me. You're going to be the only one of our group left, except Ryan and Sheri-Lynn, maybe."

"Sheri-Lynn." I scoff her name. "How are you two doing, anyway?"

He takes a moment to find his words. "She's someone deep-as-a-puddle me would date."

"Wow, what a glowing review. Why even bother with her, then?"

"Because she's a distraction."

"The wendigo thing must be stressful, I guess."

He shakes his head. "It's not that at all. I wouldn't miss a minute of being a wendigo, good and bad."

"Then what? You're holding out on me."

Mason stands up, leaving me chilled. "Come on. Let's go back to the beach."

He takes my hand, helping me to my feet, but we don't go anywhere. We just stand there, so close that the body heat becomes trapped in the tiny space between us. He brings my hand to his chest, wrapping his other one around the small of my back. He pulls me closer, his chin resting on top of my head. I want to let all my problems melt into him. In this moment, I am both far away and right here. I hear him whisper, just loud enough to be heard over the din of the forest rustle. And I understand.

"She's just a distraction—from you."

CHAPTER NINETEEN

The leaves and twigs crunch beneath my feet. The path back to the beach is a combination of overgrown ferns and moss, but I seem to find every crackling bit as I walk. Everything out here reminds me that perhaps I'm still too "city" for these woods. I jump over a patch of dried leaves on the path, trying to trek more quietly. Yet I land on the edge, mashing them so loudly I'm sure every animal in the forest can hear me. There's nothing but the sound of me stumbling along this path. Not one bird chirp. Not one cricket. The animals of the forest are out there, I'm sure they are. Maybe they're just waiting, and listening, for the silent predator behind me to make his move.

As hard as I try, I can't hear his footsteps over mine. I can feel him, though. Like a person can feel when someone is watching them. It's like his steps don't even scuff the surface where he walks. As if nothing is altered by his presence. But he does change things. He changes everything.

"I can hear you sighing." Mason's voice is smooth and calm, which is sort of annoying considering my head is swarming with thoughts. "Are you going to tell me what you're thinking about? Or are you just going to asphyxiate yourself with patchy breathing?"

I slam on the brakes, turning to face him. He should have ploughed right into me, but not Mason. He stands just inches away, on purpose no doubt. I should step back, but I don't. We're so close, but not touching. I can't help but notice him, all of him. He's a head taller than me, so sure of himself, his breathing so relaxed. There isn't a wrinkle on his pristine white T-shirt or a crease on his plaid shorts. On the surface he looks perfect. But his life is just as screwed up as mine.

"My footsteps crush the leaves," I stutter. "They break the sticks." I look down at my feet. My toes are within inches of his.

"Um . . . okay." His warm breath rolls over me. I want him to pull me in close. Tell me everything's okay. Tell me the things I've done haven't ruined absolutely everything.

"I've changed things. I've broken things. They'll never be the same," I say.

"What won't be the same?"

"Everything!" The word chokes halfway out of my throat. "Julie and Chloe will leave. Nate will leave, and you will leave.

And I will . . . I don't know. But I do know that every wish put into motion by that damn spirit box is my fault. And now everything is ruined. I screw everything up."

I am exactly where I am, and nowhere to be found. I'm floating in the eye of my own storm.

There has to be a way to come down from this. I can't have come so close to finding a place where I feel like I'm home only to lose it. This is not the way it should end. I close my eyes. I feel his closeness. I breathe the woods in deeply. The scent of green moss and clinging dew fills my lungs. The breeze brushes my cheek. The air has cooled. The sun is setting. The fading light creeps over me, and I let it. I will not let the dark frighten me tonight.

Tonight, I will stand in the space between the light and the dark, where neither exists.

"Mason," I say, with my eyes still shut.

"Yes?"

"Do you think, if no one had made those wishes . . . Do you think any of this would have happened? I mean, jobs would have eventually come back to this town. The community center eventually would have been built. Would the lottery money still have been won? Would you still—be like this?" My voice trails off.

"It doesn't really matter if it would've happened or not,

because it did. And if you weren't the one to put these things in motion, something else would have. Or not. Things happen for a reason. Maybe reasons we'll never understand. That's life." I feel the tips of his fingers brush softly against my arm. "It's unpredictable, chaotic, tragic . . . beautiful."

"Mason."

We inch closer, the space between us disappearing. "Yes?"

I might float away if he wasn't here. "If you weren't a wendigo, would you still try so hard to be my friend?"

"Being a wendigo has nothing to do with that. In fact, I've never tried harder to not be categorized as a 'friend' than I have with you. But you know that. You'd have to be blind not to notice."

My gaze flickers up to the unmistakable *want* in his crystal blue eyes. Eyes that mirror mine. A few dark hairs have fallen over his brow. I can't help but touch them. The feel of his skin is euphoric, my own personal happy drug.

This is wrong. I can't use him for some drug-induced high. He's the only person who understands how broken I am. The one who really knows me—probably better than I do myself—and still wants to be with me.

He's been my best friend, a better one than I deserve.

I let my body draw into his. I let my thoughts crawl past

the friend zone to a place where want overrides thought. The light brush of his fingertips against my arm turns to a solid hold, as his other hand traces around to the small of my back.

The electricity of anticipation is almost too much.

I let the air from my breath mingle with the sweetness from his, just a fraction from his lips. Every molecule of me screams *yes*.

Except one.

A barely audible whisper comes from my lips. "No." It comes from the last bit of conviction left in me, the part that hasn't forgotten what dark lurks just below his perfect surface. The part that remembers I'm currently dating the sweetest guy on the planet.

Mason's warmth draws away and my comforting numbness leaves me.

"I'm sorry. I thought—"

"Don't be." I let my forehead rest on his chest. I feel his body relax as his arms envelop me in a hug. He pecks a soft kiss on the top of my head.

"Come on. Let's go back to the lake."

The three-minute walk back seems to trudge on forever.

Hearing voices and music coming from the water's edge, I know we're almost there. I'm relieved and a little sick to my stomach at the same time. Is Mason going to hang out with the girls and me? Is Sheri-Lynn still with them? Nate said he'd be out at the lake tonight too. Is he here already?

Mason. I almost kissed him. Now I'm going to hang out with his girlfriend. And it's always a bit uncomfortable when Nate and Mason are in each other's vicinity but, hey, let's throw in a slice of I-almost-kissed-Mason into the mix. Ugh, I can't do this. Any of this.

Mason's dark, charismatic presence. Nate's job offer. Julie's departure. I want to go back to the lake about as much as I want to go back into that darkening forest. I should just cop out of the rest of the night and go home. I'll make something up. I'm done tonight. I stop, turning to face him.

"Mason. I think I'm just going to—"

"Shh." He cuts me off before I can finish.

His face has a look of terror. Sidestepping me, he bolts towards the docks. The shock of him leaving fades and I notice now what he must have sensed. The vibe from the crowd of people has changed. Their voices are hushed. Someone has turned down the music. People are craning their necks towards the shore of the lake. There are people yelling.

Running towards the crowd gathered at the dock, I see Mason at the water's edge. He's drenched from head to toe in frigid lake water. In his arms is a very limp, very blue Sheri-Lynn.

I squeeze between two girls to get closer.

"What happened?" I ask one of them.

"Some girls got drunk on the docks. I think a couple of them fell in."

"Do you know who it was?"

"I don't know. I heard they're seniors, though. Someone said it was that girl who won the lotteries and two of her friends."

I push further through the crowd, breaking through to the front. Mason has laid Sheri-Lynn on the ground beside Julie. Both of them are blue and silent. I can't tell if they're breathing or not. They are so still. Too still. Chloe is soaking wet, shivering, and leaning over Julie. Beads of freezing water drip from her tangled hair right onto Julie's face. Julie doesn't even flinch.

Chloe's grip on Julie's arm is piercing. It's going to leave a bruise. I try to say something but choke on the words. Chloe brushes her twisted mop of hair away from her face with her hand, revealing what should be an angry bruise on Julie's arm, but there isn't one. Instead, ghostly white splotches in the shape of fingerprints linger on her skin.

I'm watching like some innocent bystander, but I'm not innocent. I shouldn't have lingered coming back to the beach. I shouldn't have wanted to kiss Sheri-Lynn's boyfriend. I should have never let us make those wishes.

This shouldn't be happening, but the scene is unfolding right before my eyes and I have no control over it. I hear every word around me, but they barely reach me. I'm just . . . here. Doing nothing. Because that's what I do.

Chloe's voice is shrill in my ears, scratching at the broken parts of me. She calls for Julie in a frantic, wet scream. No one comforts her. There's a place inside me that knows no one can.

"Rachel?" I hear Mason's calm voice, almost a whisper over the cries, over the wretched breathing, over the horror. It doesn't come from inside my head, though. It's like the volume on the rest of the world just got turned down. His lips move again as I hear him speak. "I can't hold this forever. You're going to have to choose."

And that's when it clicks. Chloe isn't screaming anymore. Her face is contorted into an anguished cry, but nothing comes out. Even the water drops from her hair have stilled mid-air. Everything is still except for me and Mason. Suspended time. Just another bit of the supernatural I never thought could exist.

"Choose what?" My voice cracks. I feel my own hot tears streaming down my face. "What are you waiting for? Help them!" I'm not even sure what I'm asking him to do. The expressions on Julie and Sheri-Lynn are peaceful, placid. I know Mason has many powers that I can't begin to understand, but is reversing death one of them?

"I'm letting you see this because you have a choice." He

motions for me to kneel beside him. My body is on autopilot. I think my legs might give out from the shaking, but they hold as I lower myself beside him. The ground is cold and wet from the water they brought ashore. Or maybe it's raining again. *I'm so numb. I can't tell what the weather is anymore.*

"Sheri-Lynn is . . . I can't save her." His words hit me like a rock to the gut. "I can feel her energy leaving her, trying to find its way back into the network that surrounds us. She'll be lost within it if we do nothing." He directs his gaze towards Julie and my eyes follow. "Julie is still here. She's fighting to stay. I know she hears Chloe calling her. She doesn't want to go, but she's too weak to hold on all by herself. Julie needs my help."

"So do it, help her! Whatever you're going to do, just do it!"

"There's a consequence to everything. Know what you are asking me to do before you ask it." The silence of the world around us closes in. "Sheri-Lynn will die. Or at least her body will. Her energy is what I need to help Julie. I can . . . jump-start Julie, so to speak. It will give her a chance, at least."

I begin to consider that Sheri-Lynn is already dead, or will be, but bile creeps up the back of my throat. I'm rationalizing using one person's energy, one person's soul, to save someone else's.

"There's one more thing." Mason's voice sails across the silence between us. "My powers don't come for free. The source of my powers comes from the energy I collect. I'll need to replenish."

I remember the story Nate's grandpa told. Wendigos collect souls. That's what gives a them their powers.

And there's the catch. The big catch. Do nothing, Sheri-Lynn dies and Julie too. Choose, and Julie lives. Sheri-Lynn helps save her, and someone else, some random person, loses their life too.

"Just do it. I won't do nothing," I whisper over the pounding of my aching heart.

He doesn't ask whether I'm sure. He just goes to work. The frozen stillness of everything starts to melt away, but not all at once. The distant sounds come back first, the far-away murmur of people, and the wind moving through the trees.

Before the area that surrounds us starts to move again, I see it. It was right in front of me the whole time, but invisible until Mason's fingers touched it. Sheri-Lynn's soul, floating inches above her lifeless chest. Its pale blue glow illuminates the stilled faces around us. Mason grasps it between two fingers, plucking it from the air, severing whatever spider-thin thread kept it from floating away.

The sound of the lake water lapping against the shore returns.

Mason takes what was Sheri-Lynn and places it in Julie's

ash-grey hand. He wraps her hand around the tiny light until all that can be seen is the pulsing, blue glow between her fingers. It fades as quickly as the peachy colour returns to Julie's fingers, hand, wrist, arm . . .

I did it. Or, he did it. She'll be okay. Chloe's sobbing cries return. Would she have made the same choice as I did? Sheri-Lynn lies motionless and cold beside me. "I'm sorry," I mouth to her, barely a whisper. "And thank you."

Chloe's sobs turn to tears of joy. Julie has opened her eyes and is looking right at me between the tangled ropes of Chloe's wet hair. Her eyes are a warm brown, just like they've always been, but for a moment, I swear they look different, like someone else is peering out.

The crowd still hovers around our scene of horror. They have no idea what really happened. They have no knowledge of the monster among them. Maybe I don't have any idea myself.

Maybe I'm the monster.

I take Sheri-Lynn's ice-cold hand in mine. I know she's not in there anymore, but somehow it makes sense to hold her hand. Or maybe I want her to hold mine—to give me a sign that things will be okay. But she doesn't, and they're not. All I feel is the muted chill of her lifeless hand.

I don't know how long I've been sitting here when the paramedics move me. The ambulance's twirling lights flash harshly as they load Julie into the back. Chloe is arguing with a paramedic, trying to ride with her friend. Sheri-Lynn is covered with a sheet now. It's white. The water from her clothes soaks through it, making it cling to her like a second skin. She is loaded into a second ambulance, which arrives more quietly than the first. No lights flash on this one. Like a universal signal for everyone to leave, the two ambulances close their doors and drive off. People gather their things and wander away to their cars. Except me.

Where do I go from here?

I'm at the hospital. One minute I can remember how I got here, and the next it's all a blur. The scene plays over and over in my head. Sheri-Lynn's hand leaving mine. Everyone walking away. I'm all alone by the edge of the water. That's where Nate finds me, looking out at the glassy surface of the lake. There is barely a ripple, like nothing horrible just happened there.

When Nate found me, I didn't tell him what happened. He knew already. I let him wrap his arms around me as I crumpled into him. I didn't deserve any of his comfort or sympathy, but I took it. The truck ride to the hospital was a blur of numbing tears, but I know Nate drove me here.

Mason wasn't beside me when the ambulances arrived. I don't think he's at the hospital either. He sort of . . . disappeared.

I'm not sure if I want to see him right now anyway. I can't decide if he reminds me of my friend who's still alive or the one who isn't.

The clock on the wall of the hospital waiting room reads 11:32 p.m. I should probably go home. Julie was admitted past visiting hours and they won't let me see her tonight because I'm not family. This chair is killing my back, but the pain is almost welcome. Nate's gone to talk to the nurses again for an update on Julie. I'm both glad and afraid to have this moment with myself . . . I have no idea who that is anymore.

The chair beside me creaks. I don't bother to look up. I know Nate's going to try and convince me to go home.

"Rachel?" comes a familiar voice from the seat beside me.

I look over to find Nate's grandpa sitting beside me. He's dressed in blue pajama bottoms, leather slippers, and one of those hospital gowns that ties in the back.

"I thought that was you," he says matter-of-factly. "What brings you here? You don't look so good, like you just lost your best friend or something."

No, she's still here. I'm not entirely sure if I am, though. The waterworks start to flow again. I thought my reservoir had run dry. Guess not.

"Ah, shit. I'm sorry. Don't cry. This old brain of mine has no filter sometimes."

"It's okay," I sniff back. "I'm fine. It's just been a long day." Why do people feel the need to assure people they are okay? I'm not okay.

"All right . . . Good," he replies, shifting in his chair. "I can go if you want me to. I was just wandering the halls because I can't sleep. Hospitals give me the creeps. They smell funny."

"You can stay." I try to smile, but it won't come. "Nate will be back in a few minutes to take me home, though. Does he know you're here?"

"Oh yeah. I think I told him. I'm in here pretty regular these days. Nothing major, just getting old is all. They like to run tests on me. Make sure I'll live another hundred years." He playfully nudges my shoulder. Probably trying to get a smile out of me. I look up and oblige with a small one before we settle into an awkward silence.

"So I saw you earlier today at the community center. You're a pretty lucky girl to have seen a white bear that close. There aren't very many people who have." He adjusts in his seat, as if anyone could be comfortable in a hospital waiting room. "I've seen one before," he goes on. "Did you know that white bears are called Kermode bears, or spirit bears?"

I so don't want to make small talk right now. I answer with a muffled, "Um-hm."

"Some people believe that spirit animals are omens. A white bear can mean many things." I half-listen to what he's saying, but I'm not up for his stories right now. "It portrays qualities of fearlessness and leadership, but mostly it's an omen of death and rebirth." His voice trails off on the last few words.

Death and rebirth. You could say that's what happened to Julie. The bear was her spirit animal.

He clears his throat before starting again. "That bear wasn't meant for you, though, was it?" Was that a question? "A white deer brings the same omen, too—the part about death and rebirth at least. If one was meant for you, that one would suit you better."

 Like a rock hitting the surface of a glassy lake and sinking to the silty bottom, it hits me. He knows. He knows about the wendigo. He knows about the spirit box, and he knows about the white animals. Maybe he's guessing or piecing something together, but I'm sure Nate's Grandpa knows more than he says. Or maybe he's been saying it all along, but no one ever believed him.

Before I get the chance to say anything, Nate's voice calls from down the fluorescent-lit hallway.

"Grandpa? I didn't know you'd be in here tonight," he says as he strides towards us.

"Yeah. Just getting some tests done. I'll be out in the morning, it's no big deal."

Concern etches fine lines into the smooth skin of Nate's

face. "Okay. You should probably get some rest though. It's late." Nate offers his hand to me. "I'll take you home, Rachel. There's no sense in spending the night here. Visiting hours start at eleven tomorrow. The nurse told me Julie might even be released before that. She's okay. They're just keeping her here overnight to be sure."

I take Nate's hand. I guess I'm leaving here whether I want to or not.

"I'll come to your place tomorrow, Grandpa. I'll bring you lunch, see how you're doing." Nate wraps his arm around me as we start down the long hallway.

"See you again, Rachel," Grandpa calls after us with a small wave.

Nate gives my shoulder a little squeeze as we walk away. "I think my grandpa has a bit of a soft spot for you."

I don't say anything back. Everything that's gone on today is too much to process. My brain feels like it's breaking down as I walk, with too few cells remaining to form any words. Most doors we pass down the long, sterile hallway are shut, except for one near the end. It's open a foot or two and the lights inside are all on, spilling light into the dim hallway. My world slows again as we pass. It's not magic doing it this time. It's just me, taking in the images I'm seeing.

I see a girl in a bright pink hoodie. The same girl, the same hoodie, as the one at the lake when I first arrived tonight.

My footsteps drag as we pass the open door. The girl is sobbing, clinging to the person in the chair next to her. The few words I hear her say snap the last unshattered piece of me.

"Andrew was looking right at me, Mom. There were people all around us. He was looking right at me." Her rattled sobs shake me. "And then he was dead."

CHAPTER TWENTY

It's the third time I've had this dream since Nate brought me home from the hospital. It follows me day and night, every time I close my eyes. It starts the same each time: with me, in the field of totems. Daylight is slowly descending. I see the spirit totem up ahead. I'm walking towards it like my feet have a mind of their own. The totem's gnarled, grey roots search the earth around it, breaking through the stony surface. There's a haunting, blue glow coming from its deeply carved grooves. I know it's found what it's looking for, and that's when I fall. Into what, I don't know, but the sensation is real. I've heard that if you fall in dreams and hit the bottom, you can actually die. The first two times I had the dream, I didn't hit bottom. The third time I did. The first two times I woke up in a cold sweat, gasping in panic.

This last time was different. I woke with a gasp, sucking in air as if my life was escaping me. Yet my mind stayed calm and focused on one thought only.

A fall that should have shattered all my broken parts . . . has healed me.

Eeereeek.

My old bed creaks in protest as I roll over to readjust. I should get up, but why bother? After what happened at the lake on Saturday night, I feel like I'm as much a monster as that wendigo thing that hides inside Mason.

My whole body aches. I've been lying in my bed since Saturday night. It's Monday now. My mom and my grams came into my room yesterday to check on me. I didn't have to tell them much about what happened at Ross Lake. They already knew. One thing about small towns: news isn't always accurate, but it spreads like wildfire.

When Grams came in to see me, she told me what she'd heard about Andrew Harris's death. He's in my English class, or *was*. He had a girlfriend, he was smart, he wanted to go into the military after high school, and now he's dead. If I'd chosen not to save Julie, Andrew would still be here. But instead, he's been added to what will be a growing list of wendigo victims.

"There's talk that he might have been taking some sort of stimulant drug that put a strain on his heart. He was a pretty big, athletic kid, and in that competitive soccer league. Maybe that's why his heart stopped?" I didn't correct her. I just let her words scrape over the raw parts of me. "It's very sad that a nice boy like that just up and died. He had so much life ahead of him," she said.

Her words still echo around me, and no amount of tossing in my bed rids me of them. Andrew did have a life ahead of him. And now it's gone, or collected, or whatever happens to a person when a wendigo takes them. All I know is that no soul resides in Andrew's body anymore.

I want so badly to forget, to ignore what's happening. I wonder how long I can hide here, under my covers, before someone makes me get up.

But it's Monday. I still have a week of classes left before exams. I've missed at least the first two periods of class today. Grams and Mom must have assumed I'd gone to school, but I'm still lying here. The house is oddly quiet. Not that there should be any noise—I am the only one home. It feels too silent, though, like the house is holding its breath, waiting for something, just like I am.

Swish, creak, slam.

The sound of the screen door snaps me from my haze. It must be my Grandma or Mom, come home to see why I'm not at school.

"Rachel?" a voice calls softly from the kitchen. "Hey, are you home?"

It's Julie. I decide that if I pretend to sleep she might leave me be. It's a feeble attempt, but that's where my creativity resides today. I hear the soft groan as my bedroom door opens and I try my best to look asleep. There's a tension in the air as I feel her pause in the doorway.

"You can open your eyes now. I know you're faking it."

Okay. Now I feel stupid. "What gave me away?" I ask, opening my eyelids just a crack. Julie is standing square in front of me, hands on her hips.

"You're a crappy actor. Besides, I stopped by to see you twice yesterday, and your mom said you were sleeping—both times. How much sleep do you need?" Her mouth twists into that angry little pouty face she makes when she's pissed off. "You should be the one checking on *me*, you know. I'm the one who just got out of the hospital yesterday. And Mason . . . Sheri-Lynn's dead, Rachel. Have you even talked to him since Saturday night?"

I want to turtle under my blanket and silently fade away. Unfortunately for me, I do not possess this power. This is my reality. Two people are dead because of decisions I made. No second chances. No turning back.

"I'm sorry." My voice comes out cracked and dry. I sit up on my bed and peel back the covers. Who am I kidding, anyway? Smothering myself in blankets is like trying to put a Band-Aid over a gaping wound.

I haven't even changed my clothes or showered since Saturday. I wonder if she notices.

"I should have come to see you yesterday. I followed the ambulance to the hospital, but they wouldn't let me see you there. So Nate brought me home, and I've been here ever since." I suck in the stale air of my bedroom, filling my reluctant lungs. "How are you? Are you okay?" I can feel the tears welling in my eyes.

She stares at me hard, probably deciding if she should have come here or not. "Physically, I'm fine." There's an edge to her words. "Which seems to baffle the doctors at the hospital. They said that they'd never seen someone take in so much water . . . and live." Her hands slide from her hips as she sits beside me on the bed. "But I'm still here, and Sheri-Lynn's not." Her last words falter, tears beginning to stream down her cheeks.

I put my arms around her shoulders, holding tight. I've been so selfish, thinking that what's happening affects only me.

"And when the doctors checked me over before they let me go," Julie continues, "they said it looked like nothing had even happened. That there'd been no damage to my lungs, and that I'm probably healthier than I was before I drowned. Before I fucking drowned, Rachel! 'Cuz I did. I remember it. I was dead. Why am I still here and she's not?" Julie's shoulders crumple as she leans into me. We sit together like this on the edge of my bed, crying into one another, looking off at nothing and everything all at once.

My voice cracks, holding back my burning tears. "Life isn't fair. Life is random, and it doesn't make sense. And the parts we think we have control over"—my eyes wander back to the spirit box on my shelf—"we don't." My breathing is ragged. She leans into me a little more.

"It's okay to cry. Sheri-Lynn is dead. We weren't super close, but she was a friend." She keeps talking, but all I hear is *Sheri-Lynn* and *friend*. I may not be a wendigo, but I am truly a monster.

I feel the first hot tear streak down my face like it's running from what's inside me, followed by so many of its little friends.

By the time I'm done showering, Julie has laid an outfit on the bed for me: faded jeans and a plain grey T-shirt. She isn't trying to dress me up today. Has she given up? But she insists on driving me to school, probably to make sure I get there. She's right. Stepping out of my house into the brightness of the day, I notice my car parked in the driveway. I forgot I'd left it at the lake Saturday night.

"Mason and I brought it home for you yesterday," she answers, before I ask the question. "We got the keys from your mom when we stopped by to see you."

"Thanks," I say, not looking directly at her. Maybe if I keep my eyes down and don't look at anybody, I can make it through this day.

We plunk ourselves unceremoniously into her car and buckle our seatbelts, but she doesn't start it right away. I can see her knuckles turning white on the steering wheel as she grips it tightly.

"I came to see you yesterday." She pauses, letting her words hang. "I wanted to tell you something. I wanted you to hear it from me before anyone else told you." She breathes out her tension before speaking. "I'm leaving with Chloe after finals are done. Our first stop is California. After that, I don't know. And . . . I'm not sure when I'll be back." Is she trying to apologize for leaving? "I know we just had this big talk about how I thought I was a lifer here and staying forever, but—"

"Yeah, I know, Julie."

"How? I mean, who told you? I thought you haven't talked to anybody since Saturday?" I can hear the irritation in her voice.

"Mason. He told me."

"Oh. Well— " Julie shakes her head slowly. "Why would he tell you? I've known Mason forever. I mean, he should have known to let me tell you. What an ass."

An ass who saved your life. "I wouldn't be too hard on the guy. He just overheard you and Chloe talking. And he told me because—" Do I say anything? *Aw, fuck it.* "He wants me to leave town too."

Her expression is a bit lost. "What do you mean, *leave town*?" A nervous giggle escapes her lips. "This isn't the old west. Nobody's chasing you away for doing bad things."

Maybe they should. "No." I swallow the lump in my throat. "No one is making me leave, but it kind of makes sense to go when there isn't going to be anyone left here."

"What are you talking about? Just Chloe and I are going."

"And Mason. And Nate. I guess that leaves me with Sheri-Lynn. If she was still alive. Not that she'd want to hang out with me anyway. Not after her boyfriend asked me to run away with him." I just said that out loud. "Mason told me you were leaving, and that Nate is leaving. I haven't confirmed about Nate yet, but I suspect he is. Everyone. Leaves. Eventually. It's been my story so far. Why should it ever change?" I can feel my face getting hot. "The only thing that's changing is me. 'Cuz I actually considered it."

"Considered what?" Her words are tentative.

"I considered running off with a person who shines light on the dark parts of me, just so I wouldn't be left behind." I let my head fall back on the headrest. "Or maybe I wanted to do the leaving for once."

I see her expression through the corner of my eye. Her mouth opens slightly, giving breath to her disbelief. She knows she's missing pieces to the story. I can tell by her distant look. She probably hates me now. Good, someone should.

Her hands loosen on the steering wheel as she stretches the tension out of them.

"So you and Mason—and you and Nate?" She gestures with her hands as if to say I'm dating both.

"No, just Nate."

"So . . ." Her forehead creases as she tries to piece together the puzzle. "Why did Mason ask you to go with him?"

I've lied and held secrets from everyone for too long, I can't even begin to explain. Even if I wanted to, I'm not brave enough to tell the truth.

My mouth stalls to find the words. "I don't know. He— It's complicated."

She looks over at me, studying my face. "It's been a hell of a few days, hasn't it?" She offers a weak smile. "I'm sorry I got you out of bed today, but you can't sleep forever. You have to get up some time."

It is a long, quiet ride to school with Julie, and an even quieter day at school. I avoid speaking to Mason even though I see him everywhere, trying to get my attention. He could just get in my head and talk to me that way, or find me alone and say what he wants. He could, but he hasn't. He's being patient. He's waiting for me. I admit, I want to talk to him, but what would I say?

Thank you.

How could you?

Get away from me.

Don't leave me.

Why can't I hate you?

I skip going to my locker after class. I don't really need anything out of there anyway, and I have a better chance of avoiding . . . *everyone* if I just leave now. *Eyes down, straight for the exit, you're almost there.* The steely crunch of the school's doors closing behind me, sealing the noises inside, sends a shiver of relief through me. But my feeling of being home free soon disappears when I notice my car isn't in the school parking lot. That's right, Julie drove me here. Looks like I'm walking home today.

I head for the street, but walking doesn't seem to cut it. I need to get away from here faster. My feet hit the pavement, quickening with every step. I don't have a jacket or my backpack, just a binder from my last class clutched under my arm, and the edges are cutting into me. It crosses my mind that it might actually break skin, but I don't care. I just go. The air feels sticky against me. *I just need to get away.*

What am I going to do when I get home—sit in my room again? I can't get away from the thoughts in my own head. Like it's all my fault. It always has been. People are dead because of me. My best friend is a monster, and so am I. How could I let it get this far? I'm a liar. I need to get control. I have choices. *Figure it out.*

Honk honk.

Nate has pulled up beside me in his truck. He's leaning over the seat to the open passenger window.

"Hey," he says, putting the truck in park. "Sorry for honking at you. I tried calling for you out the window, but you must not have heard me."

My thoughts were screaming so loud I couldn't hear life whispering. "Um, yeah. Sorry." I try to steady my voice. "I must have been thinking about something else." There's an awkward pause. Is he waiting for me to say more?

"Can I give you a ride?"

"Yes. Please."

He slides over to the passenger door and opens it from the inside. I put my binder down on the floor of the truck as I get in, but the deep red creases left from its edge sting. Rubbing them with my hand only makes them worse.

"Are you okay?" Nate's warm hand covers mine. Why does he have to be so nice? I don't deserve nice.

"I'm not okay, Nate." I look up at him, really seeing him, his kind eyes searching for me to say more. But that's just it: I never say more. I just box things up it my corrugated cardboard vault, putting them away forever.

His hand strokes mine for a while before he puts it on the steering wheel. "Where can I take you?" he finally asks, breaking the silence.

I'm about to say *home*, but I change my mind. "You pick," I say, letting out a breath. "Just take me away from here."

Nate signals and gets back on the road. I don't pay attention to where we're going, just that we are going. He reaches across and takes my hand in his. My hand in his is not enough. I want to get lost in his arms, to hide in that safe place that is *Nate*. But I can't hide or run. What I know to be true will always be in my head, haunting me.

We've been driving for a while when Nate breaks the silence. "The day after you met my grandpa I went to visit him again." He doesn't glance towards me as he speaks, focusing on the road ahead. "He told me, 'That girl of yours—she's like a deer. She steps lightly and scares easy. Don't you say anything stupid to scare her off.'"

"Huh." I huff out a breath, remembering what Mason said to me the night we all made wishes on the spirit box animals: *"Nah, you keep that one. It suits you better. Besides, you have to play. It's your game."*

Nate's hand leaves mine as he puts it back on the steering wheel to turn the truck off the road. I think we're on the other side of the river and a ways out of town. I do remember passing over a timber-framed bridge to get here.

After pulling into a clearing, he shifts the truck into park and turns off the ignition. The cheery sounds of outside invade my safe bubble inside the truck. The sun is warm and shining, the grass sways in the breeze, and the sunlight drifts through the spaces between the trees, but it's all wrong.

This is not a nice day.

"I try so hard to say the right things around you," Nate says, letting his truck keys tumble into one of the empty cup holders. "I try to give you your space, not to ask questions and to just *understand* you. But I don't. So, please, help me. Tell me something. Anything, so I don't go crazy trying to figure it out. Anyone who pays any attention can see there's something going on with you."

I should be surprised, maybe shocked, that Nate is finally asking me this, but I'm not. All I do is hide things from my friends. He's just brave enough to call me on it. I turn towards him and take him in. His soft, grey T-shirt is wrinkled and faded. Like mine. He's still looking straight ahead out the windshield, even though we've parked and he's talking. And for the first time ever, I notice he looks tired.

"Sometimes, I think maybe you'd rather be around

Mason than me. Do you even like me?"

"What? Of course I like you." My words tumble out quickly. Is that it? Do I even *have* emotions anymore? "What I mean to say is, you're the best thing that's ever happened to me." My words come out rusty, like it's been too long since I've spoken. "Every time I see you, you take me away from everything horrible in my life."

He finally looks at me. "I'm happy to be your distraction, but . . ." His lips part slightly, as if he doesn't know if he should say the words. "I want more than that. I want to know you."

I am a deer caught in headlights.

"I don't know me." Saying the words makes it more real, and I don't know if that's any better.

He takes a deep breath in and out. "Can we go for a walk? There's something I want to show you."

Nate is undoubtedly the sweetest person I know. Why am I so afraid to open up to him? To anybody? Maybe because they might see what's really inside, and it's all kinds of fucked up. Looking out the dusty windshield, I see the line of tall pine trees knit so closely they barely allow enough sunlight for the few small plants to grow on the forest floor. I don't recognize this place at all.

"Okay. Where are we?"

"We're on the other side of the river. It's a bit of a tricky place to find. You have to take a few back roads to get here. I found it about a week ago when I was doing some fieldwork for Allen Drilling. I've wanted to show you all week."

"You've been working for Allen Drilling?" I know he's been working for them, of course. I'm just too chicken to ask him outright if he's taken a job with them in Vancouver.

"Yeah. You remember, don't you? When we were at the municipal office." His voice trails off. "I've been doing some fieldwork for them, trying to find better locations for their drilling projects."

"Oh yeah, I remember. I was just . . . thinking out loud." Maybe he doesn't want to talk about it right now. A taste of my own medicine, I guess. "So," I say, looking back out the window, "is there a path or anything?"

A quiet smile spreads across his face. "A small one. Come on, I'll show you."

I don't see it until we are right in front of it. A narrow trail of trampled pine needles and yellowed grass snakes through the trees. I try not to trip over the exposed roots that cross the path. Nate walks in front of me, leading the way. The path starts to get steep, weaving back and forth against the side of the hill—or mountain, I guess.

"It's not much farther." His graceful strides never seem to tire. Meanwhile, I'm starting to breathe heavily. I'm trying my best not to let him hear, but I'm failing. "Do you want to stop and take a break or keep going?" My lungs are burning from the muggy, hot air. He doesn't wait for me to answer. He sits on a fallen tree near the path, patting the space beside him. I sit close enough to him that our knees just touch.

"I should have said something back at the truck when you asked me," he starts. "I've been doing some work with Allen Drilling, and they've offered me a job." His voice heightens a little. "And I took it. I've already talked to my uncle about my piece of the ownership in the garage. He said that him and Sam can handle things. That Sam might even buy it off me." From the look on Nate's face, he's been bottling up this conversation for a while. "This job will give me experience in what I went to college for . . . I just think I need to take this opportunity." With one last sigh, he lets the bomb drop. "I have to move away."

I knew this was coming. So why does my heart drop out of my chest?

"I'll be moving to Vancouver, where you're from. And I know this is crazy to ask because we've only been dating a few weeks, but I thought—since you're from there—maybe you miss it? Maybe you'd want to move there too, with me?"

I can't do this right now. "You want me to go with you?" The look on his face falls flat. Crap.

I look up and let my lips find his. I kiss him like I'm searching for something. I *am* searching for something. I want to be less broken.

He gives a cautious smile. "So does that mean you want to come with me?"

"It means . . ." My brain needs a second to sort out my jumbled thoughts. "It means, when I first came here, I thought it was just going to be another meaningless stop on the road. But I was wrong. I've met you here, and all my friends. This place has been . . . unexpected. And, although I want to be with you, I'm not ready to leave here yet. That doesn't mean I won't. I just can't say yes right now."

"Okay." His smile has faded to a look of confusion. "I guess I kind of sprung the question on you." Ugh. Nate is the last person I want to hurt.

I go on before he can say more. "I'm sorry, I'm a crappy girlfriend. There's just so much to figure out if I'm going to leave. I just—I don't know what I want yet."

"I know what I want." He says the words with such confidence. I envy that. "And we could figure out the rest together."

I let go of a deep breath I didn't know I was holding. "I don't know how I got a guy like you to like me."

"I love you, Rachel." My whole world goes still upon hearing those words. I'm pretty sure I love him too, but I can't say it back. He touches my lips with one finger. "I'll patiently wait for your answer on Vancouver. And I want you to know. You—are like no one I've ever met. It's obvious you've had some stuff go on in the past, and maybe even still. But you are a fighter, more so than I think you know. I think it's what makes everyone take notice of you. You are a force all on your own. And you're exactly who I want. I've finally found what I'm looking for."

Even if I could say the words, I'm not sure my lips could make the sounds. He knows what he wants, and he's found what he's looking for. But that's my wish. The jumbled thoughts are starting to sort themselves out.

What do I want? Not to be confused. Not to be afraid. I want to put everything back to the way it was, before Eric died, before my parents divorced, before my friend became a monster and before I did too. I want to be un-broken. I think I know what I have to do. I let his warm finger press against my lips for a moment longer before taking his hand away. Without saying anything, I kiss him again, and he kisses me back. We finally break, coming up for air.

"I did actually bring you here to show you something. Still up for hiking the rest of this hill? It's not far. I promise. In fact, I think I can see it through the trees."

I look off in the direction he's pointing. "What are you looking at? All I see are trees."

"There's a totem pole up here, all by itself. It's the weirdest thing." I follow behind him on the trail. "I've hiked all over this area and I've never come across it before. And I've never heard anybody talking about a totem way out here either." Nate keeps on talking without missing a step. "Remember that story my grandpa told you about the wendigo?"

"I do."

"In the story, there were two tribes and two spirit boxes. It would only make sense that there were two spirit totem poles." No sooner does he finish speaking than we are there.

The path plateaus into a small clearing surrounded by pine trees. At the center of an undisturbed layer of dried pine needles stands a towering spirit totem pole. It looks very similar to the other one. I recognize the wendigo carved at the bottom. A shiver goes through me to think there could be more wendigos, and another box.

"The animals are different on this one," Nate says. "From the top it goes, owl, fox, frog, and then wendigo."

I stare at the totem, taking in its every detail. My foot brushes over a bump on the needled forest floor. A root. It has roots just like the other spirit totem. They're gnarled and grey, weathered smooth from the elements. "I haven't told anyone about this yet," Nate finally says. "I'm not sure if I should."

Is he asking me if he should? He stands next to me, looking up at the totem. He's silent and beautiful, and so innocent of everything. "What would happen if you told people about this?" I ask, just above a whisper.

"This is where the drilling projects are slated to begin.

Not exactly in this spot, but close. If people found out about this"—he gestures to the totem—"it would change everything."

I look up, examining the features chiseled into this ancient wood. The carved eyes of the wendigo stare back at me. I know what happens to people who tamper with wendigo wishes.

"But you told me," I say.

"I did. But if anyone can keep a secret, it's you. And I think this one is better left untold."

CHAPTER TWENTY-ONE

"I need a shovel and the spirit box. That's all, right?" I say aloud, even though I'm the only one here, standing at the back of my car, staring into the oblivion of its trunk. Nate dropped me off after our little walk, and I know what I need to do. It's reckless, but I've made up my mind.

The open trunk gapes at me. No more sitting, doing nothing, watching people die. I no longer believe that everything happens by chance. I have a hand in this. And I can change it.

I load the spirit box and the shovel I took from Grams' shed into the trunk. This is the right thing to do. For once, I'll be brave enough. I'm going to send this box back where it came from, back to where it never should have existed. A breeze brushes a few stray hairs across my face.

The hot summer has arrived. With it, a buzz of what's to come.

Letting the trunk hood slip from my fingers, I hesitate a

moment before slamming it closed. I check my phone for the time. Seven o'clock. There should be enough time to get this done before it gets dark.

At least I hope so.

The road to the spirit totem field feels old hat, like I've driven it countless times before. Every turn is more a reflex than a thought, even though I've only been there once in real life. How many times in my dreams?

The parking lot at the hall is empty, yet I still park around back. I'd have a hell of a time explaining myself if anyone stopped to ask what I'm doing. The nervous butterflies in my stomach flap their tiny wings too fast. *Oh, I'm just digging a hole—burying an ancient box that grants wishes and ruins lives.*

The shifter sticks a little as I put the car in park. *Just breathe. You aren't burying somebody in the woods. It's a box.* I plan to bury it under the spirit totem. I'm "returning it to the earth from which it came." The words of Nate's grandpa echo in my head. I'll put the box back, and everything will go back to the way it was. Like pressing rewind. A do-over. A second chance.

Cha-chunk.

The truck latch lurches open as I press the release. My heart aches like it's running a race, skipping a beat, long enough to clear the first hurdle of many. The river churns close by. Its shushing flow of water sounds impatiently rushed.

It's now or never.

I haven't forgotten what Mason said about putting this thing back in the ground. He said that all the wishes would be taken back and that it would come at a cost: one soul. I haven't forgotten that last part, but I've thought this through and I know how to beat it. I will come out of this alive and so will Mason. It will fix everything.

I balance the spirit box on my hip, cradling it under my left arm. It's much heavier than it looks. As it slips further down my leg, I reach with my other hand for the shovel. Balancing the two, I close the trunk, barely managing to hold them both. I see it then, not thirty feet from me. Its huge brown eyes, its antlers grown to host at least seven points, and its stark white fur, a beacon against the dark curtain of the trees. My white deer. He stands alert, head up, proud. He doesn't move an inch, even when my shovel slips from my hand, clattering to the ground. His gaze on me doesn't waver.

"All the wishes will be taken back if the box is returned." Mason's warning plays again in my head. Chloe will lose her millions and her fame. Julie will lose the town rec center. Mason will lose all the progress his father's company has made. And I will lose . . . the knowledge of what I want. I won't find what I'm looking for. I know what I want now: I want the gaping hole inside me where my brother used to be to scar over. I don't want to hurt anymore. Perhaps I've always known that.

I let the air heave out of me. "I'm the only one who hasn't been granted a complete wish, but you keep showing up like I have," I yell at the white deer. All he does is stare back at me. The sting of a lone tear rolls down my cheek. "I know what I want, deer." The heat in me is rising. "But I still don't know what I'm looking for." Reaching down, I pick up the shovel. "If you're going to show me, do it now." *Come on, you stupid deer.* But he's grazing quietly at the edge of the dark trees. Perhaps he's lost interest in this crazy girl's ranting.

Pulling my phone out of my pocket, I check the time. 7:42. Mason's details glare at me in the harsh glow of the screen. Last chance.

I press the call button. *This has to work. It's going to work.* Mason answers with just my name. The ways he says it tugs at the strings that keep me together, like whole sentences have sprung from just one word: *Are you okay? I was worried. Where are you? Please talk to me.*

"Before you say anything, just listen," I say, interrupting him before he can go on. "I've figured it out, Mason. I know how to fix everything, and you can't change my mind. So don't try. I need you to come out to the field of totems where the spirit totem is. I'll explain when you get here." I want to hang up. I want to be mad and angry at everything he is, but I'm not. "Please."

The finality of what I've set in motion hits me. I have no idea how long it will take him to get here. Is he coming from his place? Will he drive? Can he use his wendigo speed to travel long distances? Or is that just for quick maneuvers? Maybe he's close by, watching me. The whole world seems to have eyes that watch.

Making my way to the totem while dragging a shovel and holding the heavy spirit box takes longer than I thought. Damn it. I should have dug the hole first and then called him. I rest the box on the grass, far enough away from the spirit totem that it won't get dirty from the digging. Which is kind of pointless, now that I think about it.

"Okay. Where to dig?" The spirit totem towers over me, a few dizzying storeys high. At its base, gnarled roots spread out, snaking through the surface of the rocky earth at least ten feet in every direction. I pick a spot near the base of the wendigo carving, trying to ignore its eyes as I dig where the roots have parted. Heaving my shovel into the dirt, it collides with hard pack, barely making a scratch. I try again. This time, it's like hitting cement. A shock of pain runs through me as I let the shovel clatter to the ground.

"Fuck!" Whoever says screaming profanities isn't productive is wrong. Screw the shovel, I'll dig with my hands. I fall from standing to kneeling on the hard ground, and it should hurt like hell, but I don't feel it. At least, not yet. I don't feel anything right now.

The top inch of soil flakes away, revealing more hard ground between petrified roots. Two of my fingernails have torn back and started to bleed, but I can't stop. I force my legs to bend, stumbling over to the box. The pain comes back to me now, real and present. It's more than just the pain of falling to my knees. It's everything: my brother, my parents, my friends. My heart isn't breaking. It feels like it's being crushed, flattened by everything that weighs on it so heavily until it's only a tenth of the size it should be, only able to feel the most primitive things.

The hole I've dug looks like nothing more than animal scratchings, but it will have to do. Placing the box where I've cleared the dirt, I wait, and . . . nothing. Nothing happens. I gather a handful of loose dirt and throw it on top, grinding it into the carved grooves. There are no blue flames, no theatrics, nothing. Why didn't I check to see if I could actually dig a hole before I did this? Stupid! One simple detail and my whole plan is ruined.

There is nothing left in me. I am empty. I have failed with this just like everything else. I sit back against the spirit totem. I drag the box onto my lap and wrap my arms around it. "I'm sorry," I whisper to it. "I'm sorry I couldn't fix everything." I want to hug the box and strangle it at the same time. "Don't you understand that you have to go back? Go back to where you came from!"

My whole body aches like a bad dream from which I can't wake up. I press my cheek against the box and close my eyes. I'll just wait here. Mason will find me, and then—whatever.

The lid of the box feels warm. It feels nice. It's comforting. I could almost go to sleep, but there's something that keeps me awake. What is that noise?

Ca-caw . . . Caw caw caw.

My head feels too heavy to lift, but I crack my eyes open. On a tree not far from me, sitting on a low branch, perches the white crow. His feathers are ruffled, and his wings are outstretched. His call sounds more like a scream than a bird call. My white deer has come closer too. I lift my head and the world spins. I don't like this spinning, or that bird, or that deer.

"Rachel!"

Mason. He's running towards me. At least I think it's him. The ground tilts and loses focus. "No!" I hear him say. "What have you done?"

Nothing. I've done nothing. I hear my words in my own head, but they won't come out of my mouth. "I had a plan, Mason." My throat is sore, as if I've been talking for hours. "I tried to return it to the spirits, but they wouldn't take it. I'm stuck with it." I give the box a shove. I want it off my lap, but it's too heavy. Everything is thick, coated with haze. "And that white crow has come to laugh at me. Look at him."

"You're not making any sense. Just hold on, I'll get you out of this."

Hold on to what? Now *he's* not making sense. My knees

don't ache as much anymore. There's something approaching behind Mason, but my words still aren't working. I try to point to show him. My hand leaves a trail in slow motion. *It's the white bear, Mason, come to laugh at me too.*

"You were supposed to save me before the spirits took back the box. So the box, and wishes, and wendigo would be gone. I don't want to go with it, Mason. You're supposed to save me. But it doesn't matter. Just take me home. I want to go home, Mason."

Out of nowhere, Mason's face, pale and frightened, is right in front of me. It looks blue. Everything looks blue.

I'm tired. Just take me home.

"How am I supposed to save you, Rachel?"

"Take my life before they do—and give it back. Just like Sheri-Lynn and Julie."

His words sound garbled but I manage to sort out a few. "Can't cheat the spirits . . . wendigos take . . . no giving back . . . How can I give you back if the spirits take my powers? I won't be a wendigo anymore."

Wait. If he isn't a wendigo anymore, he can't bring me back. If he can't bring me back . . . The chaos of what surrounds me sharpens into this moment.

Game over.

Then I feel it: that last part of me fighting, screaming,

grasping at what ties me to this existence.

My neck goes slack. I let my head fall back against the spirit totem and look up. Every carved groove and crack is lit up like a blue Christmas tree. The light trickles and flows into the indigo night sky.

"It's beautiful," I whisper.

For a moment I'm floating too, up into the sky. Then I realize that Mason is carrying me. The totem is still glowing but we are moving away from it. Too bad, it was nice there. But there's that nagging feeling again at the back of my mind. It's important . . . What is it?

"Stay with me, Rachel," I hear Mason say.

I'm not going anywhere. I'm right here. I want to say the words, but they stay in my head. We've stopped somewhere in the trees. It's dark and quiet here. I'm not afraid of the dark anymore. Let it come.

I see Mason's luminescent blue eyes. They are the same colour as the blue totem lights. I think they've always been that colour. Maybe they shine a little brighter tonight.

I feel it again. Nag, nag. It keeps nudging me, wanting an answer: *How are you going to survive this, Rachel?*

"I'll do it." Mason's blue eyes look sad. "But this isn't like Julie and Sheri-Lynn. I don't know if it will work. This could—"

I breathe in, letting the cool night fill my lungs. I feel the life it gives me, filling me then slowly ebbing away. This wasn't how I planned it. I was supposed to cheat this part. I know the price of returning the spirit box. One soul. Even Mason warned me. But I thought I had it all figured out. This wasn't how it was supposed to go. Now I know the answer to the nagging question of how I will survive.

I won't.

"Will it hurt?" I breathe out.

"No. Not for you. I'd never hurt you." The words barely escape his lips before I'm kissing him. The rush of his lips touching mine is electric, like a shock to my heart, almost strong enough to keep me here.

My world is fading. I'm caught in that space between light and dark, where nothing exists except me. It's just me, and him. His lips leave mine, and then it's just me. The lights fade. The sounds fade, except for one distant sound. *Ba-boom—whoosh. Ba-boom—whoosh. Ba-boom—*

And that's when I fall.

It's dark and cold. Am I dead? If I were, would I even been able to think that? This place is so empty. The darkness is so black. I think that no matter how long I'm here, my eyes will never adjust. It is just me and my thoughts. I have brought nothing with me.

My legs are bare. That's why I'm cold. I'm barefoot, standing on wet pavement. It's just rained, I think. I can smell it. I remember this smell: wet moss, dirt, and puddled water on concrete.

I see my pale reflection in the puddle I'm standing in. No shoes, skinny bare legs. I'm wearing a pair of light pink boxer shorts and a nightshirt with a picture of an orange kitten on it. I remember these pyjamas. I wore them all the time when I was . . . fourteen.

I see the rest of the scene around me now. The ambulance. The police car. The fire truck. Their lights are flashing, but there's no sound. Their reflections pulse in the puddle. Red, blue, white, orange. I've been to this place too many times to count. In my dreams, mostly—only once in real life. The flashing makes my thoughts swirl.

So this is where I go. Even in death it haunts me.

My legs are unsteady. Stepping back, I lose my balance. A twisted, steely guardrail running along the rain-soaked road catches me. It keeps me from falling into the gaping void of the ravine below. The rail curves where the road curves, but beside me, just one step to the right, it's broken. The opening is torn and jagged. It gapes, sending curling, twisted steel into the darkness. The trees and vines overgrown in the ravine are barely visible in the semi-darkness. I see them, though, their strange shadows casting blotches on what's plunged over the edge. I know what's down there. I've tried a million times to change the reality of what is down there. My brother and the car he rode to his death. The taillights glow red. They glow, fade, and then it's dark, like it was never there, but I know different. I only have to remember the guardrail and the distorted, torn hole in it. Just like the scar I carry, it never lets me forget.

"You always come back to this place. Why?" I know that voice. It's been too long since I've heard it.

"Eric?" At first I see his hand beside me, gripping the cold, steel guardrail. The cuff of his faded grey jean jacket is torn at the buttonhole, just like I remember it. My eyes follow his arm, his shoulder. His face! He's standing right beside me. "How? You're dead."

"So are you." His words escape in a puff of warm breath. I watch in amazement as his breath rises and dissipates into the dark.

"But you breathed. I just saw you."

"I breathe because you want me to. All this"—he gestures with his hand like this is some ordinary day—"is exactly what you want to see, or need to see. It's what you're looking for, Rachel."

I wished to know what I want, and to find what I'm looking for.

The words burn in my thoughts as though permanently

etched.

"Why do you keep coming back here, Rachel?" he asks again.

"Because . . ." My words are slow at first, but once they find their momentum it's like a weight has been lifted. "Before you died, I was strong and I knew that my future was happy. I was happy. After you died, I just broke. I crumbled into myself and stayed there. I tried to fix things and sort out the pieces, but nothing would stick. Nothing would fix. I couldn't fix me. Or you. Anything. That's why I come back here. This is the place between 'before' and 'after.' This is the place where I lost everything. I come back here to find it. To find what I'm looking for."

"And have you found it?" Eric's voice is as I remember it, but with at least one hundred years of wisdom behind it. This is both the Eric I knew and someone totally different.

My mind teeters between *yes* and *no*. The answer is there. I can feel it, but it still remains just beyond me.

I look up to Eric's face, as if some epiphany might be hidden there. I see his hazel eyes. His nose, much like mine except for the bump where he broke it years ago. His dark brown hair with sun-bleached tips is a tousled mess. Some might consider it too long, but it suits him. He even smells the same. I always thought his cologne smelled too sweet, but now it couldn't smell better. He is just as I remember him, and totally different.

"Is it—you? Are you what I'm looking for?"

"No, Rach. It's not me." His voice is kind, like my brother, but there is frustration behind it.

"But you're here. And I'm happy. And . . ." Eric's face creases in concern, a look I don't think I've ever seen cross his face. Eric never worried.

"He's been trying to explain it to you all along, Rach. He's been trying to explain how things really work. You just need to open your eyes."

"My eyes are open! I see you, Eric. I see you like you still exist. Like you're not dead."

"I do exist. I existed before I was me, while I was me, and after I died. What we are never stops existing." He pauses. "We just are. We are neither created nor destroyed. We are always moving, always changing. I just went somewhere else when I died, and I'm sorry I had to go, but I've never really left. I just changed. You need to understand. Open your eyes." And with those last words, my world morphs again.

Pictures flash around me, drowning out the ravine, the guardrail, and the emergency vehicles. Surrounding me, I now see the blue light Mason used to ignite the wet firewood on the beach. I see how he made the plants grow, and I understand. I see the control he had over the bear. I understand. I see how he saved

Julie, and let Sheri-Lynn go. I see how he can talk to me without speaking.

I see everything.

More scenes flash. More blue lights. I get it. The rush. In this moment, every part of me that was hurt, confused, and scared falls away like ashes. I am new. I am awakened to all that surrounds me, and it fills me up. Everything looks different now. It *is* different. Like everything has taken on a whole new shine. I am different.

The spot where Eric's death had left a hole in me starts to close. My hurt is gone. I am strong. I understand the connection between life and death. I understand the connections among everything.

"Do you see now? Have you found it?"

"I have." I look around to see the blue-lit images fading, leaving only a dull glow in the distance. There is only Eric and I left in this place.

"This is what he's been trying to show you." Even Eric's hands, face, and neck—the spots where I can see exposed skin— have changed, although not really. He is still Eric. The brother I knew. The brother I know, but I see the blue that glows just below the surface of his skin. "You've found what heals you. You've found what makes you strong. Don't be afraid of it. Open your eyes and take it with you. You've found what you're looking for."

"My eyes are open." Glancing down, I see the same blue glow inside my hands, under my skin, inside me. Looking back at Eric, I see he is drifting way. Where is he going? He can't go yet. "Stay with me!" I call after him.

"You'll be fine. I know you will. Just open your eyes."

He's gone, leaving me with only the soft blue glow under my skin to keep me company. I don't feel alone, though. I don't think I even will again. And Eric is right, I'll be just fine. All I need to do now is open my eyes.

"Holy crap, you're alive! I thought I killed you and you were gone forever." I wake up on my back, lying on the cold, damp ground. Mason's face hangs just inches over mine.

"You did kill me," I croak. "But you of all people know that I wasn't gone."

I need no time to adjust to the darkness of the night. I can see right away everything that surrounds me. The box rests beside me. He must have saved it. It makes sense. If the box was gone, his powers would be too, and he couldn't have put me back in my body. Perhaps the box does have a place in this world. Maybe wendigos do, too.

Pushing myself up to a sitting position, I feel the new strength in my arms, in my whole body. I am strong now. Not just in body, but in mind too. I let the warmth of a smile flood across my face, and it feels—good.

Our gazes meet again, but this time it's different. I've seen his eyes a thousand time and never really understood what was behind them. But I do now. I let the new glow from within me flare, producing the same light I've seen may times behind his gaze. Does he understand what's happened? Does he understand how I've changed?

"Oh my God. Your eyes. Does this mean you're . . . ?"

A playful giggle escapes me, while nervousness radiates off him so thick I can almost taste it. "No. I'm not a wendigo."

Stretching my arms out wide, I feel a few deep-rooted kinks release. It's like I've been tied up in knots for years. I taste salt on my lips, remnants from the kiss I took from Mason just before I died. I taste the notes of passion in it, the fireworks, the desire . . . and his heartache.

"I'm something else entirely. And I think—I'm going to like it."

About the Author

Katherine Dell is a young adult fiction author fascinated by the supernatural and the stories that surround them. She began her writing endeavours in 2011 when she wanted to reinvent herself from her previous career as an event planner. When she's not writing, she can be found in cold hockey arenas sipping coffee, working on her tan at little league games, or trying to keep her dog out of her many gardens. She lives with her husband, two boys, and fur babies, in Calgary, Alberta, Canada.

Acknowledgments

The journey of writing this story and getting it to publication has taken years, and it's taken a village to get here. So I pledge my thanks to all those who've played a part in this. I couldn't have done it without you.

My husband, Orrin, and our boys have always been there to encourage me and pick up the slack when I'm neck-deep in my writing.

To my mom for being patient and believing this book would be out one day.

Bri, Frank, Ali, you are my army of artists, designers, photographers, and web professionals who take my work to the next level and put up with my insistent need for perfection.

Amanda, you took my manuscript from good to great. It's so polished I can see my face in it.

Kelly, Sheri, Chris, Jackie, Charlene, you've all read my rough drafts and asked the detailed questions that helped me refine this story. You left no stone unturned. Thanks for believing in me.

And Adam, I've truly won the lottery when it comes to your mentorship, friendship, and help on this project. This wouldn't have seen the world without you.

Finally, to all those who've helped but are too numerous to name. Your support has inspired me to keep writing.

Write a Review!

Sharing your thoughts and feelings about the book you just read lets the world know that there are people reading this book. Without genuine reviews many awesome titles can go unnoticed. So if you have a bit of time, write a review. There 's an author out there who greatly appreciates it.

Many thanks,

Katherine